GEPT

初試1次過

全民英檢

初級 閱讀測驗

每日刷題 10 分鐘，1 天 2 頁
1 個月後高分過關！

國際語言中心委員會——著

準備初級英檢閱讀，
為什麼每天只要花 10 分鐘就可以了？

　　相信多數參加過各種英文檢定考試的考生都可以認同，考前「大量刷題」是一件必須做的事情 — 因為訓練考試的手感很重要！在真正考試時，由於時間緊迫，很多都是瞬間反應，當手感熟悉後選對題目幾乎成為反射動作，但如果每天都寫完整的考題，加上檢討得花費大量時間，對於忙碌的現代生活來說，最後往往中途而廢，或敗在力不從心了。因此，本書將所有初級閱讀常考的題型，設計成 1 天 10 題，每天不但都可以練習到每一個 PART，且能熟悉作題的感覺又不必花費太多時間。每日短時練習注重的是效率，不僅減輕學習壓力，也確保你在短時間內集中精神學習，學習效果最佳。

　　透過每天 10 分鐘的學習，能夠讓你養成良好的學習習慣，而日積月累的實力將可發揮滴水穿石的效果。這種細緻的積累比耗費金錢與通勤時間，更具持久效果且不容易倦怠。最後，這樣的學習方式不僅讓你應對考試不害怕，還能夠持續提高語言水平。這種持續進步的學習方式，使你在更高級的英語學習中也能夠輕鬆應對挑戰。

這套訓練計畫的架構不僅緊密貼合新制初級英檢閱讀的考試內容，更注重每一位學習者的日常時間管理。每日各 PART 的練習題都經過精心挑選，旨在循序漸進地提升學習者的詞彙量、語境理解力以及閱讀分析能力。透過這 28 天的有計畫學習，包含 2 回完整測驗，以及每一道題目的中文翻譯及答題詳解，這樣的豐富資源確保讀者不僅能應對考試挑戰，還能深入理解每道題目，強化英語閱讀技能，學習者也能夠在短時間內感受到明顯的進步，不僅為英檢初級閱讀考試做好準備，更在英語學習的長遠道路上建立起穩固的基石。系統性的學習結構讓讀者能夠有效安排學習時間，輕鬆培養英語閱讀習慣，迎接下一個等級的挑戰。

國際語言中心委員會

本書特色與使用說明

1

請在每一個 Day 的最上方填入當天的自我測驗日期，除 Day 14 與 Day 28 之外，測驗時間皆為 10 分鐘。

Part 1 詞彙練習：建議您自我要求 1 分鐘之內作答完畢。這個測驗可加強你的用字能力：每天只需解答 2 個詞彙練習題，你就能夠迅速提升詞彙量，使你的語言更豐富、表達更準確。

Day 01　　月　日

我的完成時間＿＿＿＿分鐘
標準作答時間 10 分鐘

Part 1 詞彙

1. A ＿＿＿＿＿＿ is someone who is engaged in buying and selling.
   - A. cook
   - B. businessman
   - C. seller
   - D. customer

2. Mary was skinny last year, but she is ＿＿＿＿＿＿ now.
   - A. tall
   - B. fat
   - C. smarter
   - D. fast

Part 1 詞彙

Q1 考題重點〉認識職業的英文單字

A ＿＿＿＿＿＿ is someone who is engaged in buying and selling.
- A. cook
- **B. businessman**
- C. seller
- D. customer

| 翻譯 | 從事買賣的人為商人。

| 詳解 | buying（買）跟 selling（賣）是本題的關鍵，會同時做買跟賣的非商人莫屬，所以正確答案為選項 B。

| 詞彙 | cook [kʊk] 廚師　seller [ˋsɛlə] 賣家　customer [ˋkʌstəmə] 顧客

Q2 考題重點〉①注意語氣的轉折　②了解反義字

Mary was skinny last year, but she is ＿＿＿＿＿＿ now.
- A. tall
- **B. fat**
- C. smarter
- D. fast

| 翻譯 | 瑪莉去年身材瘦削，但她現在變胖了。

| 詳解 | skinny 指「瘦削的」，關鍵字在 but（但是）。去年很瘦，而連接詞用 but 代表現在的狀況要跟胖瘦等身材有關，所以正確答案為選項 B。

| 詞彙 | skinny [skɪnɪ] 瘦骨如柴的　fast [fæst] 快的

Part 2 段落填空

Questions 3-7

David likes __(3)__ mountain climbing. He has climbed mountains __(4)__ almost twenty years. Now he plans to climb the Taipei 101. Do you know __(5)__ he wants to climb the building? People say that he wants to be __(6)__ , but David says that __(7)__ .

3. A. to
   B. to go
   C. to went
   D. enjoy

4. A. for
   B. in
   C. since
   D. already

5. A. what
   B. how
   C. why
   D. when

6. A. angry
   B. famous
   C. dumb
   D. blamed

7. A. I do it just for fun
   B. he does it just for fun
   C. he has done it just for fun
   D. I has done it just for fun

Part 2 段落填空

David likes **(3) to go** mountain climbing. He has climbed mountains **(4) for** almost twenty years. Now he plans to climb the Taipei 101. Do you know **(5) why** he wants to climb the building? People say that he wants to be **(6) famous**, but David says that **(7) he does it just for fun**.

| 翻譯 | 大衛喜歡去爬山。他已經爬了將近二十年的山了。現在他打算要攀登上台北 101。你知道他為什麼想要爬上那棟大樓嗎？人們說他是想要出名，不過大衛說他做這件事只是為了好玩。

2

Part 2 段落填空：每天解答一個題組，每個題組包含 5 小題。建議您自我要求 3~4 分鐘之內作答完畢。這部分訓練你在上下文中找到合適的詞語。透過這個訓練，瞬間強化你在前後文中找到合適詞彙的能力，並培養良好的閱讀理解能力

3

Part 3 閱讀理解：每天做一個題組，含 3 個小題，建議您自我要求 5~6 分鐘之內作答完畢。這個訓練將有助於提升你對文章整體結構的把握，培養分析和推斷的能力。

Q9 What kind of side effects might the medicine have on the patient?
這個藥品對於病人可能會產生什麼樣的副作用？
A. Dry eyes　眼睛乾澀
B. Headache　頭痛
C. Skin problem　皮膚問題
D. Sleepiness　嗜睡

| 詳解 | 這個題目要綜合兩篇文章來解題。題目問此藥品可能會產生甚麼副作用，在第一篇文章中我們可以看到 If you don't feel well after using the medicine, consult your doctor immediately，要求使用者如果感覺到不舒服要諮詢醫生，不過並沒有講到會產生什麼症狀。我們從第二篇諮詢醫生的信件中可以看到 my skin gets lot of red rashes，表示病人在使用後起了紅疹，綜合這兩個線索，我們就知道這個藥品的副作用是產生皮膚問題，因此正確答案為 C。

| 詞彙 | side effect 副作用　patient ['pefənt] 病人　headache ['hrd,ek] 頭痛

Q10 Which is NOT true about the medicine?
關於藥品的描述何者不實？
A. It can be taken without seeing a doctor.
　沒有看過醫生也可使用。
B. It may hurt your eyes.　它可能會傷害眼睛。
C. It may make you not feel good.　它可能會讓你不舒服。
D. You can take it a few times a day.　你一天可以吃數次。

| 詳解 | 答案提示在 Use the medicine only under the doctor's directions.（只可在醫生指示下使用。）表示此藥品要有醫生許可才能用，很顯然選項 A 說的並非事實，而題目剛好要選的是「不實的描述」，所以答案為 A。從第一個文本的「(E) If the medicine goes into your eyes...」可知，選項 B 是正確的敘述；從「(D) If you don't feel well after using the medicine...」可知，選項 C 是正確的敘述；從「(A) Use the medicine every four hours.」可知，選項 D 是正確的敘述。

Part3 閱讀理解

Questions 8-10
Here are the directions on the medicine.
(A) Use the medicine every four hours.
(B) Keep the medicine away from kids.
(C) Use the medicine only under the doctor's directions.
(D) If you don't feel good after using the medicine, consult your doctor immediately.
(E) If the medicine goes into your eyes, wash them with water right away.
....

Dear Doctor,
After using the medicine for three days, my skin gets lot of red rashes.
Should I continue to use it?

　　　　　　　　　　　　　　　　John

8. Where should you put the medicine?
　A. You should put it near the children.
　B. You should put it in the refrigerator.
　C. You should put it on the bookshelf.
　D. You should put it in a place where the children can't reach it.

9. What kind of side effects might the medicine have on the patient?
　A. Dry eyes
　B. Headache
　C. Skin problem
　D. Sleepiness

10. Which is NOT TRUE about the medicine?
　A. It can be taken without seeing a doctor
　B. It may hurt your eyes.
　C. It may make you not feel good.
　D. You can take it a few times a day.

| Day **14** | 月　日 | 我的完成時間　　分鐘 標準作答時間 35 分鐘 |

Part1 詞彙

1. Her goal is _____ financially independent.
　A. being　　　　　C. been
　B. to be　　　　　D. to being

2. She had a car _____ on her way to work this morning.
　A. accident　　　C. umbrella
　B. library　　　　D. celebration

3. The room was so hot that everyone was sweating due to the intense _____
　A. heat　　　　　C. snow
　B. rain　　　　　D. wind

4

結束 13 天的練習之後，可以在第 14 天訓練一回完整的測驗，驗證自己的能力提升。

解答與詳解　上頁簡答

1. (B) 2. (A) 3. (A) 4. (D) 5. (B) 6. (D) 7. (C) 8. (D) 9. (C)
10. (A) 11. (B) 12. (A) 13. (C) 14. (C) 15. (D) 16. (B)
17. (A) 18. (B) 19. (D) 20. (D) 21. (C) 22. (B) 23. (A)
24. (D) 25. (B) 26. (A) 27. (D) 28. (D) 29. (C) 30. (A)

Part1 詞彙

Q1 考題重點 一定要用不定詞（to-V）的情況
Her goal is _____ financially independent.
A. being　　**B. to be**　　C. been　　D. to being

| 翻譯 | 她的目標是財務自由。
| 詳解 | goal（目標）代表一件未完成、未達到的事，所以要用表示「目的」或「未來」的不定詞作為補語，正確答案是選項 B。不定詞的結構是「to + 原形動詞」，所以 D 是錯誤的。
| 詞彙 | goal [gol] 目標　financially [faɪ'næntʃəlɪ] 財務上　independent [,ɪndɪ'pɛndənt] 獨立的，自主的

Q2 考題重點 選擇符合句意的名詞
She had a car _____ on her way to work this morning.
A. accident　B. library　C. umbrella　D. celebration

5

閱讀測驗 答對題數與分數對照表

本書最後面提供「答對題數與分數對照表」，讓你在每天進步的過程中，激發動力，不僅增強信心，還讓學習變得更有趣。

答對題數	分數	答對題數	分數	答對題數	分數
30	120	20	80	10	40
29	116	19	76	9	36
28	112	18	72	8	32
27	108	17	68	7	28
26	104	16	64	6	24
25	100	15	60	5	20
24	96	14	56	4	16
23	92	13	52	3	12
22	88	12	48	2	8
21	84	11	44	1	4

CONTENTS

目錄

GEPT 全民英檢初級閱讀測驗初試 1 次過

Part 1 詞彙

1. A _____ is someone who is engaged in buying and selling.

   A. cook

   B. businessman

   C. seller

   D. customer

2. Mary was skinny last year, but she is _____ now.

   A. tall

   B. fat

   C. smarter

   D. fast

Part 2 段落填空

Questions 3-7

David likes (3) mountain climbing. He has climbed mountains (4) almost twenty years. Now he plans to climb the Taipei 101. Do you know (5) he wants to climb the building? People say that he wants to be (6) , but David says that (7) .

3. A. to

   B to go

   C to went

   D enjoy

4. A. for

   B. in

   C. since

   D. already

5. A. what

   B. how

   C. why

   D. when

6. A. angry

   B. famous

   C. dumb

   D. blamed

7. A. I do it just for fun

   B. he does it just for fun

   C. he has done it just for fun

   D. I has done it just for fun

Day 01
Day 02
Day 03
Day 04
Day 05
Day 06
Day 07

Part 3 閱讀理解

Questions 8-10

Here are the directions on the medicine.

(A) Use the medicine every four hours.

(B) Keep the medicine away from kids.

(C) Use the medicine only under the doctor's directions.

(D) If you don't feel good after using the medicine, consult your doctor immediately.

(E) If the medicine goes into your eyes, wash them with water right away.

....

Dear Doctor,

After using the medicine for three days, my skin gets lot of red rashes.

Should I continue to use it?

John

8. Where should you put the medicine?

    A. You should put it near the children.

    B. You should put it in the refrigerator.

    C. You should put it on the bookshelf.

    D. You should put it in a place where the children can't reach it.

9. What kind of side effects might the medicine have on the patient?

    A. Dry eyes

    B. Headache

    C. Skin problem

    D. Sleepiness

10. Which is NOT TRUE about the medicine?

    A. It can be taken without seeing a doctor

    B. It may hurt your eyes.

    C. It may make you not feel good.

    D. You can take it a few times a day.

Part 1 詞彙

Q1 考題重點〉認識職業的英文單字

A _____ is someone who is engaged in buying and selling.

A. cook   C. seller

B. businessman   D. customer

| 翻譯 | 從事買賣的人為商人。

| 詳解 | buying（買）跟 selling（賣）是本題的關鍵，會同時做買跟賣的非商人莫屬，所以正確答案為選項 B。

| 詞彙 | **cook** [kʊk] 廚師   **seller** [`sɛlɚ] 賣家    **customer** [`kʌstəmɚ] 顧客

Q2 考題重點〉①注意語氣的轉折   ②了解反義字

Mary was skinny last year, but she is _____ now.

A. tall   C. smarter

B. fat   D. fast

| 翻譯 | 瑪莉去年身材瘦削，但她現在變胖了。

| 詳解 | skinny 指「瘦削的」，關鍵字在 but（但是）。去年很瘦，而連接詞用 but 代表現在的狀況要跟胖瘦等身材有關，所以正確答案為選項 B。

| 詞彙 | **skinny** [skɪnɪ] 瘦骨如柴的   **fast** [fæst] 快的

Part 2 段落填空

David likes **(3) to go** mountain climbing. He has climbed mountains **(4) for** almost twenty years. Now he plans to climb the Taipei 101. Do you know **(5) why** he wants to climb the building? People say that he wants to be **(6) famous**, but David says that **(7) he does it just for fun**.

| 翻譯 | 大衛喜歡去爬山。他已經爬了將近二十年的山了。現在他打算要攀登上台北 101。你知道他為什麼想要爬上那棟大樓嗎？人們說他是想要出名，不過大衛說他做這件事情只是為了好玩。

Day 01

Day 02

Day 03

Day 04

Day 05

Day 06

Day 07

Q3 考題重點〉①like + 不定詞（to-V）/ 動詞-ing　②go + 動詞-ing

A. to

C. to went

B. to go

D. and goes

|詳解| 「like +不定詞（to-V）/ 動名詞（Ving）」表示「喜歡做某事」，所以正確答案為 B。

Q4 考題重點〉完成式搭配「for + 一段時間」

A. for

C. since

B. in

D. already

|詳解| has climbed 是現在完成式，表示持續時間時必須用 for 介系詞代表「已持續」幾年，所以正確答案為 A。

Q5 考題重點〉疑問副詞的運用

A. what

C. why

B. how

D. when

|詳解| 要注意前後文，後面沒有提到如何爬上台北 101，所以選項 B 不對。沒有提到什麼時候爬，所以 D 不對。A 邏輯不通，所以正確答案為 C。

Q6 考題重點〉填入符合文意的形容詞

A. angry

C. dumb

B. famous

D. blamed

|詳解| 前文提到大衛想攀登台北 101，因此這句話要表達的應該是「他想出名，但大衛說…」，故正確答案是 B。選項 A、C、D 意思分別是「生氣的」、「愚蠢的」、「被責備的」，皆不符文意。

Q7 考題重點〉①文章整體時式判斷　②直接引述與間接引述

A. I do it just for fun　我做這件事只是為了好玩

B. he does it just for fun　他做這件事只是為了好玩

C. he has done it just for fun　他做了這件事只是為了好玩

D. I has done it just for fun　我做了這件事只是為了好玩

|詳解| 整篇文章為現在式，也就是說大衛「打算」爬 101 而非「已經」爬了 101，所以選項 C、D 不符。另外 said 後面沒有逗點，前後也沒有引述符號「"…"」，所以可以知道是間接引述，因此直接引述的選項 A 也錯誤，所以正確答案為 B。

Here are the directions on the medicine.

(A) Use the medicine every four hours.

(B) Keep the medicine away from kids.

(C) Use the medicine only under the doctor's directions.

(D) If you don't feel good after using the medicine, consult your doctor immediately.

(E) If the medicine goes into your eyes, wash them with water right away.

⋯⋯⋯⋯⋯⋯⋯⋯⋯⋯⋯⋯⋯⋯⋯⋯⋯⋯⋯⋯⋯⋯⋯⋯

Dear Doctor,

After using the medicine for three days, my skin gets lot of red rashes.

Should I continue to use it?

John

| 翻譯 | 藥品使用指示。(A) 每隔四小時使用一次。(B) 請將藥品遠離小孩。(C) 只可在醫生指示下使用。(D) 使用藥品後如感到不適，請立即諮詢醫生。(E) 如藥品進入眼睛，請立即用清水清洗。

⋯⋯⋯⋯⋯⋯⋯⋯⋯⋯⋯⋯⋯⋯⋯⋯⋯⋯⋯⋯⋯⋯⋯⋯

親愛的醫生，在用了這個藥物三天後，我的皮膚長了很多紅疹。我應該繼續使用它嗎？　約翰

| 詞彙 | **keep... away from** 使⋯遠離、不接近　**consult** [kən`sʌlt] 諮詢
immediately [ɪ`midɪɪtlɪ] 立即　**wash with** 以⋯清洗

Q8 Where should you put the medicine?
你應該把藥品放在哪裡？

A. You should put it near the children.　你應該放在小孩旁邊。

B. You should put it in the refrigerator.　你應該放在冰箱裡。

C. You should put it on the bookshelf.　你應該放在書架上。

D. You should put it in a place where the children can't reach it.
你應該放在小孩拿不到的地方。

| 詳解 | 答案提示在 Keep the medicine away from kids.，意思是「請將藥品遠離小孩」，所以答案為 D。

| 詞彙 | **children** [`tʃɪldrən] 小孩（child 的複數）　**refrigerator** [rɪ`frɪdʒəˌretə] 冰箱
bookshelf [`bʊkˌʃɛlf] 書架　**reach** [ritʃ] 觸及

Day 01

Day 02

Day 03

Day 04

Day 05

Day 06

Day 07

Q9 What kind of side effects might the medicine have on the patient?
這個藥品對於病人可能會產生什麼樣的副作用？

A. Dry eyes　　眼睛乾澀

B. Headache　　頭痛

C. Skin problem　　皮膚問題

D. Sleepiness　　嗜睡

| 詳解 | 這個題目要綜合兩篇文章來解題。題目問此藥品可能會產生甚麼副作用，在第一篇文章中我們可以看到 If you don't feel well after using the medicine, consult your doctor immediately，要求使用者如果感覺到不舒服要諮詢醫生，不過並沒有講到會產生什麼症狀。我們從第二篇諮詢醫生的信件可以看到 my skin gets lot of red rashes，表示病人在使用後起了紅疹，綜合這兩個線索，我們知道這個藥品的副作用是產生皮膚問題，因此正確答案為 C。

| 詞彙 | **side effect** 副作用　　**patient** [ˋpeʃənt] 病人　　**headache** [ˋhɛdͺek] 頭痛

Q10 Which is NOT true about the medicine?
關於藥品的描述何者不實？

A. It can be taken without seeing a doctor.
沒有看過醫生也可使用。

B. It may hurt your eyes.　　它可能會傷害眼睛。

C. It may make you not feel good.　　它可能會讓你不舒服。

D. You can take it a few times a day.　　你一天可以吃數次。

| 詳解 | 答案提示在 Use the medicine only under the doctor's directions.（只可在醫生指示下使用。）表示此藥品要有醫生許可才能用，很顯然選項 A 說的並非事實，而題目剛好要選的是「不實的描述」，所以答案為 A。從第一個文本的「(E) If the medicine goes into your eyes...」可知，選項 B 是正確的敘述；從「(D) If you don't feel well after using the medicine...」可知，選項 C 是正確的敘述；從「(A) Use the medicine every four hours.」可知，選項 D 是正確的敘述。

Part 1 詞彙

1. This book gives a good _____ of daily life in Taiwan.

   A. picture

   B. person

   C. season

   D. describe

2. My boss told me to do the checking _____ .

   A. right away

   B. on the go

   C. far away

   D. in the past

Part 2 段落填空

Questions 3-7

  (3) people don't write letters to their friends nowadays, but they (4) by e-mail. It's very easy for them to communicate (5) each other on the Internet. More often, they coutact each other (6) cell phone. Technology has made communication (7) today.

3　A Better and better

　　B Less and less

　　C More and more

　　D Bigger and bigger

4　A think twice

　　B take care

　　C stay in touch

　　D make better use

5　A and

　　B with

　　C in

　　D at

6　A with

　　B by

　　C at

　　D on

7　A easiest and easiest

　　B more easy

　　C more and more easy

　　D easier and easier

Questions 8-10

Flight	From	To	Departure Time	Arrival Time
CX1000	Taoyuan Airport	Sydney	7:00	9:30 the next day
BR818	Taoyuan Airport	Tokyo	10:30	15:00
NX963	Kaohsiung Airport	Seoul	14:00	18:20
AW755	Kaohsiung Airport	New York	11:30	15:30 the next day
N220	Taoyuan Airport	Bangkok	19:00	22:30

 ◁ Hi, Martin. What time will you arrive?

I'll arrive at 3 p.m. ▷

8. Sam is from Kaohsiung. He has to go to Korea on business trip next month. What flight should he take?

A. BR818

B. AW755

C. NX963

D. None of the above

9. Which city does Martin probably go?

A. Sydney

B. Tokyo

C. New York

D. Bangkok

10. What time will you get to New York if you take the flight on June 4th?

A. Half past 3 in the afternoon

B. Half past 11 the next day

C. A quarter after 3 on June 5th

D. Half past 3 in the afternoon on June 5th

Part 1 詞彙

Q1 考題重點〉詞性的認識

This book gives a good _____ of daily life in Taiwan.

A. picture　　　　　　　　　　C. season

B. person　　　　　　　　　　　D. describe

| 翻譯 | 這本書對於台灣的日常生活有很好的寫照。

| 詳解 | 形容詞 good 後面放名詞，所以選項 D 不對。describe 的名詞為 description，所以正確答案為選項 A。picture 在此指「描述，寫照」。

| 詞彙 | person [`pɝsn̩] 人　　season [`sizn̩] 季節

Q2 考題重點〉選出適當的副詞片語

My boss told me to do the checking _____.

A. right away　　　　　　　　C. far away

B. on the go　　　　　　　　　D. in the past

| 翻譯 | 我的老闆要我馬上進行檢查。

| 詳解 | 句意是「老闆要我立即進行檢查」，故正確答案是選項 A。B、C、D 意思分別是「遠離地」、「進行中」、「在過去」，皆不符句意與邏輯。

| 詞彙 | checking [`tʃɛkɪŋ] 檢查，查看

Part 2 段落填空

(3) More and more people don't write letters to their friends nowadays, but they **(4) stay in touch** by e-mail. It's very easy for them to communicate **(5) with** each other on the Internet. More often, they contact each other **(6) by** cell phone. Technology has made communication **(7) easier and easier** today.

| 翻譯 | 現在，越來越多人不寫信給他們的朋友，但他們用電子郵件來保持聯繫。在網路上彼此溝通對他們而言相當容易。更多時候，他們會用手機聯絡彼此。科技讓今天的通訊變得越來越容易。

Q3 考題重點〉「比較級 and 比較級」句型的用法

A. Better and better   **C. More and more**

B. Less and less   D. Bigger and bigger

| 詳解 | more and more 指越來越多人,所以答案為 C。如果要說越來越少人,是 fewer and fewer,故雖然選項 B 看似正確,其實不然。

Q4 考題重點〉stay in touch 片語的熟悉

A. think twice   **C. stay in touch**

B. take care   D. make better use

| 詳解 | stay in touch 是「保持聯繫」的意思,故答案為 C。A、B、D 的意思分別是「再次考量」、「保重身體」、「做更好的利用」,皆不符語意。

Q5 考題重點〉communicate with 片語的熟悉

A. and   C. in

B. with   D. at

| 詳解 | communicate(溝通)是個不及物動詞,後面必須先有介系詞之後才能接受詞,而要表達「與…(某人)溝通」時,只能用 with,所以正確答案為 B。

Q6 考題重點〉表示方法的介系詞 by

A. with   C. at

B. by   D. on

| 詳解 | 空格所在句子的大意是「以手機聯繫彼此」,這裡介系詞要用 by,所以正確答案是選項 B。本題中的 by cellphone = on their cellphones。

Q7 考題重點〉「比較級 and 比較級」句型的用法

A. easiest and easiest

B. more easy

C. more and more easy

D. easier and easier

| 詳解 | 「越來越容易」正確用法是 easier and easier,easy 的比較級只要去 -y 改成 -ier 就好。more easy and easy 是經常犯的錯誤,別被騙了,正確答案為 D。

Flight	From	To	Departure Time	Arrival Time
CX1000	Taoyuan Airport	Sydney	7:00	9:30 the next day
BR818	Taoyuan Airport	Tokyo	10:30	15:00
NX963	Kaohsiung Airport	Seoul	14:00	18:20
AW755	Kaohsiung Airport	New York	11:30	15:30 the next day
N220	Taoyuan Airport	Bangkok	19:00	22:30

 Hi, Martin. What time will you arrive?

I'll arrive at 3 p.m.

| 翻譯 |

班次	起程地	目的地	起飛時間	抵達時間
CX1000	桃園機場	雪梨	7:00	隔天 9:30
BR818	桃園機場	東京	10:30	15:00
NX963	高雄機場	首爾	14:00	18:20
AW755	高雄機場	紐約	11:30	隔天 15:30
N220	桃園機場	曼谷	19:00	22:30

 嗨，馬丁。你什麼時候抵達？

我會在下午 3 點時到。

| 詞彙 | flight [flaɪt]（飛機的）班次　airport [`ɛr͵port] 機場　Seoul [sol] 首爾（韓國首都）
departure time 起飛時間　arrival time 抵達時間

Q8 Sam is from Kaohsiung. He has to go to Korea on business trip next month. What flight should he take?
山姆是高雄人。他下個月必須到韓國出差。他應該坐哪一個航班？

A. BR818

B. AW755

C. NX963

D. None of the above　　以上皆非

| 詳解 | 既然是高雄人，山姆應該是從高雄機場搭飛機，所以答案鎖定 AW755 和 NX963，而其中 NX963 是去韓國的首都首爾，所以正確答案為選項 C。

| 詞彙 | **business trip** 差旅

Q9 Which city does Martin probably go? 馬丁可能會去哪個城市？

A. Sydney　　雪梨

B. Tokyo　　東京

C. New York　　紐約

D. Bangkok　　曼谷

| 詳解 | 這個題目要綜合兩篇文章來解題。題目問馬丁可能會去哪個城市，在第一篇文章中我們看不到任何有關馬丁的訊息，但是在時間表中，我們可以發現到飛機抵達東京的時間是 15:00，也就是下午三點。在第二篇文章，我們也可以從即時通訊軟體的對話中找到馬丁抵達的時間是下午三點。結合這兩個線索，可以推斷出馬丁所去的城市就是東京，所以正確答案為選項 B。

| 詞彙 | **probably** [`prɑbəblɪ] 可能地

Q10 What time will you get to New York if you take the flight on June 4th?
如果你搭乘六月四日的班機到紐約，你何時會到達？

A. Half past 3 in the afternoon　　下午 3:30

B. Half past 11 the next day　　隔天 11:30

C. A quarter after 3 on June 5th　　六月五日 3:15

D. Half past 3 in the afternoon on June 5th　　六月五日下午 3:30

| 詳解 | 本題針對班機時刻表的部分找答案即可。首先，在目的地為 New YorK 的這一行可以看到抵達時間是「15:30 the next day」，而題目指明要搭「六月四日的班機」，所以抵達時間是六月五日的下午 3:30，正確答案為選項 D。

Part 1 詞彙

1. _____, we'll go hiking this Saturday.
   A. If it rains　　　　　　　　　C. No matter rains
   B. Whether it rains or not　　　D. Though it will be raining

2. Your car might be _____ away if you parked it illegally.
   A. drawn　　　　　　　　　C. caught
   B. denied　　　　　　　　　D. arrested

Part 2 段落填空

Chris decided _(3)_ to work because there was heavy traffic. He spent too much time _(4)_ to move. And when he got to the office, he _(5)_ find a parking space. Afterwards Chris went to work by the MRT. It is very comfortable for him to _(6)_ in the clean, quiet and air-conditioned cars. Most important of all, _(7)_ .

3. A. not driving
   B. not to drive
   C. to not drive
   D. to drive not

4. A. waiting
   B. to wait
   C. waited
   D. and waited

5. A. couldn't hardly
   B. hardly couldn't
   C. hardly could
   D. could hardly

6. A. take
   B. ride
   C. drive
   D. walk

7. A. there are no more traffic jams
   B. there are no more traffic accidents
   C. Chris can buy a whole new car
   D. Chris can go home more quickly and smoothly

> Welcome to the WaterLand!
>
> Opening Hours: 9:00~18:00 (Closed on Monday)
>
> Ticket Office Hours: 8:30~16:00
>
> Adults: $560 | Students: $280
>
> Children Aged Twelve and Under: $150
>
> Parking: $20 per hour

Shows	Time
Live Band	13:00~15:00; 16:00~18:00
Dolphin Show	10:30~11:30; 13:30~14:30; 16:30~17:30
3D Cartoon show	9:30~10:00; 12:30~13:00; 14:30~15:00

8. Jenny went to the WaterLand at about 9 in the morning and left at noon. What event did she miss?

   A. Dolphin Show   C. Live Band

   B. 3D Performance   D. She didn't miss any of them.

9. Mr. and Mrs. Chen, together with their two seven-year-old daughters drove to the WaterLand. They stayed for three hours. How much did they spend?

   A. $1420   C. $1330

   B. $1480   D. $1740

10. If someone wants to see the last Dolphin Show, what is the latest time they have to get tickets?

    A. Half past 4:00 in the afternoon   C. Before 4:00 P.M.

    B. One thirty in the afternoon   D. Nine o'clock in the morning

Day 01
Day 02
Day 03
Day 04
Day 05
Day 06
Day 07

Part 1 詞彙

Q1 考題重點〉副詞子句的正確使用

_____, we'll go hiking this Saturday.

A. If it rains   C. No matter rains

B. Whether it rains or not   D. Though it will be raining

| 翻譯 | 無論是否下雨，我們這星期六都會去健行。

| 詳解 | 選項 A 無文法錯誤，但是下雨反而去健行不合常理邏輯，故不選。選項 C 少了主詞，所以不符。選項 D 的未來進行式 will be raining 必須有一個未來的時間點，所以錯誤，應改成 will rain。所以本題正確答案為選項 B。

| 詞彙 | hiking [`haɪkɪŋ] 健行，徒步旅行

Q2 考題重點〉填入符合邏輯的動詞

2. Your car might be _____ away if you parked it illegally.

A. drawn   B. denied   C. caught   D. arrested

| 翻譯 | 如果你違規停車，你的車可能會被吊走。

| 詳解 | 句意是「違法停車的話，車子會被拖走」，即使不懂句尾 illegally 的意思，僅以 Your car might be... away 這句來看，也只是 be drawn away 符合邏輯，所以答案為選項 A。

| 詞彙 | draw [drɔ] 拉，拖   illegally [ɪ`ligəlɪ] 非法地

Part 2 段落填空

Chris decided **(3) not to drive** to work because there was heavy traffic. He spent too much time **(4) waiting** to move. And when he got to the office, he **(5) could hardly** find a parking space. Afterwards Chris went to work by the MRT. It is very comfortable for him to **(6) ride** in the clean, quiet and air-conditioned cars. Most important of all, **(7) there are no more traffic jams**.

| 翻譯 | 克里斯決定不開車上班了，因為交通太壅塞。他花費了太多時間等著前進。而當他到了辦公室，他又很難找到停車位。後來克里斯搭捷運上班。坐在乾淨、安靜又有冷氣的捷運車廂裡他覺得非常舒適。最重要的是，不會再有塞車問題了。

Day 01
Day 02
Day 03
Day 04
Day 05
Day 06
Day 07

Q3 考題重點〉decide + 否定不定詞（to-V）的用法

A. not driving　　**B. not to drive**　　C. to not drive　　D. to drive not

| 詳解 | 「決定…（做某事）」是 decide to-V，decide 後面要用不定詞（to-V）作為其受詞，而當這裡的 to-V 是否定意思時，not 要擺在 to 的前面，所以正確答案為選項 B。

Q4 考題重點〉「spend + 金錢／時間 + Ving」的句型

A. waiting　　B. to wait　　C. waited　　D. and waited

| 詳解 | 本題考點是 spend 這個動詞的慣用句型。及物動詞 spend 表示「花費」，後面的受詞可能是時間或金錢，然後接上去的「動作」就必須以「動詞 - ing」來表現，所以正確答案為選項 A。

Q5 考題重點〉否定副詞的用法

A. couldn't hardly　　　　　　C. hardly could

B. hardly couldn't　　　　　　**D. could hardly**

| 詳解 | 「否定副詞」hardly 表示「幾乎不」，本身就具有否定意味，所以不能再加上 not 了，與助動詞連用時，須放在 could 後面，所以正確答案是選項 D。

Q6 考題重點〉填入適當的動詞

A. take　　**B. ride**　　C. drive　　D. walk

| 詳解 | 空格要填入的這個動詞，判斷依據是句尾的 cars，而這裡的 cars 並非「汽車」，而是捷運的「車廂」或「有軌電車」（即「捷運」）。ride 也有「搭乘」的意思，句型是「ride in the +『可在內走動的交通工具』」，所以正確答案是選項 B。

Q7 考題重點〉填入符合文意的句子

A. there are no more traffic jams　　不會再有塞車問題

B. there are no more traffic accidents　　不會再有交通意外了

C. Chris can buy a whole new car　　克里斯可以買一輛全新的車子

D. Chris can go home more quickly and smoothly
　　克里斯可以更快且更順利地回到家

| 詳解 | 因為短文前面提到塞車的情形，克里斯後來選擇坐捷運上班也是為了避開此情況，所以最後一句總結時，要表達的就是「不會再有塞車的問題」，正確答案為選項 A。

Welcome to the WaterLand!

Opening Hours: 9:00~18:00 (Closed on Monday)

Ticket Office Hours: 8:30~16:00

Adults: $560 | Students: $280

Children Aged Twelve and Under: $150

Parking: $20 per hour

Shows	Time
Live Band	13:00~15:00; 16:00~18:00
Dolphin Show	10:30~11:30; 13:30~14:30; 16:30~17:30
3D Cartoon Show	9:30~10:00; 12:30~13:00; 14:30~15:00

| 翻譯 |

歡迎來到水上樂園！

開放時間：9:00~18:00（星期一休息）

售票時間：8:30~16:00

成人票價：$560 | 學生票價：$280

十二歲以下兒童票價：$150

停車費：每小時$20

表演節目	演出時間
現場演唱	13:00~15:00; 16:00~18:00
海豚秀	10:30~11:30; 13:30~14:30; 16:30~17:30
3D 動畫	9:30~10:00; 12:30~13:00; 14:30~15:00

| 詞彙 | **opening hour** 開放時間　**office hour** 上班時間　**live** [laɪv] 現場的，即時的　**band** [bænd] 樂團　**dolphin** [`dɑlfɪn] 海豚　**cartoon** [kar`tun] 卡通

Day 01
Day 02
Day 03
Day 04
Day 05
Day 06
Day 07

Q8 Jenny went to the WaterLand at about 9 in the morning and left at noon. What event did she miss?

珍妮大約在早上九點到水上樂園，並在中午離開。她錯過了什麼表演？

A. Dolphin Show　　海豚秀

B. 3D Cartoon Show　　3D 動畫

C. Live Band　　現場樂團演唱

D. She didn't miss any of them.　　她沒有錯過任何演出。

| 詳解 | 直接看第二篇的行程表。因為珍妮中午就離開水上樂園，所以下午的表演沒辦法觀看，而其中現場樂團演唱只有在下午一點後才有表演，故本題正確答案為選項 C。

| 詞彙 | miss [mɪs] 錯過

Q9 Mr. and Mrs. Chen, together with their two seven-year-old daughters drove to the WaterLand. They stayed for three hours. How much did they spend?

陳先生跟陳太太跟他們兩個七歲的女兒開車到水上樂園。他們逗留了三小時。他們總共花了多少錢？

A. $1420　　　　**B. $1480**　　　　C. $1330　　　　D. $1740

| 詳解 | 直接看第一篇文章的公告。票價：2 大人加 2 小孩 =（560 x 2）+（150 x 2）=1420。停車費：20 x 3 = 60。總共：1480，所以正確答案為選項 B。

| 詞彙 | together with 還有，連同…

Q10 If someone wants to see the last Dolphin Show, what is the latest time they have to get tickets?

如果想看最後一場的海豚秀，最晚必須買票的時間是什麼時候？

A. Half past 4:00 in the afternoon　　下午 4:30

B. One thirty in the afternoon　　下午 1:30

C. Before 4:00 P.M.　　下午 4 點前

D. Nine o'clock in the morning　　早上 9 點

| 詳解 | 這個題目要綜合兩篇文章來解題。首先，題目問的是看最後一場海豚秀最晚買票的時間，在第二個文本中我們可以看到最後一場海豚秀是 16:30～17:30，但是在第一個文本的水上樂園的公告中，可以發現賣票最晚到 16:00，也就是說不能在海豚秀的最後一場開始的時間才買票，而是要提前到 16:00 買票進場，所以正確答案為選項 C。

| 詞彙 | latest [`letɪst] 最晚的，最近的

Part 1 詞彙

1. My car needs _____. Can you help?

   A. wash

   B. to wash

   C. washing

   D. washed

2. I can't _____ you well. Could you speak slowly?

   A. hear

   B. listen to

   C. sound

   D. listen

Part 2 段落填空

If you are an adult and rent an apartment outside, you can lead _(3)_ life and _(4)_ . _(5)_ , if you are still living with them at home, you may need to be mindful _(6)_ your parents' views and feelings _(7)_ in their house.

3. A. you

   B. yours

   C. yourself

   D. your own

4. A. rely on your parents for every decision

   B. ask for a lot of money from your parents

   C. your parents should respect your privacy

   D. your parents need not take care of you

5. A. However

   B. Therefore

   C. Indeed

   D. After all

6. A. in

   B. of

   C. with

   D. at

7. A. while

   B. like

   C. before

   D. be

Online Shopping Survey of Single Women Aged 25-30					
item \ frequency	seldom	daily	weekly	monthly	within half an year
food/drinks		99%	1%		
clothes/shoes			35%	60%	5%
books/magazines	1%	3%	39%	52%	5%
sports items	10%		3%	10%	77%
cosmetics	4%		5%	35%	56%
jewelry/luxury goods	20%		2%	20%	58%
household appliances	38%		2%	25%	35%

 I just bought a good lipstick online. It was on sale!

Really, Jessica? Send me the website address and I'll check it out.

8. Who could be the target of this survey?

    A. University female students

    B. Married women aged over 30

    C. Unmarried women aged 25-30

    D. Women whose annual income is over NT$1 million

9. How often is Jessica most likely to buy lipsticks?

    A. Every day

    B. Every week

    C. Every month

    D. Every 5 months

10. Which item do most single women aged 25-30 seldom buy?

    A. cosmetics

    B. sports items

    C. jewelry/luxury goods

    D. household appliances

Part 1　詞彙

Q1　考題重點〉need 後面接 Ving 表示被動

My car needs _____. Can you help?

A. wash

C. washing

B. to wash

D. washed

| 翻譯 | 我的車得洗一下了。你可以幫忙嗎？

| 詳解 | need 後面如果接動名詞，表示「被動」，因為車子是「被洗」，所以正確答案為選項 C。need washing = need to be washed。

| 詞彙 | **wash** [wɑʃ] 洗

Q2　考題重點〉表示「聽」的動詞用法

I can't _____ you well. Could you speak slowly?

A. hear

C. sound

B. listen to

D. listen

| 翻譯 | 我聽不清楚你說的話。你可以說慢一點嗎？

| 詳解 | 「hear + 人」是「聽見某人說的話」的意思，最符合句意，所以正確答案為選項 A。listen to 後面要接「正在聽的東西」，如 music、radio、podcast…等；而「soud（聽起來）」是感官動詞，後面不能直接接受詞，且其主詞通常為「事物」，所以錯誤。

| 詞彙 | **listen to** 聆聽　**slowly** [`slolɪ] 緩慢地

Part 2　段落填空

If you are an adult, you can lead **(3) your own** life and **(4) your parents might respect your privacy**. **(5) However**, if you are still living with them at home, you may need to be mindful **(6) of** your parents' views and feelings **(7) while** in their house.

| 翻譯 | 如果你是個成年人，你能夠過著自己的生活，且你的父母就應該尊重你的隱私。然而，如果你仍然和他們住家裡，那在家裡的時候，就得在乎你父母的意見。

Day 01
Day 02
Day 03
Day 04
Day 05
Day 06
Day 07

Q3 考題重點〉名詞前面經常放形容詞

A. you   C. yourself

B. yours   **D. your own**

| 詳解 | 空格後面是名詞 life（生活），前面是 lead，lead... life 表示「過著⋯的生活」，應填入一個形容詞，所以正確答案是 D。own 當形容詞，表示「自己的」。人稱代名詞的 you、反身代名詞 yourself 以及所有格代名詞 yours 皆不符文法規則。

Q4 考題重點〉填入符合前後文意的句子

A. rely on your parents for every decision   每一次的決定都依賴你的父母

B. ask for a lot of money from your parents   跟你的父母要很多錢來花用

C. your parents might respect your privacy   你的父母可能會尊重你的隱私

D. your parents need not take care of you   你的父母不必照顧你

| 詳解 | 連接詞 and 前面提到成年人可以過著自己的生活，且父母可能比較會「尊重隱私（respect one's privacy）」是最適當的說法，答案為 C。其餘選項內容皆前後矛盾或不符句意。

Q5 考題重點〉填入符合文意的連接副詞

A. However   C. Indeed

B. Therefore   D. A.ter all

| 詳解 | 前面提到過著自己的生活以及個人隱私，空格後面是「if you are still living... respect your parents' views...」，顯然前後語意相反，所以正確答案是 A。其餘 Therefore（因此）、Indeed（的確）、After all（畢竟）皆不符語境。

Q6 考題重點〉填入適當的介系詞

A. in   C. with

B. of   D. at

| 詳解 | mindful 是「在意的，介意的」意思，常見於 be mindful of sb./sth.（在意，顧慮到⋯）的用法中，為固定用語，故正確答案為選項 B。

Q7 考題重點〉連接詞前後主詞相同的省略用法

A. while   B. like   C. before   D. be

| 詳解 | 空格前是個完整句子，後面是個介系詞片語，且依句意是「住在家裡時就得在乎父母的意見」，故應填入後面省略 you are (living) 的連接詞 while，答案是選項 A。

Online Shopping Survey of Single Women Aged 25-30					
item \ frequency	seldom	daily	weekly	monthly	within half an year
food/drinks		99%	1%		
clothes/shoes			35%	60%	5%
books/magazines	1%	3%	39%	52%	5%
sports items	10%		3%	10%	77%
cosmetics	4%		5%	35%	56%
jewelry/luxury goods	20%		2%	20%	58%
household appliances	38%		2%	25%	35%

 I just bought a good lipstick online. It was on sale!

Really, Jessica? Send me the website address and I'll check it out.

| 翻譯 |

25-30 歲單身女性的網路購物調查					
項目 \ 頻率	很少會	每天	每週	每個月	每半年內
衣服／鞋子			35%	60%	5%
書本／雜誌	1%	3%	39%	52%	5%
運動用品	10%		3%	10%	77%
化妝品	7%		5%	35%	53%
珠寶／奢侈品	20%		2%	20%	58%
家電用品	38%		2%	25%	35%

 嗨，潔西卡！我剛在網路買了一支很棒的口紅。正在特價呢！

真的嗎？把網址傳給我，我看一下。

| 詞彙 | **survey** [ˋsɝˌve] 調查　**single** [ˋsɪŋɡl] 單身的　**frequency** [ˋfrikwənsɪ] 頻率
cosmetics [kɑzˋmɛtɪks] 化妝品　**jewelry** [ˋdʒuəlrɪ] 珠寶　**luxury** [ˋlʌkʃərɪ] 奢侈，豪華
household [ˋhaʊsˌhold] 家庭的，家用的　**appliance** [əˋplaɪəns] 電器

Day 01

Day 02

Day 03

Day 04

Day 05

Day 06

Day 07

Q8 Who could be the target of this survey?
以下何者可能是這項調查的對象？

A. University female students　大學女生

B. Married women aged over 30　30 歲以上的已婚婦女

C. Unmarried women aged 25-30　25 到 30 歲的未婚女性

D. Women whose annual income is over NT$1 million　年薪百萬以上的女性

| 詳解 | 從表格上方的標題「Online Shopping Survey of Single Women Aged 25-30」可知，對象就是 single women aged 25-30（25-30 歲單身女性），所以正確答案為選項 C。

| 詞彙 | **target** [ˈtɑrgɪt] 目標　**annual** [ˈænjʊəl] 每年的　**income** [ˈɪnˌkʌm] 收入

Q9 How often is Jessica most likely to buy lipsticks?
潔西卡最有可能多久買一次口紅？

A. Every day　每天

B. Every week　每個星期

C. Every month　每個月

D. Every 5 months　每五個月

| 詳解 | 這個題目要綜合兩篇文章來解題。首先，從對話中可以知道第一位說話者（Jessica）表示剛買了一支口紅，再來從表格中找到口紅（lipstick）是屬於化妝品（cosmetics）的項目，最高比率是選「每半年內」的有 53%（表示「最有可能」），所以正確答案是選項 D。

| 詞彙 | **how often** 多久一次　**lipstick** [ˈlɪpˌstɪk] 口紅

Q10 Which item do most single women aged 25-30 seldom buy?
哪一個項目是最多 25 至 30 歲單身女性幾乎不會買的？

A. cosmetics　化妝品

B. sports items　運動用品

C. jewelry/luxury goods　珠寶／奢侈品

D. household appliances　家電用品

| 詳解 | 本題關鍵字是 seldom，對照表格中 seldom 這欄下方的最高比率的是 38%，也就是說，家電用品是這個年齡層女性很少會去購買的東西，正確答案是選項 D。

| 詞彙 | **seldom** [ˈsɛldəm] 很少，幾乎不

Part 1 詞彙

1. He is six years old and is going to _____ this September.

   A. university
   B. elementary school
   C. kindergarten
   D. high school

2. Can you help me _____ the address of the new restaurant on the internet?

   A. turn on
   B. look forward to
   C. look up
   D. take care of

Part 2 段落填空

Last Saturday, I went to the (3) with my friends. (4) The menu had a variety of options, and I finally chose the expensive pasta, (5) was delicious. After (6) our meals, we walked to the nearby park (7) a music show.

3. A. cinema
   B. beach
   C. library
   D. museum

4. A. I woke up very early and brushed my teeth then.
   B. We decided to order some delicious food from a local restaurant.
   C. We practiced playing the piano for hours while it rained hard outside.
   D. On our way to the restaurant, all of us had felt very hungry.

5. A. that
   B. who
   C. which
   D. when

6. A. finishing
   B. finished
   C. to finish
   D. finish

7. A. enjoy
   B. enjoyed
   C. enjoying
   D. to enjoy

Day 01
Day 02
Day 03
Day 04
Day 05
Day 06
Day 07

Part 3 閱讀理解

Train Schedule			
Train	Departure	Destination	Arrival
Train 101	08:00 AM	Taichung	10:30 AM
Train 102	11:15 AM	Taichung	01:45 PM
Train 103	02:30 PM	Kaohsiung	06:30 PM
Train 104	06:45 PM	Kaohsiung	10:45 PM
Train 105	08:00 PM	Tainan	11:00 PM

 What time should we meet at the train station?

Let's aim to meet there by 2:00 PM so that we have some time to grab snacks before boarding.

8. According to the train schedule, which train are the speakers planning to take?
   A. Train 101
   B. Train 102
   C. Train 103
   D. Train 104

9. What will they do before getting on the train?
   A. take a walk near the train station
   B. buy something to eat
   C. meet a close friend
   D. grab some breakfast

10. How long does it take for them to arrive at their destination?
    A. 2.5 hours
    B. 3 hours
    C. 3.5 hours
    D. 4 hours

Part 1 詞彙

Q1 考題重點〉選擇正確的詞彙

He is six years old and is going to _____ this September.

A. university   C. kindergarten

B. elementary school   D. high school

| 翻譯 | 他六歲了，而且九月的時候將要去上小學。

| 詳解 | 雖然「六歲上小學」算是常識，但本題考的是對於單字本身的認知與否。只要知道 elementary school 是「小學」的意思就能選出正確答案的選項 B。另外，「小學」的另一種說法是 primary school。

| 詞彙 | **elementary** [ˌɛlɪˈmɛntrɪ] 初級的，基本的   **kindergarten** [ˈkɪndəˌɡɑrtn] 幼稚園
high school 高中

Q2 考題重點〉選擇正確的動詞片語

Can you help me _____ the address of the new restaurant on the internet?

A. turn on   B. look forward to   **C. look up**   D. take care of

| 翻譯 | 你能幫我在網上查找新餐廳的地址嗎？

| 詳解 | 這個句子要選擇一個合適的動詞片語，使句子結構通順且符合語境，因此只有 look up（查找）符合句意，故正確答案是選項 C。

| 詞彙 | **turn on** 開啟   **look forward to** 期望   **take care of** 照顧，處理

Part 2 段落填空

Last Saturday, I went to the **(3) beach** with my friends. **(4) We decided to order some delicious food from a local restaurant.** The menu had a variety of options, and I finally chose the expensive pasta, **(5) which** was delicious. After **(6) finishing** our meals, we walked to the nearby park **(7) to enjoy** a music show.

| 翻譯 | 上星期六，我和朋友一起去海灘玩。我們決定從當地一家餐廳點一些美味的食物。菜單上有各種選擇，最後我選擇了昂貴的義大利麵，味道非常棒。用餐結束後，我們走到附近的公園去欣賞一場音樂表演。

Q3 考題重點〉選擇符合文意的名詞

A. cinema   **B. beach**   C. library   D. museum

| 詳解 | 4 個選項都是與「地方」有關的名詞，後面提到在這個地方吃著美味的義大利麵，所以正確答案應為選項 B，其他選項的地方一般都是禁止食物的。

Q4 考題重點〉填入符合語境的句子

A. I woke up very early and brushed my teeth then.
我很早就醒來，然後刷了牙。

B. We decided to order some delicious food from a local restaurant.
我們決定從一家當地餐廳訂一些美味的食物。

C. We practiced playing the piano for hours while it rained hard outside.
我們花了好幾個小時練習彈鋼琴，當時外面下著大雨。

D. On our way to the restaurant, all of us had felt very hungry.
在去餐廳的路上，我們都感到非常餓。

| 詳解 | 空格後面提到「菜單上有各種選擇，最後我選擇了⋯」，顯然空格句子應與在餐廳點餐有關，所以正確答案為選項 B。

Q5 考題重點〉關係代名詞的用法

A. that   B. who   **C. which**   D. when

| 詳解 | 空格後面非完整句，要填入的是關係代名詞，且前有逗號，先行詞是物（pasta），故應選代替物的 which，正確答案為選項 C。that 當關係代名詞時，前面不能有逗號。

Q6 考題重點〉分詞的用法

A. finishing   B. finished   C. to finish   D. finish

| 詳解 | 「After _____ our meal」這部分是簡化副詞子句的分詞構句，而「吃完餐點」是「主動」，所以要選表主動的現在分詞 finishing，正確答案為選項 A。

Q7 考題重點〉表示目的的不定詞（to-V）

A. enjoy   B. enjoyed   C. enjoying   **D. to enjoy**

| 詳解 | 空格前的句意是「走去附近公園」，空格後是「欣賞一場音樂表演」，顯然後者是前者的「目的」，應以不定詞（to-V）表示，故正確答案是選項 D。

Day 01
Day 02
Day 03
Day 04
Day 05
Day 06
Day 07

Part 3 閱讀理解

Train Schedule			
Train	Departure	Destination	Arrival
Train 101	08:00 AM	Taichung	10:30 AM
Train 102	11:15 AM	Taichung	01:45 PM
Train 103	02:30 PM	Kaohsiung	06:30 PM
Train 104	06:45 PM	Kaohsiung	10:45 PM
Train 105	08:00 PM	Tainan	11:00 PM

 What time should we meet at the train station?

Let's aim to meet there by 2:00 PM so that we have some time to grab snacks before boarding.

| 翻譯 |

火車時刻表			
列車編號	出發	目的地	抵達
101 號列車	08:00 AM	台中	10:30 AM
102 號列車	11:15 AM	台中	01:45 PM
103 號列車	02:30 PM	高雄	06:30 PM
104 號列車	06:45 PM	高雄	10:45 PM
105 號列車	08:00 PM	台南	11:00 PM

 我們要約幾點在火車站碰面？

我們約下午兩點在那見，這樣我們上車前還有一點時間買些零食吃。

| 詞彙 | **train schedule** 火車時刻表 　**departure** [dɪˈpɑrtʃɚ] 出發 　**arrival** [əˈraɪvəl] 抵達 **destination** [ˌdɛstəˈneʃən] 目的地 　**aim to** 致力於，設法要 　**grab** [græb] 攫取，抓取 **snack** [snæk] 點心 　**board** [bɔrd] 登上（車、船、飛機等）

Day 01
Day 02
Day 03
Day 04
Day 05
Day 06
Day 07

Q8 According to the train schedule, which train are the speakers planning to take?
根據火車時刻表，說話者們預計要搭乘哪一班火車？

A. Train 101　　101 號列車

B. Train 102　　102 號列車

C. Train 103　　103 號列車

D. Train 104　　104 號列車

| 詳解 | 這個題目要綜合兩篇文章來解題。首先，第二位說話者提到，他們要約下午兩點在火車站，如此還有一些時間買吃的東西。然後對照第一個文本的火車時刻表可知，他們應搭乘下午 2:30 的 Train 103，所以正確答案是選項 C。

| 詞彙 | according to 根據

Q9 What will they do before getting on the train?
他們在上火車之前會做什麼？

A. take a walk near the train station　　在火車站附近散步

B. buy something to eat　　買點吃的東西

C. meet a close friend　　與一位好友碰面

D. grab some breakfast　　吃點早餐

| 詳解 | 第二位說話者提到 grab snacks before boarding（在上車前買些零食吃），所以正確答案是選項 B。選項 D 刻意用對話中的 grab 來誘答，但那個時間點說吃早餐當然是不合理的。

| 詞彙 | get on 上（車）　　close [klos] 親近的

Q10 How long does it take for them to arrive at their destination?
他們要坐多久的火車抵達他們的目的地？

A. 2.5 hours　　兩個半小時

B. 3 hours　　三個小時

C. 3.5 hours　　三個半小時

D. 4 hours　　四個小時

| 詳解 | 承 Q8，我們知道他們搭乘 103 號列車，出發（departure）時間是 2:30 PM，抵達（arrival）的時間是 6:30 PM，所以正確答案是選項 D。

| 詞彙 | arrive at... 抵達…

Part 1 詞彙

1. This is the ＿＿＿＿＿＿＿＿＿ book I have ever read.

    A. interesting
    B. more interesting
    C. most interesting
    D. interested

2. It's almost ＿＿＿＿＿＿＿＿ to rent an apartment under NT$10,000 in Taipei.

    A. important
    B. impossible
    C. impolite
    D. instant

Part 2 段落填空

In our neighborhood, the local park is a popular __(3)__ for families. Children play games on the wide green lawn, and the playground facilities are __(4)__ maintained than those in the neighboring town. Recently, there is a new rule: shoes must be __(5)__ off before entering the playground area. This rule aims to keep the play area __(6)__ . There are also signs reminding visitors to follow this rule __(7)__ .

3. A. desert
    B. habit
    C. machine
    D. spot

4. A. well
    B. badly
    C. better
    D. best

5. A. taking
    B. taken
    C. took
    D. take

6. A. cleaner
    B. cleaning
    C. to clean
    D. cleaned

7. A. after playing there to their hearts' content
    B. before starting a delicious babecue there
    C. while enjoying their time outdoors
    D. or else the playground area will be closed earlier

Single Room for Rent

- Close to bus/MRT station and supermarket

- Independent bathroom

- Furniture included

- No pets allowed

- At least 1 year period to rent

- Monthly rent: NT$15,000

Call owner: 0988-384-968

 David, what makes you decide to rent that single room?

Well, I just want to enjoy the complete privacy and comfort.

8. What is NOT mentioned as part of the rental ad?

A. The location is convenient.

B. Furniture is provided.

C. You can raise a cat.

D. The minimum rental period is one year.

9. According to the dialogue, what's the primary reason David decides to rent this room?

A. The location is convenient.

B. It has an independent room.

C. It provides some furniture.

D. Its rent is very cheap.

10. How should those interested contact the landlord?

A. by phone

B. by email

C. by text messaging

D. by fax

解答與詳解

Part 1 詞彙

Q1 考題重點〉形容詞最高級的用法

This is the _____ book I have ever read.

A. interesting　　　　　　　　**C. most interesting**

B. more interesting　　　　　　D. interested

| 翻譯 | 這是我讀過最有趣的書。

| 詳解 | book 後面的形容詞子句是 I have ever read（我曾經讀過的），所以必須搭配形容詞最高級來修飾 book，正確答案是選項 C。過去分詞 interested 用來形容「人」，而非事物。

| 詞彙 | **interesting** [`ɪntərɪstɪŋ] 有趣的

Q2 考題重點〉選擇符合句意的形容詞

It's almost _____ to rent an apartment under NT$10,000 in Taipei.

A. important　　**B. impossible**　　C. impolite　　　D. instant

| 翻譯 | 要在台北租到一萬元以下的公寓幾乎是不可能的。

| 詳解 | 這個句子要選擇一個符合句意的形容詞，使句意通順並符合邏輯，因此只有 impossible（不可能的）符合句意，故正確答案是選項 B。

| 詞彙 | **impolite** [͵ɪmpə`laɪt] 不禮貌的　　**instant** [`ɪnstənt] 即刻的

Part 2 段落填空

In our neighborhood, the local park is a popular **(3) spot** for families. Children play games on the wide green lawn, and the playground facilities are **(4) better** maintained than those in the neighboring town. Recently, there is a new rule: shoes must be **(5) taken** off before entering the playground area. This rule aims to keep the play area **(6) cleaner**. There are also signs reminding visitors to follow this rule **(7) while enjoying their time outdoors**.

| 翻譯 | 在我們的社區中，當地這個公園是家庭休閒的熱門場所。孩子們在寬闊的草坪上玩遊戲，而遊樂設施的維護比鄰近城鎮的更佳。最近，有一項新規定：進入遊樂區前必須脫鞋。這項規定的目的是為了保持遊樂區更清潔。也有告示牌提醒遊客在戶外遊樂時要遵守這個規定。

Day 01
Day 02
Day 03
Day 04
Day 05
Day 06
Day 07

Q3 考題重點〉選擇符合文意的名詞

A. desert

B. habit

C. machine

D. spot

│ 詳解 │ 空格所在句子主詞是 park，是個地方，動詞是 is，所以主詞補語也應是與地方有關的名詞，所以正確答案應為選項 D。

Q4 考題重點〉比較級的關鍵字 than

A. well

B. badly

C. better

D. best

│ 詳解 │ 空格後面有 than，且句意是「遊樂設施的維護比鄰近城鎮的更佳」，所以正確答案為選項 C。

Q5 考題重點〉語態的選擇

A. taking

B. taken

C. took

D. take

│ 詳解 │ 鞋子是被人脫掉，要用被動式（be 動詞 + 過去分詞），所以正確答案為選項 B。take → took → taken。

Q6 考題重點〉keep 的用法

A. cleaner

B. cleaning

C. to clean

D. cleaned

│ 詳解 │ keep 這個動詞用來表示「保持…（某人事物處於某種狀態）」時，句型為「keep + O. + adj.」，而句意是「保持遊樂區更清潔」，所以正確答案為選項 A。cleaned 雖然可視為過去分詞當形容詞，但句子會變成「保持遊樂區被清掃」的奇怪語意。

Q7 考題重點〉選擇符合前後文的句子

A. after playing there to their hearts' content　在那裡盡情玩樂之後

B. before starting a delicious babecue there　在那裡開始美味的燒烤之前

C. while enjoying their time outdoors　當他們在戶外遊樂時

D. or else the playground area will be closed earlier　否則遊樂區會提早關閉

│ 詳解 │ 前面提到告示牌提醒遊客要遵守規定，也就是說，提醒遊客在戶外這個遊樂區玩時要遵守規定，故正確答案是選項 C。

Single Room for Rent

- Close to bus/MRT station and supermarket
- Independent bathroom
- Furniture included
- No pets allowed
- At least 1 year period to rent
- Monthly rent: NT$15,000

Call owner: 0988-384-968

 David, what makes you decide to rent that single room?

Well, I just want to enjoy the complete privacy and comfort.

| 翻譯 |

單人房出租

- 近公車／捷運站及超市
- 獨立衛浴
- 含傢俱
- 禁止養寵物
- 最短租期 1 年
- 月租：NT$15,000

來電：0988-384-968

 大衛，什麼原因讓你決定租下那間單人房呢？

嗯，我只是想要享受完整的隱私及舒適感。

| 詞彙 | **single** [ˈsɪŋgl̩] 單一的，單身的　**rent** [rɛnt] 租金，租用　**(be) close to** 靠近，接近　**independent** [ˌɪndɪˈpɛndənt] 獨立的，自主的　**furniture** [ˈfɝnətʃɚ] 家具

include [ɪnˈklud] 包括，包含　allow [əˈlaʊ] 允許，准許

Q8 What is NOT mentioned as part of the rental ad?
以下何者是出租廣告中未提及的？

A. The location is convenient.　地點便利

B. Furniture is provided.　提供家具

C. You can raise a cat.　可以養貓。

D. The minimum rental period is one year.　最短租期是一年。

| 詳解 | 從這張出租廣告內容中的 No pets allowed 可以得知不能養寵物，所以正確答案是選項 C。

| 詞彙 | mention [ˈmɛnʃən] 提及　rental [ˈrɛntl] 租賃的　provide [prəˈvaɪd] 提供
minimum [ˈmɪnəməm] 最小的

Q9 According to the dialogue, what's the primary reason David decides to rent this room?
根據對話內容，大衛決定要租下這房間的主因為何？

A. The location is convenient.　地點便利。

B. It has an independent room.　它擁有獨立衛浴。

C. It provides some furniture.　它提供一些家具。

D. Its rent is very cheap.　它的租金很便宜。

| 詳解 | 這個題目要綜合兩篇文章來解題。首先，在第二個文本的對話中，David 提到「I just want to enjoy the complete privacy...」，表示他相當重視個人的隱私。接著我們對照第一個文本的出租廣告，找尋與這一點有關的項目，那麼顯然「Independent bathroom」符合了他的要求，所以正確答案是選項 B。

| 詞彙 | primary [ˈpraɪˌmɛrɪ] 主要的

Q10 How should those interested contact the landlord?
有興趣承租者應如何聯繫房東？

A. by phone　以打電話的方式

B. by email　以電子郵件方式

C. by text messaging　以短訊傳送方式

D. by fax　以傳真方式

| 詳解 | 從第一個文本的廣告內容最下方的 Call owner: 0988-384-968 可知，正確答案是選項 A。

| 詞彙 | contact [ˈkɑntækt] 聯絡　landlord [ˈlændˌlɔrd] 房東

Part 1 詞彙

1. We can _____ eat now or later - it's up to you.

   A. not

   B. either

   C. neither

   D. only

2. I'm required _____ a uniform to school every day.

   A. wear

   B. wearing

   C. to wear

   D. and wear

Part 2 段落填空

Listening to music is a wonderful way __(3)__ happier and relax. __(4)__ you're feeling happy or sad, music can bring comfort and joy to your day. Some people enjoy listening to their favorite songs __(5)__ , finding a sense of comfort in familiar melodies. __(6)__ , discovering fresh beats and rhythms. No matter how you choose to enjoy music, it's a _ __(7)__ language that can calm the spirit and bring people together.

3. A. to feel

   B. feeling

   C. to feeling

   D. felt

4. A. When

   B. Whether

   C. How

   D. No matter

5. A. now and then

   B. here and there

   C. again and again

   D. up and down

6. A. Many people don't have the habit of listening to music

   B. Some youngsters think music is kind of an art

   C. Some are not interested in country music

   D. Others prefer to explore new music genres

7. A. dangerous

   B. general

   C. famous

   D. national

Part **3** 閱讀理解

https://super_college.org/guitar club/welcome

Join Guitar Club!

Love playing guitar or want to learn? Join our club!
Daily activities for all levels.
Meet fellow music lovers, play together, and improve your skills.
Fun guaranteed!
Sign up now for a musical journey at https://super_college.org/guitar club/registration. Don't miss out!

Hotline for inquiry: 0958-886-688
LINE: @clubs_guitar
FB: SUPER's Guitar

 Good Morning, Mary. Did you see the website I sent you yesterday?

Yes, I did think it would be awesome to make some friends who love music. But do you think they will welcome beginners?

8　What is the main purpose of the Guitar Club mentioned in the ad?

　A. To organize a concert for all levels of guitar players

　B. To provide a platform for music enthusiasts to meet together

　C. To offer private guitar lessons for beginners

　D. To sell musical instruments online

9　How can someone find more information about signing up for the Guitar Club?

　A. By visiting a website　　　C. By making a phone call

　B. By adding this Club on LINE　　D. By adding this Club's Facebook

10　What can be a correct answer to Mary's question?

　A. Of course. The Club is primarily designed for beginners.

　B. Of course. The ad says "Daily activities for all levels."

　C. In fact, beginners need to take a small test first.

　D. I'm afraid not. Besides, the number of participants allowed is limited.

解答與詳解

1. (B) 2. (C) 3. (A) 4. (B) 5. (C)
6. (D) 7. (B) 8. (B) 9. (A) 10. (B)

Part 1 詞彙

Q1 考題重點〉either... or 的用法

We can _____ eat now or later - it's up to you.

A. not   C. neither

B. either   D. only

| 翻譯 | 我們可以現在就吃，也可以等一下再吃 — 由你決定。

| 詳解 | 本題關鍵字是後面的連接詞 or，either... or... 是個對等連接詞，連接 now 和 later 兩個同性質的字彙，所以正確答案是選項 B。

| 詞彙 | **up to** 由…（某人）決定

Q2 考題重點〉動詞 require 的用法

I'm required _____ a uniform to school every day.

A. wear   **C. to wear**

B. wearing   D. and wear

| 翻譯 | 我被要求每天穿制服去上學。

| 詳解 | require 當「要求」時，是「不完全及物動詞」，接受詞之後必須接不定詞（to-V）作為「受詞補語」（OC），而改為被動式時，就變成 be required to-V 的用法，故正確答案是選項 C。

| 詞彙 | **require** [rɪˋkwaɪr] 要求　　**uniform** [ˋjunəˌfɔrm] 制服

Part 2 段落填空

Listening to music is a wonderful way **(3) to feel** happier and relax. **(4) Whether** you're feeling happy or sad, music can bring comfort and joy to your day. Some people enjoy listening to their favorite songs **(5) again and again**, finding a sense of comfort in familiar melodies. **(6) Others prefer to explore new music genres**, discovering fresh beats and rhythms. No matter how you choose to enjoy music, it's a **(7) general** language that can calm the spirit and bring people together.

Day 01
Day 02
Day 03
Day 04
Day 05
Day 06
Day 07

| 翻譯 | 聽音樂是提振精神和放鬆的好方法。無論你是感到開心還是傷心,音樂都能給你帶來舒適和快樂。有些人喜歡一次又一次地聽著他們最喜歡的歌曲,在熟悉的旋律中找到一種慰藉感。而有些人更喜歡探索新的音樂類型,發現新的節奏和節拍。無論你如何享受音樂,它都是一種可以撫慰靈魂並團結人心的普遍語言。

Q3 考題重點〉way to-V 表示「做…的方法」

A. to feel C. to feeling

B. feeling D. felt

| 詳解 | 空格前的 way 是關鍵字,且從四個選項來看,這題要考的是「way to-V」(做某事的方法),所以正確答案應為選項 A。

Q4 考題重點〉whether... or... 的用法

A. When C. How

B. Whether D. No matter

| 詳解 | 本題考的事是「無論是 A 或 B」(whether A or B)的句型,且句意是「無論感到開心還是傷心,音樂都能…」,所以正確答案為選項 B。

Q5 考題重點〉填入符合句意的副詞

A. now and then **C. again and again**

B. here and there D. up and down

| 詳解 | 句意是「喜歡一次又一次地聽著最喜歡的歌曲」,所以正確答案為選項 C。A 的意思是「偶爾」,B 的意思是「到處」,D 的意思是「上上下下」。

Q6 考題重點〉選擇符合前後文意的句子

A. Many people don't have the habit of listening to music
  許多人沒有聽音樂的習慣

B. Some youngsters think music is kind of an art
  許多年輕人認為音樂是一種藝術

C. Some are not interested in country music
  有些人對鄉村音樂沒有興趣

D. Others prefer to explore new music genres
  有些人更喜歡探索新的音樂類型

| 詳解 | 前一句提到「有些人喜歡一次又一次地聽著他們最喜歡的歌曲…」，後一句則是「在熟悉的旋律中找到一種慰藉感」，因此空格這句話應與另外有些人基於什麼原因聽音樂有關，因此正確答案為選項 D。

Q7 考題重點〉填入符合句意的形容詞

A. dangerous   **B. general**   C. famous   D. national

| 詳解 | 句意是「音樂是一種可以撫慰靈魂並團結人心的普遍語言」，所以正確答案為選項 B。A 的意思是「危險的」，C 的意思是「有名的」，D 的意思是「國家的」。

Part 3 閱讀理解

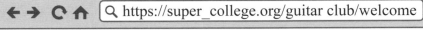

Q https://super_college.org/guitar club/welcome

Join Guitar Club!

Love playing guitar or want to learn? Join our club!
Daily activities for all levels.
Meet fellow music lovers, play together, and improve your skills.
Fun guaranteed!
Sign up now for a musical journey at https://super_college.org/guitar club/
registration. Don't miss out!

Hotline for inquiry: 0958-886-688
LINE: @clubs_guitar
FB: SUPER's Guitar

Good Morning, Mary. Did you see the website I sent you yesterday?

Yes, I did think it would be awesome to make some friends who love music. But do you think they will welcome beginners?

https://super_college.org/guitar club/welcome

加入吉他社吧！

熱愛彈吉他或想要學習彈吉他嗎？快來加入我們的社團吧！

為所有程度者提供每日的活動。

可以來結識音樂的愛好者，一起演奏，並提升你的技能。

保證樂趣十足！

快上 https://super_college.org/guitar club/registration 來報名參加一趟音樂之旅吧！別錯過了！

詢問熱線：0958-886-688

LINE：@clubs_guitar

臉書：SUPER's Guitar。

 早安，瑪莉。你看過昨天我傳給你的網站嗎？

有啊，我覺得能認識一些熱愛音樂的朋友會很棒。但你覺得他們會歡迎新手加入嗎？

| 詞彙 | club [klʌb] 俱樂部，社團　fellow ['fɛlo] 同伴的　improve [ɪm'pruv] 改善
guarantee [ˌgærən'ti] 保證，擔保　sign up for 報名參加；註冊　journey ['dʒɝnɪ] 旅程
miss out 錯過，遺漏　awesome ['ɔsəm] 極好的，了不起的
beginner [bɪ'gɪnɚ] 新手，入門者

Q8 What is the main purpose of the Guitar Club mentioned in the ad? 這篇吉他社宣傳廣告的主要目的為何？

A. To organize a concert for all levels of guitar players
為所有程度的吉他手主辦一場音樂會

B. To provide a platform for music enthusiasts to meet together
提供一個平台讓音樂愛好者聚在一起

C. To offer private guitar lessons for beginners　提供給初學者的私人吉他課程

D. To sell musical instruments online　在網路販售音樂器材

| 詳解 | 從標題底下第一句「Love playing guitar or want to learn? Join our club!」可知，這則廣告目的是提供一個平台讓音樂愛好者聚在一起，所以正確答案是選項 B。

| 詞彙 | concert [`kɑnsɚt] 音樂會　level [`lɛvl] 程度，等級　enthusiast [ɪn`θjuzɪˌæst] 熱衷者　instrument [`ɪnstrʊmənt] 樂器

Q9 How can someone find more information about signing up for the Guitar Club? 關於報名參加吉他社，應如何找到更多資訊？

A. By visiting a website　前往某個網站

B. By adding this Club on LINE　加入這個社團的 LINE

C. By making a phone call　打電話聯繫

D. By adding this Club's Facebook　加入這個社團的 FB

| 詳解 | 從第一個文本（社團廣告）中的「Sign up now for a musical journey at https://super_college.org/guitar club/registration」可知，要上該網站報名參加，所以正確答案是選項 A。

| 詞彙 | add... on LINE 將…加入 LINE 好友

Q10 What can be a correct answer to Mary's question? 對於瑪莉提出問題，哪個選項是正確的答案呢？

A Of course. The Club is primarily designed for beginners.
當然。這個社團是專為新手設計的。

B Of course. The ad says "Daily activities for all levels."
當然。廣告上寫著「每日提供適合各種程度的活動」。

C In fact, beginners need to take a small test first.
事實上，初學者需要先通過一項小測試。

D I'm afraid not. Besides, the number of participants allowed is limited.
恐怕不行。此外，允許的參加人數是有限制的。

| 詳解 | 這個題目要綜合兩篇文章來解題。首先，從第二個文本（對話）可知 Mary 提出的問題是「But do you think they will welcome beginners?」接著對照第一個文本（社團廣告）中的「Daily activities for all levels.」可知，該社團歡迎所有程度的人，當然也包括新手，所以正確答案是選項 B。

| 詞彙 | correct [kə`rɛkt] 正確的　design [dɪ`zaɪn] 設計　limit [`lɪmɪt] 限制

MEMO

Part 1 詞彙

1. My friends and I like to exercise together at the _____ after school.

   A. fence

   B. ocean

   C. gym

   D. rainbow

2. They have one book, but not have _____ notebooks.

   A. any

   B. no

   C. many

   D. some

Part 2 段落填空

I love my home. On weekends or holidays, I wake up and make __(3)__ a cup of coffee in the mornings. Then I tidy up and do some chores. Sometimes I may __(4)__ about not finishing all my tasks, but __(5)__ I start doing them, I feel better. In the evenings, __(6)__ . In short, I enjoy __(7)__ good time by myself at home.

3. A. you

   B. us

   C. myself

   D. me

4. A. worry

   B. know

   C. discover

   D. admire

5. A. as a result

   B. in no way

   C. no matter how

   D. as soon as

6. A. I like to have a cup of coffee with my best friend.

   B. I relax on the sofa with a book or watch TV

   C. I still need to be prepared for my work the next day

   D. I may go out shopping for a while

7. A. spending

   B. to spend

   C. to spending

   D. being spent

NOW HIRING! We NEED

3 restaurant waitress at Delicious Delights!

Related experience preferred.

Must be friendly, reliable, and able to work flexible shifts, including weekends and holidays.

Competitive pay starting at NT$180/hour plus tips.

Apply in person at Delicious Delights or email your resume to jobs@deliciousdelights.com.

Dear Hiring Manager,

I am writing to express my interest in the waitress position. I am always passionate about providing excellent customer service and willing to work for any changeable schedule. Though I haven't worked for any restaurant before, I am confident in my ability to learn quickly and adapt to new environments.

8. Which of the following is NOT a requirement for the waitress position at the restaurant?

    A. Friendly attitude

    B. Reliable behavior

    C. Able to work full time

    D. Willing to work on weekends or holidays

9. How can those interested apply for the position?

    A. By making a phone call

    B. By visiting the restaurant

    C. By filling out an application form on a website

    D. By mailing an application letter

10. For what reason might the email writer be turned down?

    A. He can't work flexible hours.

    B. He lives too far away from the restaurant.

    C. He does not have work experience in customer service.

    D. He lacks in related experience.

解答與詳解 | 上頁簡答

1. (C) 2. (A) 3. (C) 4. (A) 5. (D)
6. (B) 7. (A) 8. (C) 9. (B) 10. (D)

Part 1 詞彙

Q1 考題重點〉選出正確的名詞

My friends and I like to exercise together at the _____ after school.

A. fence
B. ocean
C. gym
D. rainbow

| 翻譯 | 我和朋友們放學後喜歡一起去健身房運動。

| 詳解 | 本題關鍵字是 exercise 這個動詞,「在健身房運動」是符合文意與邏輯的說法,所以正確答案是選項 C。

| 詞彙 | **fence** [fɛns] 柵欄　**ocean** [`oʃən] 海洋　**rainbow** [`ren͵bo] 彩虹

Q2 考題重點〉not... any... 的用法

They have one book, but not have _____ notebooks.

A. any
B. no
C. many
D. some

| 翻譯 | 他們有一本書,但沒有任何筆記本。

| 詳解 | any 意思是「任何」,常用於否定句中,且符合句意,故正確答案是選項 A。

| 詞彙 | **notebook** [`not͵bʊk] 筆記本

Part 2 段落填空

I love my home. On weekends or holidays, I wake up and make **(3) myself** a cup of coffee in the mornings. Then I tidy up and do some chores. Sometimes I may **(4) worry** about not finishing all my tasks, but **(5) as soon as** I start doing them, I feel better. In the evenings, **(6) I relax on the sofa with a book or watch TV**. In short, I enjoy **(7) spending** good time by myself at home.

| 翻譯 | 我愛我的家。在週末或假日,早上醒來我會為自己泡一杯咖啡。然後收拾一下之後,我會做一些家務。有時候我可能會擔心做不完所有的工作,但一旦我開始做了,我的感覺會好很多。晚上,我會在沙發上看書或看電視放鬆一下。總的來說,我喜歡獨自在家裡度過美好時光。

Q3 考題重點〉反身代名詞用法

A. you   B. us   **C. myself**   D. me

| 詳解 | 句意是「我會為自己泡一杯咖啡」，這句話主詞是 I，沒有提到別人，所以正確答案應為選項 C。

Q4 考題重點〉符合句意 的動詞

A. worry   B. know   C. discover   D. admire

| 詳解 | 句意是「有時候可能會擔心做不完所有的工作」，所以正確答案為選項 A。B 的意思是「知道」，C 的意思是「發現」，D 的意思是「羨慕」。

Q5 考題重點〉用連接詞連接兩句且符合句意

A. as a result B. in no way C. no matter how **D. as soon as**

| 詳解 | 空格需填入可以連接 I start doing them 和 I feel better 兩句的連接詞，且符合「一旦開始做了，感覺就好很多」的句意，所以正確答案為選項 D。A、B 都是副詞，不合文法；C 的意思是「無論如何…」，不合句意。

Q6 考題重點〉選擇符合前後文意的句子

A. I like to have a cup of coffee with my best friend.
 我喜歡和我最好的朋友喝杯咖啡

B. I relax on the sofa with a book or watch TV
 我會在沙發上看書或看電視放鬆一下

C. I still need to be prepared for my work the next day
 我仍必須準備隔天的工作

D. I may go out shopping for a while
 我可能外出購物一下

| 詳解 | 後面句子提到「總的來說，我喜歡獨自在家裡度過美好時光」，所以 A、D 明顯不符文意。另外，從前面提到的放假時喜歡在家做家務來看，C 也會產生矛盾，因此正確答案為選項 B。

Q7 考題重點〉enjoy + Ving 的用法

A. spending B. to spend C. to spending D. being spent

| 詳解 | 動詞 enjoy 後面需接動名詞作為其受詞，所以正確答案為選項 A。D 雖然也是動名詞，但被動式的用法不合邏輯。

NOW HIRING! We NEED

3 restaurant waitress at Delicious Delights!

Related experience preferred.

Must be friendly, reliable, and able to work flexible shifts, including weekends and holidays.

Competitive pay starting at NT$180/hour plus tips.

Apply in person at Delicious Delights or email your resume to jobs@deliciousdelights.com.

Dear Hiring Manager,

I am writing to express my interest in the waitress position. I am always passionate about providing excellent customer service and willing to work for any changeable schedule. Though I haven't worked for any restaurant before, I am confident in my ability to learn quickly and adapt to new environments.

| 翻譯 |

徵才中！我們需要

3 名「美味之樂」餐廳女服務生！

有相關經驗者優先考慮。

必須態度友善、可信賴，並能接受彈性排班，包括週末和假日。

薪酬佳，起薪 NT$180／小時外加小費。

意者請親自前往「美味之樂」，或將您的履歷 email 至 jobs@deliciousdelights.com。

人事經理 您好：

我寫信來是想表達我對女服務生職位的興趣。我是個熱衷於提供優質顧客服務的人，且願意配合任何工作時間表。雖然我從未在任何餐廳工作過，但我有信心可以快速學習和適應新的環境。

| 詞彙 | prefer [prɪˈfɚ] 偏愛，更喜歡　reliable [rɪˈlaɪəbl] 可靠的，可信賴的
flexible [ˈflɛksəbl] 靈活的，可變通的 competitive [kəmˈpɛtətɪv] 有競爭力的
in person 親自　passionate [ˈpæʃənet] 熱情的　excellent [ˈɛksələnt] 出色的，極好的
changeable [ˈtʃendʒəbl] 多變的　confident [ˈkɑnfədənt] 有信心的　adapt to 適應

Q8 Which of the following is NOT a requirement for the waitress position at the restaurant?
以下何者不是該餐廳應徵女服務生一職的必要條件？

A. Friendly attitude　友善的態度

B. Reliable behavior　可靠的行為

C. Able to work full time　能夠全職工作

D. Willing to work on weekends or holidays　願意在週末假日上班

| 詳解 | 從第一個文本的求職廣告內容「Competitive pay starting at NT$180/hour...」可知，該職務並非全職性質，所以正確答案是選項 C。

| 詞彙 | requirement [rɪ`kwaɪrmənt] 必要條件　attitude [`ætətjud] 態度
behavior [bɪ`hevjɚ] 行為

Q9 How can those interested apply for the position?
意者應如何應徵該職位？

A. By making a phone call　打電話聯繫

B. By visiting the restaurant　前往該餐廳

C. By filling out an application form on a website　在網站上填寫應徵表格

D. By mailing an application letter　郵寄應徵信函

| 詳解 | 從第一個文本（社團廣告）中的「Apply in person... or email your resume to...」可知，應徵方式是親自前往該餐廳應徵或以電子郵件，所以正確答案是選項 B。

| 詞彙 | fill out 填寫…（表格等）

Q10 For what reason might the email writer be turned down?
這位寫電子郵件的人可能因為什麼原因被拒絕？

A. He can't work flexible hours.　他無法配合彈性工時。

B. He lives too far away from the restaurant.　他住得距離該餐廳太遙遠。

C. He does not have work experience in customer service.
他沒有顧客服務的經驗。

D. He lacks in related experience.　他缺乏相關經驗。

| 詳解 | 這個題目要綜合兩篇文章來解題。首先，從第二個文本（電子郵件）的「I haven't worked for any restaurant before」可知，這位應徵者沒有在餐廳的工作經驗，接著對照第一個文本（求才廣告）中的「Related experience preferred.」可知，有相關經驗者優先考慮，意即他可能因為這一點而無法應徵上，所以正確答案是選項 D。

| 詞彙 | turn down 拒絕　work experience 工作經驗

Part 1　詞彙

1.　They _____ to the gym every day since the beginning of the year.

　　A. went
　　B. have gone
　　C. go
　　D. are going

2.　The teacher will show us a new math problem.

　　A. show
　　B. keep
　　C. take
　　D. talk

Part 2　段落填空

Every day, I wake up early (3) school. After breakfast, I (4) the bus with my friends. School starts at 8 a.m. and we have classes like Math, English, and Science. At lunchtime, we (5) in the cafeteria and chat. After school, (6) or study at the library. In the evenings, I finish my homework, watch some TV, and relax before bed. That's my (7) day as a high school student.

3.　A. at
　　B. for
　　C. in
　　D. from

4.　A. drive
　　B. express
　　C. catch
　　D. ride

5.　A. turn on
　　B. look after
　　C. show off
　　D. hang out

6.　A. I brush my teeth and take a shower
　　B. the teacher may blame me for being late
　　C. I might go to soccer practice
　　D. I need to check emails and meet some clients

7.　A. monthly
　　B. healthy
　　C. recent
　　D. typical

Dear Sir or Madam,

Are you looking to sell your products online? We've got you covered! Our platform offers a simple and easy way for anyone to start their own online stores and turn their passion into a business. With just a few clicks, you can showcase your products to a wide range of people and start making sales for a limited time. Sign up now and start your journey to success!

JOIN NOW

Hi! I'd like to inquire about how I will be charged if I want to formally become a member.

Good Morning, sir. You can click "JOIN NOW" to see what's going on there. Of course, if you decide not to use within the 14 days of trial, you don't need to pay at all.

8. What is the purpose of the email?

    A. To advertise a platform for starting online stores

    B. To introduce some new products

    C. To offer discounts on online products

    D. To promote a sales event

9. What is one benefit mentioned in the email for using the platform?

    A. Access to a wide range of products

    B. A free platform provided for at least one month

    C. Opportunity of starting making sales immediately

    D. Assurance of achieving success in business

10. What does "a limited time" mean in the email?

    A. The 14-day free trial will be canceled soon.

    B. New members can enjoy free trial of the first 14 days after signing in.

    C. There will be 14-day free trial before signing in.

    D. New members have to pay the first bill before they can enjoy the 14-day free trial.

解答與詳解 上頁簡答

| 1. (B) | 2. (A) | 3. (B) | 4. (C) | 5. (D) |
| 6. (C) | 7. (D) | 8. (A) | 9. (C) | 10. (B) |

Part 1 詞彙

Q1 考題重點〉選出正確的動詞時態

They _____ to the gym every day since the beginning of the year.

A. went   C. go

B. have gone   D. are going

| 翻譯 | 自年初以來，他們每天都去健身房。

| 詳解 | 本題雖然有 every day，但可別急著認定是現在式，因為關鍵字是 since 這個連接詞，句意是「自年初以來，他們每天⋯」所以正確答案是選項 B。

| 詞彙 | gym [dʒɪm] 健身房，體育館

Q2 考題重點〉授予動詞 show 的用法

The teacher will show us a new math problem.

A. show   C. take

B. keep   D. talk

| 翻譯 | 老師會讓我們看看一個新的數學問題。

| 詳解 | show 也可以當「授予動詞」用，後面可以接兩個受詞（間接受詞 + 直接受詞），show somebody something 表示「讓某人看到某物」，故正確答案是選項 A。

Part 2 段落填空

Every day, I wake up early **(3) for** school. After breakfast, I **(4) catch** the bus with my friends. School starts at 8 a.m. and we have classes like Math, English, and Science. At lunchtime, we **(5) hang out** in the cafeteria and chat. After school, **(6) I might go to soccer practice** or study at the library. In the evenings, I finish my homework, watch some TV, and relax before bed. That's my **(7) typical** day as a high school student.

| 翻譯 | 每天，我一早就起床要去上學。吃完早餐後，我和朋友一起搭公車。學校在早上八點開始上課，我們有數學、英文和科學等課程。午餐時，我們經常在餐廳一起聊天。放學後，我可能會去練足球或在圖書館讀書。晚上，我會做完家庭作業，看些電視，然後在睡前放鬆一下。這就是我身為一名高中生的典型日子。

Day 08
Day 09
Day 10
Day 11
Day 12
Day 13
Day 14

Q3 考題重點〉介系詞用法

A. at   C. in

B. for   D. from

|詳解| 句意是「一早起床要去上學」，就像「上學遲到（be late for school）」的 for 用法，所以正確答案應為選項 B。

Q4 考題重點〉動詞的正確用法

A. drive   **C. catch**

B. express   D. ride

|詳解| 「搭公車」如果不用 take a bus，也可以用 catch a bus，其餘動詞都不能用，所以正確答案為選項 C。

Q5 考題重點〉動詞片語的分辨

A. turn on   C. show off

B. look after   **D. hang out**

|詳解| 句意是「午餐時經常在餐廳一起聊天」，hang out 是「常去某處」的意思，所以正確答案為選項 D。A 的意思是「開啟（電器等）」、B 的意思是「照顧）」、C 的意思是「炫耀」。

Q6 考題重點〉選擇符合前後文意的句子

A. I brush my teeth and take a shower　我刷牙並洗澡

B. the teacher may blame me for being late　老師可能會責怪我遲到了

C. I might go to soccer practice　我可能會去練足球

D. I need to check emails and meet some clients
　　我得查看電子郵件並和一些客戶見面

|詳解| 空格前後分別是 After school 以及 or study at the library，顯然要填入放學後可能從事的活動，所以正確答案是選項 C。

Q7 考題重點〉填入符合句意的形容詞

A. monthly   C. recent

B. healthy   **D. typical**

Part3 閱讀理解

Dear Sir or Madam,

Are you looking to sell your products online? We've got you covered! Our platform offers a simple and easy way for anyone to start their own online stores and turn their passion into a business. With just a few clicks, you can showcase your products to a wide range of people and start making sales for a limited time. Sign up now and start your journey to success!

JOIN NOW

Hi! I'd like to inquire about how I will be charged if I want to formally become a member.

Good Morning, sir. You can click "JOIN NOW" to see what's going on there. Of course, if you decide not to use within the 14 days of trial, you don't need to pay at all.

| 翻譯 |

先生或女士 您好：

您是否有興趣在網路上販售您的產品？我們為您提供了解決方案！我們的平台為任何人提供一個簡單易用的方式，讓他們開設自己的網路商店，將自己的熱情轉化為事業。只需幾個點擊，您就能在一段有限的時間內，向廣大的民眾展示您的產品，並開始進行銷售。請立即註冊成為會員，開啟您通往成功的旅程吧！

立即加入

您好。我想詢問一下，你們對於正式的會員是如何收費的呢？

 早安，先生。您點擊「立即加入」後就可以看到詳細的說明。當然，如果您在 14 天的免費試用期之內決定不再使用，您完全不需要支付任何費用。

| 詞彙 | **platform** [ˈplætfɔrm] 平台，舞臺　　**passion** [ˈpæʃən] 熱情，熱愛
turn... into... 把…變成…　　**click** [klɪk]（用滑鼠）點擊　　**showcase** [ˈʃokes] 展示
a wide range of... 各種各樣的　　**inquire** [ɪnˈkwaɪr] 詢問，打聽　　**charge** [tʃɑrdʒ] 收費
formally [ˈfɔrməlɪ] 正式地　　**trial** [ˈtraɪəl] 試用，嘗試

Q8 What is the purpose of the email?
這封電子郵件的目的為何？

A. To advertise a platform for starting online stores
　　為一個可開啟網路商店的平台進行宣傳

B. To introduce some new products
　　為了介紹一些新產品

C. To offer discounts on online products
　　為了提供線上產品的折扣

D. To promote a sales event
　　為推廣一項促銷活動

| 詳解 | 從「Our platform offers... start their own online stores..」可知，該電子郵件的目的是宣傳一個銷售平台，所以正確答案是選項 A。

| 詞彙 | **advertise** [ˈædvɚˌtaɪz] 宣傳；廣告　　**discount** [ˈdɪskaʊnt] 折扣
promote [prəˈmot] 促銷，推廣

Q9 What is one benefit mentioned in the email for using the platform? 在電子郵件中提到使用該平台的一個好處是什麼？

A. Access to a wide range of products　　可以獲得各式各樣的產品

B. A free platform provided for at least one month　　免費提供至少一個月的平台

C. Opportunity of starting making sales immediately
　　可立即開始進行銷售的機會

D. Assurance of achieving success in business　　確保在營運中獲得成功

| 詳解 | 電子郵件中第三句提到「...easy way for anyone to start their own online stores and turn their passion into a business.」，因此使用這個平台的好處就是可以馬上開始賣東西，所以正確答案是選項 C。

| 詞彙 | **benefit** ['bɛnəfɪt] 好處，利益　**immediately** [ɪ'midiətlɪ] 立刻，馬上
assurance [ə'ʃʊrəns] 保證，確保　**achieve** [ə'tʃiv] 實現，達成

Q10 What does "a limited time" mean in the email?
電子郵件中的「有限時間」所指為何？

A. The 14-day free trial will be canceled soon.
14 天的免費試用期就快取消了。

B. New members can enjoy free trial of the first 14 days after signing in.
新會員可享有入會後 14 天免費試用期。

C. There will be 14-day free trial before signing in.
在登記入會之前就有 14 天的免費試用期。

D. New members have to pay the first bill before they can enjoy the 14-day free trial.　新會員得先支付第一筆帳單才能享有 14 天的免費試用期。

| 詳解 | 這個題目要綜合兩篇文章來解題。首先，從第一個文本（電子郵件）的「...start making sales for a limited time.」可知，只需幾個點擊就能在一段有限的時間內開始進行銷售，然後再對照兩人對話中的「within the 14 days of trial」可知，新會員可享有入會後 14 天免費試用期，所以正確答案是選項 B。

| 詞彙 | **sign in** 登記　**pay the bill** 支付帳單

Day 10

月　　日

我的完成時間＿＿＿＿分鐘
標準作答時間 10 分鐘

Day 08

Day 09

Day 10

Day 11

Day 12

Day 13

Day 14

Part 1 詞彙

1. The museum ＿＿＿＿＿＿＿＿ visitors in only during opening hours.

   A. accepts 　　　　B. allows 　　　　C. appears 　　　　D. attends

2. As the ＿＿＿＿＿＿＿＿ of the team, he is tasked with leading and guiding us towards achieving our goals.

   A. employee 　　　B. sailor 　　　C. manager 　　　D. policeman

Part 2 段落填空

Last summer, I __(3)__ an amazing trip around Taiwan. First, I visited Taipei where I saw the famous Taipei 101 and tried delicious street food at Shilin Night Market. __(4)__ , I traveled south to Kaohsiung, where I __(5)__ Lotus Lake and tasted fresh seafood. Next, I went to Tainan, where I learned about Taiwan's history by visiting Anping Old Street. Finally, I headed __(6)__ to Hualien, where __(7)__ . It was an unforgettable journey full of adventures and new experiences.

3. A. set up
   B. went on
   C. looked out
   D. ran into

4. A. Therefore
   B. Meanwhile
   C. Or else
   D. Then

5. A. explore
   B. explored
   C. was exploring
   D. have explored

6. A. east
   B. south
   C. west
   D. north

7. A. I took a leisurely walk along the Qingjing Farm.
   B. A variety of creatures in the Kenting National Park really fascinated me.
   C. I saw many beautiful MRT stations in the great city.
   D. I hiked in Taroko Gorge and enjoyed breathtaking scenery.

I need at least three more helpers, or else our new project will fail to meet the deadline.

Many people find good part-timers at this website. Just give it a try ASAP.

Seeking Temporary Workers?

Our website is able to help, totally free, tens of thousands of individuals and companies find their ideal assistants. Available nationwide! Just fill out the form below and send it to us right now.

Business Type: Furniture Company
Job description: outfield packing and handling
Number of Workers Needed: 3-4
Contact: Mr. William, at 0966-123-456
Location: Wugu Dist., New Taipei City
Wage: NT$200 / hour (8 hours a day)

SEND

8. What seems to be the problem between the speakers?

   A. They do not know how to find more helpers.

   B. Their contractor may fail to meet the deadline.

   C. They are short-handed.

   D. Their budget is too tight to find more helpers.

9. What is NOT true about the website?

   A. It connects many individuals or companies with their ideal assistants.

   B. The membership fee is needed.

   C. Its service is not provided overseas.

   D. Full-time workers are not available.

10. How much does the company possibly need to pay the temporary staff at most a day?

    A. NT$ 6,400   B. NT$ 4,800   C. NT$ 1,600   D. NT$ 6,800

Day 08
Day 09
Day 10
Day 11
Day 12
Day 13
Day 14

1. (B)　　2. (C)　　3. (B)　　4. (D)　　5. (B)
解答與詳解　6. (A)　　7. (D)　　8. (C)　　9. (B)　　10. (A)

Part 1 詞彙

Q1 考題重點〉選出正確的動詞

The museum ＿＿＿＿＿＿＿＿＿ visitors in only during opening hours.

A. accepts　　　　　　　　　C. appears

B. allows　　　　　　　　D. attends

| 翻譯 | 博物館遊客僅限開放時間才能進入。

| 詳解 | 本題句意是「允許遊客進入」，所以正確答案是選項 B。accept 雖然看似符合語意，但沒有 accept... in 的用法。

| 詞彙 | **opening hour** 開放時間　　**accept** [ək`sεpt] 接受

Q2 考題重點〉選擇正確的名詞

As the ＿＿＿＿＿＿＿＿＿ of the team, he is tasked with leading and guiding us towards achieving our goals.

A. employee　　　　　　　　**C. manager**

B. sailor　　　　　　　　　　D. policeman

| 翻譯 | 他身為這個團隊的經理，負有領導和引導我們朝著目標前進的任務。

| 詳解 | 本題關鍵部位是後面的「...leading and guiding...」，employee（員工）、sailor（水手）、policeman（警察）都不符句意，故正確答案是選項 C。

| 詞彙 | **be tasked with...** 肩負著…任務

Part 2 段落填空

Last summer, I **(3) went on** an amazing trip around Taiwan. First, I visited Taipei where I saw the famous Taipei 101 and tried delicious street food at Shilin Night Market. **(4) Then**, I traveled south to Kaohsiung, where I **(5) explored** Lotus Lake and tasted fresh seafood. Next, I went to Tainan, where I learned about Taiwan's history by visiting Anping Old Street. Finally, I headed **(6) east** to Hualien, where **(7) I hiked in Taroko Gorge and enjoyed breathtaking scenery**. It was an unforgettable journey full of adventures and new experiences.

| 翻譯 | 去年夏天，我進行了一趟令人難忘的台灣環島之旅。首先，我造訪了台北，看到了著名的台北 101，並在士林夜市品嘗了美味的街頭小吃。然後，我往南前往高雄，探索了蓮池潭，品嚐了新鮮的海鮮。接著，我前往台南，在安平老街了解了台灣的歷史。最後，我向東前往花蓮，在太魯閣峽谷徒步並欣賞了令人驚嘆的景色。這是一段充滿冒險和新體驗的難忘旅程。

Q3 考題重點〉「踏上…之旅」的用法

A. set up   C. looked out

B. went on   D. ran into

| 詳解 | 句意是「進行一趟令人難忘的台灣環島之旅」，常與 trip 搭配的動詞除了 take 之外，還有 go on，皆表示「進行一趟…之旅」，所以正確答案應為選項 B。A 的意思是「設立」，C 的意思是「往外看」，D 的意思是「遇到」。

Q4 考題重點〉連接性副詞 then 的用法

A. Therefore   C. Or else

B. Meanwhile   **D. Then**

| 詳解 | 前一句是「First, ...」，下一句是「Next, ...」，顯然在敘述一個事情進行的順序，所以正確答案為選項 D。

Q5 考題重點〉選擇正確的時態

A. explore   C. was exploring

B. explored   D. have explored

| 詳解 | 短文以 Last summer 為開頭，且可看到使用的動詞都是過去式，表示單純描述去年夏天旅行的事情，所以正確答案為選項 B。

Q6 考題重點〉選擇符合上下文的字彙

A. east   C. west

B. south   D. north

| 詳解 | 單看空格所在句子可能無法判斷正確答案，所以必須參考前後文。前一句提到旅遊到台南，因此從台灣往花蓮應為「東行」，正確答案為選項 A。

Day 08
Day 09
Day 10
Day 11
Day 12
Day 13
Day 14

Q7 考題重點〉選擇符合前後文意的句子

A. I took a leisurely walk along the Qingjing Farm.
我在清境農場悠閒地散步。

B. A variety of creatures in the Kenting National Park really fascinated me.
墾丁國家公園的各種生物真令我著迷。

C. I saw many beautiful MRT stations in the great city.
我在大城市中看見許多優美的捷運站。

D. I hiked in Taroko Gorge and enjoyed breathtaking scenery.
我在太魯閣峽谷徒步並欣賞了令人驚嘆的景色。

| 詳解 | 前面句子提到旅行到花蓮（Hualien），所以看到有 Taroko Gorge 的選項即可確定是正確答案了，故選 D。

Part 3 閱讀理解

> I need at least three more helpers, or else our new project will fail to meet the deadline.

> Many people find good part-timers at this website. Just give it a try ASAP.

Seeking Temporary Workers?

Our website is able to help, totally free, tens of thousands of individuals and companies find their ideal assistants. Available nationwide! Just fill out the form below and send it to us right now.

Business Type: Furniture Company
Job description: outfield packing and handling
Number of Workers Needed: 3-4
Contact: Mr. William, at 0966-123-456
Location: Wugu Dist., New Taipei City
Wage: NT$200 / hour (8 hours a day)

SEND

我至少需要增加三名幫手，否則我們的新專案將無法在截止日期前完成。

許多人在這個網站找到了良好的兼職人員。趕快試試看吧。

尋找臨時工？

我們的網站可完全免費幫助數萬名個人和公司找到其理想的助手。全國各地都可以找得到人！只需填寫以下表格就可以開始。馬上發送給我們吧！

企業類型：傢俱公司

工作類型：外場包裝和搬運

所需人員數量：3-4 人

聯絡人：威廉先生，電話 0966-123-456

地點：新北市五股區

工資：每小時新台幣 200 元（每天 8 小時）

| 詞彙 | **meet the deadline** 在截止日前完成　**part-timer** [`pɑrt͵taɪmɚ] 計時人員，臨時工
ideal [aɪ`diəl] 理想的　**assistant** [ə`sɪstənt] 助手　**furniture** [`fɝnɪtʃɚ] 傢俱
outfield [`aʊt͵fild] 外場，戶外區域　**packing** [`pækɪŋ] 包裝
handling [`hændlɪŋ] 搬運　**contact** [`kɑntækt] 聯絡人

Q8 What seems to be the problem between the speakers?
說話者們似乎遇到了什麼問題？

A. They do not know how to find more helpers.
　　他們不知道如何找到更多幫手。

B. Their contractor may fail to meet the deadline.
　　他們的承包商可能無法在截止日前完成。

C. They are short-handed.　　他們欠缺人手。

D. Their budget is too tight to find more helpers.
　　他們的預算吃緊，無法再找更多幫手。

Day 08
Day 09
Day 10
Day 11
Day 12
Day 13
Day 14

| 詳解 | 從第一個文本的對話內容「I need at least three more helpers...」可知，他們遇到欠缺人手的問題，所以正確答案是選項 C。

| 詞彙 | **contractor** [`kɑntræktɚ] 承包商　**meet the deadline** 在截止日前完成　**short-handed** 人手短缺的　**budget** [`bʌdʒɪt] 預算

Q9 What is NOT true about the website?
關於這個網站，何者為非？

A. It connects many individuals or companies with their ideal assistants.
它將許多個人和公司與其理想的助手連結在一起。

B. The membership fee is needed.
需支付入會費。

C. Its service is not provided overseas.　它不提供海外的服務。

D. Full-time workers are not available.　不提供全職人員。

| 詳解 | 從第二個文本（廣告）的內容可知，要找的是臨時工（非全職人員），且不提供海外的服務（Available nationwide!），至於「入會費」（membership fee）的部分，是沒有提到的（totally free），所以正確答案是選項 B。

| 詞彙 | **connect** [kə`nɛkt] 連結，連接　**individual** [ˌɪndə`vɪdʒʊəl] 個人

Q10 How much does the company possibly need to pay the temporary staff at most a day?
該公司一天可能得對多支付多少錢給臨時工？

A. NT$6,400　　　　　C. NT$ 1,600
B. NT$4,800　　　　　D. NT$ 6,800

| 詳解 | 這個題目要綜合兩篇文章來解題。首先，從第一個文本（對話）的「I need at least three more helpers...」可知，他們需要至少（at least）3 位幫手。接著再看求才廣告最後面的 Wage: NT$200 / hour（8 hours a day）可知，一天要支付 1 位臨時人員工資是 NT$ 1,600，而他們最多需要 4 位（Number of Workers needed:3-4）。請注意本題中的 at most（最多），1600×4 = 6400，所以正確答案是選項 A。

| 詞彙 | **staff** [stæf] 員工，人員

Part 1 詞彙

1. The bus stop is _____ the corner, so we don't have to walk far to catch the bus.

   A. about   B. into   C. beside   D. around

2. She had to make a difficult decision about _____ to accept the job offer or not.

   A. when   B. if   C. whether   D. whoever

Part 2 段落填空

During the long weekend, the highway was really __(3)__ . There were so many cars that they couldn't move fast. __(4)__ Some drivers looked upset, while others just listened to music, watched TV or videos, and waited __(5)__ . Some people even got out of their cars __(6)__ their legs. It was a long wait, but __(7)__ , the traffic started moving again. Everyone was relieved when they could finally drive freely.

3. A. over-crowded
   B. smooth-flowing
   C. fast-paced
   D. thick-fogged

4. A. Some drivers decided to pick up speed!
   B. It was like a big parking lot!
   C. Suddenly, a parade of heavy motor-bikes appeared!
   D. Luckily, the heavy rain stopped!

5. A. dizzily
   B. patiently
   C. excitedly
   D. hungrily

6. A. to stretch
   B. and stretched
   C. stretching
   D. to be stretching

7. A. accidentally
   B. initially
   C. eventually
   D. suddenly

Part 3 閱讀理解

King Coffee Business Hours

Weekdays: 10:00 A.M. - 8:00 P.M.
Fridays - Sundays: 10:00 A.M. - 11:00 P.M.

Come and enjoy our yummy coffee! It's made fresh and served with a friendly smile! Whether you need a morning boost or a nice evening treat, we've got what you need. Just sit back, relax, and enjoy the amazing smell of our special coffee blends. By the way, don't forget to try one of our tasty pastries or sandwiches with your coffee!

* OFF on Mondays

* Address: 1-2F, No.86, Chunghua N. St., Zenyuan City

* Hotline for reservation: 1-898-2456-88

NOTE: Reservation is not available on weekends and holidays.

 Hi, I think it's time we meet with each other after a few months of chatting online. How about tomorrow night, at King Coffee?

I'm still busy these days. Besides, that coffee shop closes tomorrow.

8. What is true about King Coffee?

   A. Customers can sit back and relax there 24/7.

   B. It is open until 8:00 P.M. on Sundays.

   C. It is closed after 11:00 P.M on Fridays.

   D. Coffee can be ordered online and be provided to-go.

9. According to the dialogue, who could be the speakers?

   A. Childhood sweethearts   C. Unfamiliar colleagues

   B. Close friends   D. Net pals

10. On what day did the dialogue take place?

    A. On Friday   C. On Sunday

    B. On Saturday   D. On Monday

Part 1　詞彙

Q1　考題重點〉固定片語 around the corner

The bus stop is ＿＿＿＿＿＿＿＿＿＿ the corner, so we don't have to walk far to catch the bus.

A. about　　　　　　　　　　C. beside

B. into　　　　　　　　　　**D. around**

| 翻譯 | 公車站就在轉角處，所以我們不必走很遠就能搭上公車。

| 詳解 | 本題關鍵是對於片語 around the corner 的認知，所以正確答案是選項 D。

| 詞彙 | **corner** [ˈkɔrnɚ] 角落

Q2　考題重點〉whether... or not 的用法

She had to make a difficult decision about ＿＿＿＿＿＿＿＿＿＿ to accept the job offer or not.

A. when　　　　　　　　　　**C. whether**

B. if　　　　　　　　　　　　D. whoever

| 翻譯 | 她必須對於是否接受這份工作來做出一個艱難的決定。

| 詳解 | 疑問詞 whether 常與 or not 連用，表示「是否…」故正確答案是選項 C。if 雖然也可以解釋為「是否」，但不能與 or not 連用。

| 詞彙 | **make a decision**　做出決定

Part 2　段落填空

During the long weekend, the highway was really **(3) over-crowded**. There were so many cars that they couldn't move fast. **(4) It was like a big parking lot!** Some drivers looked upset, while others just listened to music, watched TV or videos, and waited **(5) patiently**. Some people even got out of their cars **(6) to stretch** their legs. It was a long wait, but **(7) eventually**, the traffic started moving again. Everyone was relieved when they could finally drive freely.

| 翻譯 | 在長假期間，高速公路擁擠不堪。有這麼多車子，使得它們無法快速行進。它就像是個大型的停車場！有些駕駛看起來很生氣，但有些人則只是聽著音樂、看著電視或影片並耐心等待。有些人甚至下車伸展雙腿。這是一個漫長的等待，但最終，交通開始重新流動。當他們終於能夠自由行駛時，每個人都感到如釋重負。

Q3 考題重點〉符合前後文意的複合形容詞

A. over-crowded　　　　　　　C. fast-paced

B. smooth-flowing　　　　　　　D. thick-fogged

| 詳解 | 下一句是「...so many cars that they couldn't move fast」，顯然本句要表達的是「高速公路擁擠不堪」，所以正確答案應為選項 A。選項 B、C、D 的意思分別是「行車順暢的」、「步伐快速的」、「濃霧瀰漫的」。

Q4 考題重點〉選擇符合前後文意的句子

A. Some drivers decided to pick up speed!　有些駕駛決定加快速度！

B. It was like a big parking lot!　它就像是個大型的停車場！

C. Suddenly, a parade of heavy motorbikes appeared!
突然間，一隊重型機車出現了！

D. Luckily, the heavy rain stopped!　幸運的是，大雨停了！

| 詳解 | 前一句提到有這麼多車子無法快速行進，後面句子也有類似的敘述（It was a long wait...），顯然這一句還是在著墨著高速公路上大塞車的景象，因此正確答案為選項 B。

Q5 考題重點〉符合前後文意的副詞

A. dizzily　　　　　　　　　　　C. excitedly

B. patiently　　　　　　　　　D. hungrily

| 詳解 | 句意是「有些駕駛看起來很生氣，但有些人則…」，表示應填入與前面 upset 相反意思的修飾語，以符合「有些人不耐煩，但有些人耐心等待」的文意，所以正確答案為選項 B。A 的意思是「暈眩地」，C 的意思是「感到興奮地」，D 的意思是「飢餓地」。

Q6 考題重點〉表示「目的」的不定詞（to-V）用法

A. to stretch　　　　　　　　C. stretching

B. and stretched　　　　　　　D. to be stretching

| 詳解 | 空格前面句意是「有些人甚至下車」，搭配前面句子提到駕駛人在大塞車的路上之內容，顯然要表達的是「為了伸展雙腿」而短暫下車，所以正確答案為選項 A。

Q7 考題重點〉轉折性副詞 eventually 用法

A. accidentally   **C. eventually**

B. initially   D. suddenly

| 詳解 | 從最後一句「...when they could finally drive freely」中的 finally 可推知，這句要表達的就是「但最終，……終於能夠自由行駛」，所以正確答案為選項 C。A、B、D 的意思分別是「意外地」、「最初地」、「突然地」。

Part3 閱讀理解

King Coffee Business Hours

Weekdays: 10:00 A.M. - 8:00 P.M.
Fridays - Sundays: 10:00 A.M. - 11:00 P.M.

Come and enjoy our yummy coffee! It's made fresh and served with a friendly smile! Whether you need a morning boost or a nice evening treat, we've got what you need. Just sit back, relax, and enjoy the amazing smell of our special coffee blends. By the way, don't forget to try one of our tasty pastries or sandwiches with your coffee!

* OFF on Mondays

* Address: 1-2F, No.86, Chunghua N. St., Zenyuan City

* Hotline for reservation: 1-898-2456-88

NOTE: Reservation is not available on weekends and holidays.

 Hi, I think it's time we meet with each other after a few months of chatting online. How about tomorrow night, at King Coffee?

I'm still busy these days. Besides, that coffee shop closes tomorrow.

King Coffee 營業時間

週一至週四：上午 10:00 - 下午 8:00

週五至週日：上午 10:00 - 晚上 11:00

歡迎來品嚐我們美味的咖啡！新鮮研磨，且帶著親切的笑容服務您！不論您需要早晨提神的一杯，或是晚上的愉快小享受，都能滿足您的需求。請坐下來，放鬆心情，享受我們特製咖啡混合的美妙香氣。對了，別忘了試試我們美味的糕點或三明治，搭配您的咖啡也挺不錯的喔！

週一店休

地址：禪園市中華北街 86 號 1-2 樓

訂位專線：1-898-2456-88

注意：週末和假日不提供預約服務。

> 嗨，我想我們在網路上聊了幾個月後該見面了。明天晚上，約在 King Coffee 如何？

> 我這幾天還是要忙。此外，那家咖啡廳明天沒有營業。

| 詞彙 | **business hour** 營業時間　**boost** [bust] 提振，提神　**treat** [trit] 難得的樂事
sit back 靠背舒服地坐著　**amazing** [ə`mezɪŋ] 驚奇的　**blend** [blɛnd] 混合
pastry [`pestrɪ] 酥皮點心　**reservation** [͵rɛzɚ`veʃən] 預訂　**these days** 最近

Q8 What is true about King Coffee? 關於 King Coffee，何者正確？

A. Customers can sit back and relax there 24/7.

顧客可以全天候在那裡坐下來放鬆。

B. It is open until 8:00 P.M. on Sundays.

週日營業時間至晚上 8:00。

C. It is closed after 11:00 P.M on Fridays.

週五的營業時間至晚間 11:00。

D. Coffee can be ordered online and be provided to-go.

可以在線上點咖啡且提供外帶。

| 詳解 | 從第一個文本的網頁內容「Fridays - Sundays: 10:00 A.M. - 11:00 P.M.」可知，週五的營業時間至晚間 11:00，所以正確答案是選項 C。

| 詞彙 | order [`ɔrdɚ] 訂購　to-go [tu-`go] 外帶

Q9 According to the dialogue, who could be the speakers?
根據對話內容，說話者可能是誰？

A. Childhood sweethearts　青梅竹馬的戀人

B. Close friends　親密的朋友

C. Unfamiliar colleagues　不熟的同事

D. Net pals　網友

| 詳解 | 從第二個文本（對話）內容可知，兩人是在網路上認識且尚未見過面，所以正確答案是選項 D。

| 詞彙 | unfamiliar [ˌʌnfə`mɪljɚ] 不熟的　pal [pæl] 好友

Q10 On what day did the dialogue take place?
這則對話可能的時間是星期幾？

A. On Friday　在星期五

B. On Saturday　在星期六

C. On Sunday　在星期日

D. On Monday　在星期一

| 詳解 | 這個題目要綜合兩篇文章來解題。首先，從第二個文本（對話）的「that coffee shop closes tomorrow」可知，咖啡廳明日沒有營業，接著對照第一個文本（網頁）中的「OFF on Mondays」可知，兩人對話的時間是星期日，所以正確答案是選項 C。

| 詞彙 | take place 發生

Day 08

Day 09

Day 10

Day 11

Day 12

Day 13

Day 14

Part 1 詞彙

1. I think watching movies with friends ＿＿＿＿＿＿＿＿＿ so much fun.

   A. are
   B. is
   C. have
   D. has

2. The old church ＿＿＿＿＿＿＿＿＿ in our town for over a hundred years.

   A. will be building
   B. has built
   C. is being built
   D. has been built

Part 2 段落填空

Sometimes couples argue. It can happen when they __(3)__ on something or if they're feeling upset. __(4)__ , they might raise their voices or say things they don't mean. It's important for them to talk calmly and __(5)__ to each other's feelings. After arguing, they can apologize and make up. __(6)__ . It's sometimes a way __(7)__ through problems and understand each other better.

3. A. agree
   B. disagree
   C. decide
   D. rely

4. A. However
   B. Instead
   C. Meanwhile
   D. Fortunately

5. A. must listen
   B. have listened
   C. listen
   D. listening

6. A. Arguing doesn't mean they don't care about each other.
   B. Then, they decide to never speak to each other again.
   C. They often choose to ignore each other for days.
   D. They really need to avoid arguing again.

7. A. working
   B. to work
   C. to working
   D. and work

TOGETHER WITH OUR FAMILIES

Aileen Garcia

AND

Gordon Martinez

will exchange marriage vows

6:00 P.M., NOVEMBER 24, 2024

Le Méridien Taipei

No. 38, Songren Rd., Xinyi Dist., Taipei City

Hello, Gerry, no time no see! I'll get married next month, and I hope you can come and celebrate with us.

Hi, Aileen. Wow! That's really good news. Sure, I'll go with my wife. Congratulations!

8. What did the speakers mainly talk about?

   A. An upcoming festival   C. A wedding banquet

   B. An awkward past memory   D. A new possible relationship

9. What is NOT true about the speakers?

   A. Aileen is going to get married.   C. Garcia is Aileen's family name.

   B. Gerry is still single.   D. They will meet next month.

10. When did the dialogue take place?

   A. In September   C. In November

   B. In October   D. In December

解答與詳解

1. (B)　2. (D)　3. (B)　4. (C)　5. (C)
6. (A)　7. (B)　8. (C)　9. (B)　10. (B)

Part 1　詞彙

Q1 考題重點〉**動名詞當主詞**

I think watching movies with friends _____ so much fun.

A. are   C. have

B. is   D. has

| 翻譯 | 我認為和朋友一起看電影很好玩。

| 詳解 | 空格要填入一個動詞，而其主詞是「watching movies with friends」，為單數動詞，所以正確答案是選項 B。has 雖然也是單數動詞，但要表達「某事物」很有趣（much fun），要用 be 動詞。

Q2 考題重點〉**動詞語態與時態的綜合判斷**

The old church _____ in our town for over a hundred years.

A. will be building   C. is being built

B. has built   **D. has been built**

| 翻譯 | 我們鎮上的這棟老教堂的建立已經有超過百年之久。

| 詳解 | 主詞是 The old church，不會自己建立起來，不能用主動式。此外，句尾有「for + 一段時間（for over a hundred years）」，常與完成式搭配，故正確答案是選項 D。

Part 2　段落填空

Sometimes couples argue. It can happen when they **(3) disagree** on something or if they're feeling upset. **(4) Meanwhile**, they might raise their voices or say things they don't mean. It's important for them to talk calmly and **(5) listen** to each other's feelings. After arguing, they can apologize and make up. **(6) Arguing doesn't mean they don't care about each other.** It's sometimes a way **(7) to work** through problems and understand each other better.

| 翻譯 | 有時候情侶會吵架。這可能是因為他們在某些事情上意見不一致，或者感覺煩燥。這時候，他們可能會提高聲量，或說出一些不是他們真心的話。重要的是要冷靜地交談，聽對方的感受。吵架後，他們可以道歉和和解。吵架並不意味著他們不關心對方。有時這是一種解決問題、更佳理解對方的方式。

Q3 考題重點〉符合文意的動詞

A. agree

B. disagree

C. decide

D. rely

| 詳解 | 前後文意是，情侶會吵架，因為他們在某些事情上會意見不一致，所以正確答案應為選項 B。A、C、D 的意思分別是「同意」、「決定」、「依賴」。

Q4 考題重點〉連接前後句的連接性副詞

A. However

B. Instead

C. Meanwhile

D. Fortunately

| 詳解 | 文中提到，當情侶會在某些事情上意見不一致或彼此感覺很差時，他們可能會提高聲音（語氣不好），顯然這兩種情形不是前後因果就是同時發生的關係，所以正確答案為選項 C。

Q5 考題重點〉連接詞 and 前後結構對等

A. must listen

B. have listened

C. listen

D. listening

| 詳解 | 空格前的 and 連接「to talk calmly」以及「to listen to...」兩個不定詞，而第二個不定詞的 to 可省略，因此 and 後面直接接原形 listen 即可，正確答案為選項 C。

Q6 考題重點〉選擇符合前後文意的句子

A. Arguing doesn't mean they don't care about each other.

　　吵架並不意味著他們不關心對方。

B. Then, they decide to never speak to each other again.

　　然後，他們決定永遠不再和對方說話。

C. They often choose to ignore each other for days.

　　他們常常選擇彼此冷落好幾天。

D. They really need to avoid arguing again.

　　他們真的必須避免再吵架。

| 詳解 | 從前後句的「After arguing, they can apologize and make up.」以及「understand each other better」來看，都是對於吵架這件事的正面解讀，因此正確答案為選項 A。

Day 08
Day 09
Day 10
Day 11
Day 12
Day 13
Day 14

$Q7$ 考題重點〉way + to-V 的用法

A. working   C. to working

B. to work   D. and work

|詳解| 句意是「這是一種解決問題…的方式」，way（方法）後面接不定詞（to-V）作為其修飾語，所以正確答案為選項 B。

Part 3 閱讀理解

TOGETHER WITH OUR FAMILIES

Aileen Garcia

AND

Gordon Martinez

will exchange marriage vows

6:00 P.M., NOVEMBER 24, 2024

Le Méridien Taipei

No. 38, Songren Rd., Xinyi Dist., Taipei City

 Hello, Gerry, no time no see! I'll get married next month, and I hope you can come and celebrate with us.

Hi, Aileen. Wow! That's really good news. Sure, I'll go with my wife. Congratulations!

一起共襄盛舉

愛琳・賈西亞
與
戈登・馬丁尼茲
即將結為連理

2024年十一月二十四日
下午六時
寒舍艾美酒店（台北）
信義區松仁路38號

哈囉。格瑞，好久不見！我下個月要結婚了，我希望你可以來和我們一起慶祝。

嗨，愛琳，哇噢！那真是好消息呢！當然，我會帶我太太過去。恭喜了！

| 詞彙 | **together with** 與… 一起　**exchange** [ɪks`tʃɛndʒ] 交換，交易
marriage [`mærɪdʒ] 婚姻　**vow** [vaʊ] 誓言，誓約　**celebrate** [`sɛlə͵bret] 慶祝
congratulation [kən͵grætʃə`leʃən] 祝賀，慶賀

Day 08
Day 09
Day 10
Day 11
Day 12
Day 13
Day 14

Q8 What did the speakers mainly talk about?
說話者們主要談論什麼？

A. An upcoming festival　一個即將來到的節日

B. An awkward past memory　一段尷尬的過往

C. A wedding banquet　一場婚禮

D. A new possible relationship　一段可能的新關係

| 詳解 | 從第二個文本的對話內容可知，愛琳說她要結婚了，且邀請對方一起來慶祝，表示他們談論的是一場即將到來的婚宴，所以正確答案是選項 C。

| 詞彙 | upcoming [`ʌpˏkʌmɪŋ] 即將到來的　festival [`fɛstəvl] 節日
awkward [`ɔkwəd] 尷尬的　banquet [`bæŋkwɪt] 宴會　relationship [rɪ`leʃənʃɪp] 關係

Q9 What is NOT true about the speakers?
關於說話者們，何者為非？

A. Aileen is going to get married.　愛琳即將結婚。

B. Gerry is still single.　格瑞仍是單身。

C. Garcia is Aileen's family name.　賈西亞是愛琳的姓氏。

D. They will meet next month.　他們下個月會碰面。

| 詳解 | 從第二個文本的對話內容「I'll go with my wife.」可知，Gerry 已經結婚了，故「Gerry is still single.」的說法是錯誤的，答案是選項 B。

| 詞彙 | single [`sɪŋgl] 單身的　family name 姓氏，姓

Q10 When did the dialogue take place?
這段對話發生在何時？

A. In September　在九月

B. In October　在十月

C. In November　在十一月

D. In December　在十二月

| 詳解 | 這個題目要綜合兩篇文章來解題。首先，從第二個文本（對話）的「I'll get married next month」可知，愛琳即將在下個月結婚，接著對照第一個文本（喜帖）中的「NOVEMBER 24, 2024」可知，對話的時間應是在十月份，所以正確答案是選項 B。

| 詞彙 | take place 發生

Part 1 詞彙

1. I met a woman yesterday ＿＿＿＿＿＿＿＿＿ son is studying medicine at the university nearby.

   A. when   B. who   C. that   D. whose

2. Tom lent his jacket ＿＿＿＿＿＿＿＿＿ his girlfriend when she forgot hers at home.

   A. from   B. to   C. for   D. with

Part 2 段落填空

Mary and a friend went to a cooking class together. They learned (3) to make delicious dishes like spaghetti and meatballs, (4) creamy chicken Alfredo. Mary was excited to try new recipes, and her friend helped her cut vegetables and mix ingredients. (5) After the class, they felt proud of what they (6) and couldn't wait to cook for their families at home. They also exchanged cooking (7) with each other to improve their skills.

3. A. what
   B. how
   C. when
   D. where

4. A. away from
   B. because of
   C. no more than
   D. as well as

5. A. However, they found the cooking process tedious and boring.
   B. They accidentally burned the dish they were cooking.

   C. They had a lot of fun cooking and tasting their creations.
   D. Afterwards, they realized they forgot to turn on the oven to bake the dish.

6. A. learn
   B. learned
   C. had learned
   D. will learn

7. A. time
   B. tips
   C. recipe
   D. class

Day 08
Day 09
Day 10
Day 11
Day 12
Day 13
Day 14

Part 3 閱讀理解

Sophie can't stop coughing and she looks tired now. But she can't sleep well. I think I need to call her kindergarten teacher in the morning to take a day off.

OK. Then try the medicine that I put in the fridge. But you need to read the Usage Directions on the outer box first.

Usage Directions

◎ For kids aged over 12 and grown-ups: Take 12 c.c. after each meal. Do not go over 24 c.c. a day.

◎ For kids aged 6 to under 12: Take 6 c.c. after each meal, but don't go over 18 c.c. a day.

◎ For kids under 6: Talk to your doctor for guidance.

---

8. When could the dialogue take place?

A. In the morning

B. In the afternoon

C. At night

D. We don't know.

9. What can we learn about from the medicine direction?

A. The medicine was bought last week.

B. Only adults can take it.

C. Kids can't take it without a doctor's instruction.

D. The amount of the medicine to be taken a day is limited.

10. How much amount can Sophie take after each meal?

A. 6 c.c.

B. 12 c.c.

C. 18 c.c.

D. It depends on the doctor's advice.

Part 1　詞彙

Q1　考題重點〉關係代名詞所有格 whose 的用法

I met a woman yesterday _____ son is studying medicine at the university nearby.

A. when　　　　B. who　　　　C. that　　　　**D. whose**

| 翻譯 | 我昨天遇到一位女士，她的兒子在附近的大學念醫學。

| 詳解 | 空格後面「son is studying... nearby」是個完整句子，所以 who 和 that 都不對，應選關係代名詞所有格 whose，正確答案是選項 D。son 不能單獨存在，前面必須有冠詞或所有格，所以 A 也是錯誤的。

| 詞彙 | medicine [ˋmɛdəsn] 醫學，醫藥

Q2　考題重點〉lend... to... 的用法

Tom lent his jacket _____ his girlfriend when she forgot hers at home.

A. from　　　　**B. to**　　　　C. for　　　　D. with

| 翻譯 | 湯姆在女友把外套忘在家裡時，把他的外套借給了她。

| 詳解 | 表示「借」的 lend（過去式 lent）常搭配介系詞 to，表示「借…給…」，故正確答案是選項 B。

| 詞彙 | jacket [ˋdʒækɪt] 夾克

Part 2　段落填空

Mary and a friend went to a cooking class together. They learned **(3) how** to make delicious dishes like spaghetti and meatballs, **(4) as well as** creamy chicken Alfredo. Mary was excited to try new recipes, and her friend helped her cut vegetables and mix ingredients. **(5) They had a lot of fun cooking and tasting their creations.** After the class, they felt proud of what they **(6) had learned** and couldn't wait to cook for their families at home. They also exchanged cooking **(7) tips** with each other to improve their skills.

| 翻譯 | Mary 和一位朋友一起去上烹飪課。他們學會如何做出美味的菜餚，像是義大利麵條和肉丸子，以及奶油雞義式寬麵。Mary 很興奮地嘗試新的食譜，她的朋友幫她切蔬菜和調配食材。他們在烹飪和品嚐美食時玩得很開心。課程結束後，他們對於自己學到的技能感到自豪，並迫不及待地想要在家為家人烹飪。他們還彼此交換烹飪技巧，以提升彼此的廚藝。

Q3 考題重點〉「疑問詞 + 不定詞」用法

A. what　　　　**B. how**　　　　C. when　　　　D. where

| 詳解 | 這裡的「They learned how to...」=「They learned how they could...」，這是「疑問詞 + 不定詞＝名詞片語」的用法，而句意是「學會如何做出美味的菜餚」，其餘選項皆不合語意，所以正確答案應為選項 B。

Q4 考題重點〉對等連接詞 as well as 用法

A. away from　　B. because of　　C. no more than　　**D. as well as**

| 詳解 | 從空格前面的「...dishes like spaghetti and meatballs」來看，這裡的「creamy chicken Alfredo」也是一道餐點（dish），所以要用一個對等連接詞連接「spaghetti and meatballs」，故正確答案為選項 D。A 的意思是「遠離…」，B 的意思是「因為…」，C 的意思是「只不過是…」。

Q5 考題重點〉選擇符合前後文意的句子

A. However, they found the cooking process tedious and boring.
然而，他們發現烹飪過程冗長乏味。

B. They accidentally burned the dish they were cooking.
他們不小心把正在烹煮的菜燒焦了。

C. They had a lot of fun cooking and tasting their creations.
他們在烹飪和品嚐美食時玩得很開心。

D. Afterwards, they realized they forgot to turn on the oven to bake the dish.
後來，他們意識到他們忘了打開烤箱來烤菜。

| 詳解 | 前面句子提到「她的朋友幫她切蔬菜和調配食材」，後面提到課程結束後的滿足感，顯然這一句是對於學習烹飪時的愉悅心情，因此正確答案為選項 C。

Q6 考題重點〉過去完成式的使用時機

A. learn　　　　B. learned　　　　**C. had learned**　　D. will learn

| 詳解 | 以時間順序來說，「已經學習到」是在「感到驕傲」之前，而這裡的「感到」用過去式 felt，所以要用「過去完成式」來表達「已經學習到」，故正確答案為選項 C。

Q7 考題重點〉填入符合句意的名詞

A. time   **B. tips**   C. recipe   D. class

| 詳解 | 本題關鍵是後面的「提升廚藝（improve their skills）」，所以句子要表達的是彼此交換烹飪「技巧」，正確答案為選項 B。

Part 3 閱讀理解

 Sophie can't stop coughing and she looks tired now. But she can't sleep well. I think I need to call her kindergarten teacher in the morning to take a day off.

OK. Then try the medicine that I put in the fridge. But you need to read the Usage Directions on the outer box first.

Usage Directions

◎ For kids aged over 12 and grown-ups: Take 12 c.c. after each meal. Do not go over 24 c.c. a day.

◎ For kids aged 6 to under 12: Take 6 c.c. after each meal, but don't go over 18 c.c. a day.

◎ For kids under 6: Talk to your doctor for guidance.

| 翻譯 |

 Sophie 一直在咳嗽，看起來很累，但又沒辦法好好睡覺。我想明早得打電話給她的幼稚園老師，幫她請一天假。

好的，那就試試我放在冰箱裡的藥。但你得先看一下外包裝盒上的使用說明書。

使用方法

◎ 12 歲以上的孩童及成人：每餐後服用 12 毫升。一天不要超過 24 毫升。

◎ 6 至 12 歲的孩童：每餐後服用 6 毫升，但一天不要超過 18 毫升。

◎ 6 歲以下的孩童：請諮詢您的醫生。

Day 08
Day 09
Day 10
Day 11
Day 12
Day 13
Day 14

| 詞彙 | cough [kʌf] 咳嗽　tired [ˈtaɪrd] 疲倦的　kindergarten [ˈkɪndəˌɡɑrtṇ] 幼稚園　take a day off 休假一天　fridge [frɪdʒ] 冰箱　usage [ˈjuzɪdʒ] 使用方法　direction [dəˈrɛkʃən] 指示　outer [ˈaʊtə] 外面的　grown-up [ˈɡron-ʌp] 成人　guidance [ˈɡaɪdəns] 指導

Q8 When could the dialogue take place? 這段對話可能發生在何時？

A. In the morning　在早上

B. In the afternoon　在下午

C. At night　在夜晚

D. We don't know.　無法得知。

| 詳解 | 從第一個文本的對話內容「...she can't sleep well... call her kindergarten teacher in the morning...」可知，孩子當時正在睡覺，而這位家長打算隔天早上打電話給老師請假，所以對話時間應為夜晚，正確答案是選項 C。

Q9 What can we learn about from the medicine direction? 我們可以從用藥指示中得知什麼？

A. The medicine was bought last week.　藥是上星期才買的。

B. Only adults can take it.　只有成年人可以服用。

C. Kids can't take it without a doctor's instruction.　孩童未經醫師指示不得服用。

D. The amount of the medicine to be taken a day is limited.
一天的用藥的量是有限制的。

| 詳解 | 從第二個文本（Usage Directions）中的「Do not go over 24 c.c. a day.」以及「Do not go over 18 c.c. a day.」可知，一天的用藥的量是有限制的，所以正確答案是選項 D。

| 詞彙 | instruction [ɪnˈstrʌkʃən] 指示，說明　limit [ˈlɪmɪt] 限制

Q10 How much amount can Sophie take after each meal? 蘇菲每一餐後應服用多少量的藥？

A. 6 c.c.　6 毫升

B. 12 c.c.　12 毫升

C. 18 c.c.　18 毫升

D. It depends on the doctor's advice.　要看醫生的建議。

| 詳解 | 這個題目要綜合兩篇文章來解題。首先，從第一個文本（對話）的「call her kindergarten teacher」可知，孩子正在上幼稚園，接著對照第二個文本的「For kids under 6: Talk to your doctor for guidance.」可知，6 歲以下的孩童病患應諮詢醫生，所以正確答案是選項 D。

| 詞彙 | depend on 在於⋯，端視⋯，依靠⋯

Part 1 詞彙

1. Her goal is ＿＿＿＿＿＿＿＿ financially independent.

   A. being　　　　　　　　C. been
   B. to be　　　　　　　　D. to being

2. She had a car ＿＿＿＿＿＿＿＿ on her way to work this morning.

   A. accident　　　　　　　C. umbrella
   B. library　　　　　　　　D. celebration

3. The room was so hot that everyone was sweating due to the intense ＿＿＿＿＿＿＿＿.

   A. heat　　　　　　　　　C. snow
   B. rain　　　　　　　　　D. wind

4. Every night before going to bed, she likes to ＿＿＿＿＿＿＿＿ a diary to record her thoughts and experiences.

   A. have　　　　　　　　　C. write
   B. play　　　　　　　　　D. keep

5. She was ＿＿＿＿＿＿＿＿ tired that she couldn't stay awake during the movie.

   A. such　　　　　　　　　C. too
   B. so　　　　　　　　　　D. very

6. She is getting ready for the meeting. She is ＿＿＿＿＿＿＿＿ to start her presentation.

   A. unwilling　　　　　　　C. being
   B. having　　　　　　　　D. about

7. My sister always talks to ＿＿＿＿＿＿＿＿ in the mirror when she practices her speech.

   A. her　　　　　　　　　　C. herself
   B. she　　　　　　　　　　D. theirs

8. I need _____ sugar to make this cake.

    A. many   C. a few

    B. several   D. a lot of

9. The new bridge _____ by the construction company last year.

    A. builds   C. was built

    B. built   D. is built

10. Jenny enjoys playing _____ the piano and the violin.

    A. both   C. only

    B. much   D. even

Part 2 段落填空

Last summer, my friends and I decided to take a road trip across the country. We were excited to see many famous (11) and experience different cultures. One day, we visited a small town where we had the chance (12) with the locals and try traditional dishes. (13) We hiked for hours, reaching the summit and enjoying most beautiful views I had (14) seen.

11. A. films

    B. landmarks

    C. documents

    D. postcards

12. A. interacting

    B. collecting

    C. appearing

    D. forgiving

13. A. We were too tired , so we went back to our hotel early.

    B. I was surprised that people there were few and far between.

    C. The next stop was a breathtaking mountain range.

    D. Because of having a fight with my friends, I focused on exploring the town alone.

Day 08
Day 09
Day 10
Day 11
Day 12
Day 13
Day 14

14. A. even

    B. often

    C. ever

    D. never

Questions 15-18

In today's fast-paced world, (15) technology rapidly advancing, people are constantly using their smartphones for various tasks. Many find these (16) really helpful and convenient. (17) , there is a growing concern about the amount of time spent on cell-phones. People often wonder (18) or they are living in a virtual world.

*virtual 虛擬的

15. A. when

    B. because

    C. from

    D. with

16. A. actions

    B. devices

    C. bundles

    D. materials

17. A. However

    B. Therefore

    C. Instead

    D. Besides

18. A. how to cook a delicious meal

    B. if they are truly communicating with others

    C. why the sky is blue

    D. when the next bus will arrive

Questions 19-21

From:	Service@home_tech.com.tw
To:	Undisclosed Recipients
Subject:	Special Offer

Dear Customer,

We hope this email finds you well. For a limited time, we are excited to offer you a special discount on our latest home appliances collection. From smart kitchen aids to energy-efficient appliances, we have things for every home.

Don't miss out on this special promotion! Visit our website at www.home_tech. com.tw and use the code HOMEDEAL20 to get an extra 20% off your purchase. This offer is only valid until the end of this month.

Best regards,
HomeTech Team

Alex
Hey, did you check your email today?

Yeah, I got a promotional email from HomeTech and I've browsed through the content.
Lisa

Alex
So? Is there anything catching your eyes?

Yes, I'm considering the Smart Coffee Maker.
Lisa

Alex
Really? How much does it cost?

They offer a time-limited discount code and you only have to spend NT$2,400 to get it. What do you think?
Lisa

Alex
That sounds like a deal.

19. What is the purpose of this email?

    A. A discount on indoor furniture

    B. A customer satisfaction survey

    C. A new collection of smart kitchen aids

    D. A limited-time offer on home appliances

20. What is the original price of the Smart Coffee Maker?

    A. NT$ 2040   C. NT$ 2800

    B. NT$ 2400   D. NT$ 3000

21. What does Alex think about the discounted price of the coffee maker?

    A. It's not a good deal.   C. The price is not bad.

    B. He will deal with it later.   D. It's too expensive.

Questions 22-24

Attention

Dear visitors! We're happy to have you here. To ensure the well-being of our animals and your safety, kindly adhere to the following rules:

- ○ Respect the Animals: Please avoid loud noises and sudden movements. It helps keep our animal friends happy.

- ○ No Feeding: Please refrain from feeding them to maintain their health.

- ○ Stay on Paths: Stick to designated paths to protect both you and the animals. Climbing barriers is not allowed for everyone's safety.

- ○ Enjoy the Show: Join us for scheduled animal shows. It's a great way to learn and have fun!

Thank you for your cooperation. Have a fantastic time exploring the wonders of the animal kingdom!

22. What is the sign intended for?

    A. To welcome visitors   C. To promote animal shows

    B. To provide safety guidelines D. To sell tickets

23. Why should visitors avoid feeding the animals?

    A. It's good for the health of the animals.

    B. There may be loud noises.

    C. The animals are on a diet.

    D. Feeding is only allowed during shows.

24. What is NOT allowed for visitors' safety?

    A. Making sudden moves   C. Taking photos of the animals

    B. Making loud noises   D. Climbing barriers

Questions 25-27

This is the menu of "Happy Hour Fast Food Restaurant". This restaurant is next to Kelvin's school. Kelvin and his classmates go there to have lunch frequently. Today Kelvin is going to "Happy Hour" again.

Happy Hour Menu			
SOUPS		**SANDWICHES**	
[✓] Chicken Noodle $1.95		[ ] Tuna	$3.25
[ ] Beef and Vegetable $2.50		[ ] Turkey	$3.75
MAIN DISHES		[ ] Beef	$4.25
[✓] Hamburger	$2.95	**BEVERAGES**	
[ ] Fried Chicken	$3.95	[✓] Coffee	$0.75
[ ] Steak	$4.95	[ ] Tea	$0.75
SIDE ORDERS		[ ] Orange Juice	$1.00
[✓] French Fries	$1.25	[ ] Apple Juice	$1.00
Baked Potato	$1.00	[ ] Milk	$0.85
SALAD		[✓] Coke	$0.75
Italian Salad	$2.25	[ ] Mineral Water	$0.75
[✓] Caesar Salad	$2.50	Total	$10.15

25. How many items does Kelvin order?

    A. Seven items   C. Five items

    B. Six items   D. Four items

26. How much does Kevin spend on drinks?

    A. $1.50   C. $2.95

    B. $2.50   D. $10.15

27. Which of the following combination is good for a vegetarian?

    A. Beef and vegetable soup, Italian salad and coke.

    B. Hamburger, baked potato and milk.

    C. Tuna sandwich, French fries, and apple juice.

    D. French fries, Caesar salad and mineral water.

Questions 28-30

Once upon a time, there were three little pigs named Peter, Paul, and Penny. They each built their own houses. Peter built his house with straw, Paul with tree branches, and Penny with bricks. One day, a big bad wolf came to their neighborhood. He made a great physical effort to blow Peter's straw house, and it fell down easily. Peter ran to Paul's house, but the wolf, deciding to have a snack, blew the tree-branch house down too. Now, the scared siblings ran to Penny's brick house. The wolf tried his hardest to blow down the strong brick house, but it didn't move at all. The three little pigs were safe. The wolf gave up and went away hungry. From that day on, Peter, Paul, and Penny knew the importance of hard work and making wise choices.

28. What material did the three pigs NOT use to build their houses?

    A. Tree branches   C. Bricks

    B. Straw   D. Wood

29. Whose house did the wolf fail to destroy?

    A. Peter's   C. Penny's

    B. Paul's   D. None of the above

30. What does the story intend to teach us?

    A. The importance of working hard and making proper choices

    B. The value of friendship and cooperation

    C. The positive attitude toward difficulties

    D. Learning from past mistakes and experiences

Day 08
Day 09
Day 10
Day 11
Day 12
Day 13
Day 14

上頁簡答

解答與詳解

1. (B) 2. (A) 3. (A) 4. (D) 5. (B) 6. (D) 7. (C) 8. (D) 9. (C)
10. (A) 11. (B) 12. (A) 13. (C) 14. (C) 15. (D) 16. (B)
17. (A) 18. (B) 19. (D) 20. (D) 21. (C) 22. (B) 23. (A)
24. (D) 25. (B) 26. (A) 27. (D) 28. (D) 29. (C) 30. (A)

Part 1 詞彙

Q1 考題重點〉一定要用不定詞（to-V）的情況

Her goal is _____ financially independent.

A. being　　　　**B. to be**　　　　C. been　　　　D. to being

| 翻譯 | 她的目標是財務自由。

| 詳解 | goal（目標）代表一件未完成、未達到的事，所以要用表示「目的」或「未來」的不定詞作為補語，正確答案是選項 B。不定詞的結構是「to + 原形動詞」，所以 D 是錯誤的。

| 詞彙 | **goal** [gol] 目標　**financially** [faɪˈnænʃəlɪ] 財務上
independent [ˌɪndɪˈpɛndənt] 獨立的，自主的

Q2 考題重點〉選擇符合句意的名詞

She had a car _____ on her way to work this morning.

A. accident　　B. library　　　　C. umbrella　　　　D. celebration

| 翻譯 | 她今天早上去上班途中出了車禍。

| 詳解 | 句子大意是在上班的路上發生了一場車禍，而 accident 指的是不慎發生的意外事件，所以正確答案是選項 A。

| 詞彙 | **accident** [ˈæksədənt] 意外事件　**umbrella** [ʌmˈbrɛlə] 雨傘　**library** [ˈlaɪbrɛrɪ] 圖書館
celebration [ˌsɛləˈbreʃən] 慶祝

Q3 考題重點〉heat 與 hot 的連結

The room was so hot that everyone was sweating due to the
intense _____.

A. heat　　　　　　　　　　C. snow

B. rain　　　　　　　　　　　D. wind

| 翻譯 | 房間太熱了，每個人都因為強烈的熱氣而流汗了。

| 詳解 | 因為前面有 hot，表示房間很熱，因此每個人都因為「熱」而流汗。hot 的名詞是 heat。因此，選項 A 是正確的答案，

| 詞彙 | **sweat** [swit] 流汗　**due to** 因為　**intense** [ɪnˈtɛns] 強烈的

Q4 考題重點〉「寫日記」的「寫」不是 write

Every night before going to bed, she likes to _____ a diary to record her thoughts and experiences.

A. have   C. write

B. play   **D. keep**

| 翻譯 | 每天晚上睡前，她喜歡寫日記來記錄她的想法和經歷。

| 詳解 | 「keep a diary」是一個常見的慣用語，因為「寫日記」是一種持續的習慣，因此動詞要用 keep（保持），正確答案是選項 D。

| 詞彙 | **thought** [θɔt] 想法，思想　**experience** [ɪk`spɪrɪəns] 經驗

Q5 考題重點〉「so... that...」句型

She was _____ tired that she couldn't stay awake during the movie.

A. such   C. too

B. so   D. very

| 翻譯 | 她太累了，以至於在看電影時無法保持清醒。

| 詳解 | 空格後面是形容詞（tired）接 that 引導的完整句子，因此可聯想到「so... that...」（如此⋯以至於⋯）句型，故正確答案是選項 B。「so + adj + N. + that」＝「such a + adj. + N. + that」。

| 詞彙 | **tired** [taɪrd] 感到疲累的　**awake** [ə`wek] 醒著的

Q6 考題重點〉「be about to」的使用時機

She is getting ready for the meeting. She is _____ to start her presentation.

A. unwilling   C. being

B. having   **D. about**

| 翻譯 | 她正在為會議做準備。她即將開始她的簡報。

| 詳解 | 前面句子提到為了會議做好準備了，所以第二句應該是「即將開始做簡報」，正確答案是選項 D。

| 詞彙 | **presentation** [ˌprizɛn`teʃən]　演示，簡報的發表　**unwilling** [ʌn`wɪlɪŋ] 不願意的

Day 08

Day 09

Day 10

Day 11

Day 12

Day 13

Day 14

Q7 考題重點〉「反身代名詞」的用法

My sister always talks to _____ in the mirror when she practices her speech.

A. her
C. **herself**

B. she
D. theirs

| 翻譯 | 我妹妹總是對著鏡子裡的自己練習演講。

| 詳解 | 在這個句子中，My sister 是主詞，而當她對著鏡子說話時，要用反身代名詞 herself 表示「她自己」。因此，正確的選項是 C。

| 詞彙 | **mirror** [`mɪrɚ] 鏡子　**practice** [`præktɪs] 練習

Q8 考題重點〉後面可以接不可數名詞的限定詞

I need _____ sugar to make this cake.

A. many
C. a few

B. several
D. **a lot of**

| 翻譯 | 我需要很多糖來做這個蛋糕。

| 詳解 | sugar 是不可數名詞，因此要用可以修飾可數名詞及不可數名詞的 a lot of （很多），故正確答案是選項 D。其他選項如 many、several 和 a few（一些）僅能用於修飾可數名詞。

| 詞彙 | **sugar** [`ʃʊgɚ] 糖

Q9 考題重點〉時態＋語態的雙重考量

The new bridge _____ by the construction company last year.

A. builds
C. **was built**

B. built
D. is built

| 翻譯 | 這座新橋在去年由這家建築公司所建造。

| 詳解 | 句意是「新橋被建築公司建造」，且句尾有表過去的時間副詞（last year），因此要用被動式的 was built，正確答案是選項 C。

| 詞彙 | **construction** [kən`strʌkʃən] 建造，建設

Q10 考題重點〉both 的用法

Jenny enjoys playing _____ the piano and the violin.

A. both   C. only

B. much   D. even

| 翻譯 | 珍妮喜歡彈奏鋼琴和小提琴。

| 詳解 | 空格後面有「A and B」，符合「both A and B」的句構，表示「A 與 B 兩者」，因此正確答案是選項 A。

| 詞彙 | violin [ˌvaɪə`lɪn] 小提琴

Part 2 段落填空

Questions 11-14

Last summer, my friends and I decided to take a road trip across the country. We were excited to see many famous **(11) landmarks** and experience different cultures. One day, we visited a small town where we had the chance **(12) interacting** with the locals and try traditional dishes. **(13) The next stop was a breathtaking mountain range.** We hiked for hours, reaching the summit and enjoying most beautiful views I had **(14) ever** seen.

| 翻譯 | 去年夏天，我和我的朋友們決定進行一次縱貫全國的自駕遊。我們對於造訪許多著名地標和體驗不同文化感到興奮。有一天，我們造訪了一個小鎮，在那裡我們有機會與當地人互動，品嚐傳統美食。下一站是一座令人驚嘆的山脈。我們徒步爬山數小時，登上山頂欣賞到我所見過最美麗的風景。

Q11 考題重點〉選擇符合前後文意的名詞

A. films   C. documents

B. landmarks   D. postcards

| 詳解 | 文章內容與旅遊有關，而句意是造訪許多著名地標和體驗不同文化，所以正確答案為選項 B。A、C、D 選項的意思分別是「電影」、「文件」、「明信片」。

Q12 考題重點〉選擇正確的動詞片語

A. interacting   C. appearing

B. collecting   D. forgiving

| 詳解 | 句意是，有機會與當地人互動，所以正確答案為選項 A。其餘 collect、appear 以及 forgive 的意思分別是「收集」、「出現」、「原諒」，皆不符合語意。

Day 08
Day 09
Day 10
Day 11
Day 12
Day 13
Day 14

Q13 考題重點〉選擇符合前後文意的句子

A. We were too tired , so we went back to our hotel early.
我們太累了，所以我們提早回到飯店。

B. I was surprised that people there were few and far between.
我很訝異那裡人煙稀少。

C. The next stop was a breathtaking mountain range.
下一站是一座令人驚嘆的山脈。

D. Because of having a fight with my friends, I focused on exploring the town alone. 因為和朋友吵架了，我專注於獨自探索這個小鎮。

| 詳解 | 後面句子提到 We hiked for hours, reaching the summit...，所以空格句子應與山脈有關，正確答案為選項 C。

Q14 考題重點〉搭配完成式的副詞

A. even   **C. ever**

B. often   D. never

| 詳解 | 空格前後分別是 had 以及 seen，可見要填入一個搭配完成式的副詞，故正確答案是選項 C。「the most... I had ever seen」表示「我所見過最…的…」

Questions 15-18

In today's fast-paced world, **(15) with** technology rapidly advancing, people are constantly using their smartphones for various tasks. Many find these **(16) devices** really helpful and convenient. **(17) However**, there is a growing concern about the amount of time spent on cellphones. People often wonder **(18) if they are truly connecting with others** or they are living in a virtual world.

| 翻譯 | 在當今快節奏的世界中，隨著科技快速發展，人們經常使用他們的智慧型手機進行各種任務。許多人發現這些裝置確實很有幫助且方便。然而，對於在手機上花費的時間，人們越來越擔憂。人們常常想知道他們是否真正與他人建立聯繫，還是被深陷在虛擬世界中。

Q15 考題重點〉表原因或附帶條件的介系詞 with

A. when   C. from

B. because   **D. with**

| 詳解 | 句子要表達的是「在當今快節奏的世界中，隨著／因為科技快速發展…」，所以可以表示「原因」的 with，即選項 D 是正確答案。空格後面不是完整句子，不能填入連接詞，所以 A、B 文法錯誤。

Q16 考題重點〉選擇正確的名詞

A. actions   C. bundles

B. devices   D. materials

| 詳解 | 前面提到智慧型手機的使用，而這句又說「很有幫助且方便」，顯然空格這個名詞就是指手機本身，所以正確答案是表示「裝置」的選項 B。

Q17 考題重點〉連接性副詞的使用

A. However   C. Instead

B. Therefore   D. B.sides

| 詳解 | 空格前面的內容主要關於手機的便利與優點，而後面卻是人們的憂慮，故應填入表示語意轉折或相反意義的 However，正確答案是選項 A。

Q18 考題重點〉選擇符合前後文意的句子

A. how to cook a delicious meal   如何烹飪美味的餐

B. if they are truly communicating with others   是否真正與他人交際

C. why the sky is blue   為什麼天空是藍色

D. when the next bus will arrive   下一班公車何時到

| 詳解 | 空格後面是對等連接詞 or（或者），顯然這一句應與 they are living in a virtual world（他們正住在虛擬世界中）相同意義，因此正確答案是選項 B。

Questions 19-21

From:	Service@home_tech.com.tw
To:	Undisclosed Recipients
Subject:	Special Offer

Dear Customer,

We hope this email finds you well. For a limited time, we are excited to offer you a special discount on our latest home appliances collection. From smart kitchen aids to energy-efficient appliances, we have things for every home.

Don't miss out on this special promotion! Visit our website at www.home_tech. com.tw and use the code HOMEDEAL20 to get an extra 20% off your purchase. This offer is only valid until the end of this month.

Best regards,
HomeTech Team

Alex
Hey, did you check your email today?

Yeah, I got a promotional email from HomeTech and I've browsed through the content.

Lisa

Alex
So? Is there anything catching your eyes?

Yes, I'm considering the Smart Coffee Maker.

Lisa

Alex
Really? How much does it cost?

They offer a time-limited discount code and you only have to spend NT$2,400 to get it. What do you think?

Lisa

Alex
That sounds like a deal.

寄件者：	Service@home_tech.com.tw
收件者：	匿名收件者
主旨：	特別優惠

親愛的顧客：

展信愉快。在有限的時間內，我們很高興提供您我們最新家電產品系列的特別優惠。從智慧型廚房輔助器到節能家電，我們為每個家庭都準備了一些東西。

請勿錯過這次特別促銷！上我們的網站 www.home_tech.com.tw 看看，然後用代碼 HOMEDEAL20 可以獲得 20% 的折扣。這項優惠有效期限僅至本月底。

謹啟
HomeTech 團隊

嗨，你今天有收郵件嗎？
艾力克斯

有啊，我收到 HomeTech 的優惠消息，我已經瀏覽過內容了。
麗莎

所以呢？有什麼東西吸引你注意的嗎？
艾力克斯

有啊，我正在考慮買一台智慧型咖啡機。
麗莎

真的嗎？多少錢？
艾力克斯

他們提供一個限時的折扣碼，只需要花台幣 2,400 元就可以買到。你覺得呢？
麗莎

我覺得還不錯。
艾力克斯

Day 08
Day 09
Day 10
Day 11
Day 12
Day 13
Day 14

| 詞彙 | undisclosed [ˌʌndɪsˈklozd] 未公開的　recipient [rɪˈsɪpɪənt] 接收者　offer [ˈɔfɚ] 提供
limited [ˈlɪmɪtɪd] 有限的　home appliance [hoʊm əˈplaɪəns] 家用電器
collection [kəˈlɛkʃən] 收藏，收集　aid [ed] 輔助器
energy-efficient [ˈɛnɚdʒi əˈfɪʃənt] 節能的　miss out on 錯失，錯過
promotion [prəˈmoʃən] 促銷　valid [ˈvælɪd] 有效的　promotional [prəˈmoʃənl] 促銷的
browse through 瀏覽　catch one's eyes 引起某人的注意

Q19 What is the purpose of this email?
這封電子郵件主要的目的為何？

A. A discount on indoor furniture.　室內傢俱折扣優惠

B. A customer satisfaction survey.　顧客滿意度調查

C. A new collection of smart kitchen aids.　一批新款的智慧廚房輔助設備

D. A limited-time offer on home appliances.　家電產品限時優惠

| 詳解 | 從一開始的「...we are excited to offer you... home appliances collection.」可知，正確答案是選項 D。

| 詞彙 | purpose [ˈpɚpəs] 目的　satisfaction [ˌsætɪsˈfækʃən] 滿意（度）

Q20 What is the original price of the Smart Coffee Maker?
這台智慧型咖啡機原價是多少

A. NT$ 2040　　　　　　　C. NT$ 2800

B. NT$ 2400　　　　　　　**D. NT$ 3000**

| 詳解 | 這個題目要綜合兩篇文章來解題。對話中 Lisa 提到，他只需要花 NT$2,400，因為店家有提供折扣碼，接著我們再參考電子郵件中說用代碼 HOMEDEAL20 可以獲得 20% 的折扣（打八折），所以原始價格應是「2400/0.8 = 3,000」，正確答案是選項 D。

| 詞彙 | original [əˈrɪdʒənl] 原始的

Q21 What does Alex think about the discounted price of the coffee maker? 艾力克斯覺得這咖啡機折扣後的價格如何？

A. It's not a good deal.　價格不是很好。

B. He will deal with it later.　他將於稍後進行處理。

C. The price is not bad.　這價格還不錯。

D. It's too expensive.　它太貴了。

| 詳解 | 從對話中最後一句 Alex 說「That sounds like a deal.」可知，他認為那是個不錯的交易，所以正確答案是選項 C。

| 詞彙 | discounted [dɪsˈkaʊntɪd] 有折扣的

Attention

Dear visitors! We're happy to have you here. To ensure the well-being of our animals and your safety, kindly adhere to the following rules:

- Respect the Animals: Please avoid loud noises and sudden movements. It helps keep our animal friends happy.

- No Feeding: Please refrain from feeding them to maintain their health.

- Stay on Paths: Stick to designated paths to protect both you and the animals. Climbing barriers is not allowed for everyone's safety.

- Enjoy the Show: Join us for scheduled animal shows. It's a great way to learn and have fun!

Thank you for your cooperation. Have a fantastic time exploring the wonders of the animal kingdom!

| 翻譯 |

注意

親愛的遊客們！我們很高興您的光臨。為了確保我們的動物健康和您的安全，請遵守以下規則：

- 尊重動物：請避免大聲喧嘩和突然的動作。這有助於讓我們動物朋友們感到快樂。

- 請不要餵食牠們，以維護牠們的健康。

- 保持行走在指定路徑上：請遵循指定的路徑，以保護您和動物。爬越欄杆是不允許的，這是為了大家的安全。

- 觀賞表演：來參加我們安排的動物表演。這是一個學習和娛樂的好方法！

感謝您的合作。祝您在探索這個動物王國的驚奇中度過愉快的時光！

| 詞彙 | **ensure** [ɪnˈʃʊr] 確保　**well-being** [ˈwɛlˈbiɪŋ] 安康，幸福　**adhere to** 遵守
respect [rɪˈspɛkt] 尊重　**sudden** [ˈsʌdn̩] 突然的　**feed** [fid] 餵食
refrain from 避免，克制　**maintain** [menˈten] 維持　**stick to** 堅持，遵循
designated [ˈdɛzɪgˌnetɪd] 指定的　**protect** [prəˈtɛkt] 保護
barrier [ˈbæriɚ] 障礙，圍欄　**scheduled** [ˈskɛdʒʊld] 預定的
cooperation [koˌɑpəˈreʃən] 合作　**fantastic** [fænˈtæstɪk] 精彩的，極好的
wonder [ˈwʌndɚ] 奇蹟，驚奇　**kingdom** [ˈkɪŋdəm] 王國

Q22 What is the sign intended for? 告示牌的設立目的為何？

A. To welcome visitors　為了歡迎遊客前來

B. To provide safety guidelines　為了提供安全指南

C. To promote animal shows　為了推廣動物表演

D. To sell tickets　為了販售門票

|詳解|　從一開頭的「To ensure the well-being of our animals and your safety...」（為了確保我們動物的健康和您的安全）可知，告示牌主要目的是提供安全指南，所以正確答案是選項 B。

|詞彙|　intended [ɪnˋtɛndɪd] 打算中的　guideline [ˋgaɪdˏlaɪn] 指南，指引

Q23 Why should visitors avoid feeding the animals?
為何遊客應避免向動物餵食？

A. It's good for the health of the animals.　那對動物健康有益。

B. There may be loud noises.　可能會有大聲的噪音。

C. The animals are on a diet.　動重正在進行節食。

D. Feeding is only allowed during shows.　餵食僅限表演時才能進行。

|詳解|　從第二項規定的內容「No Feeding: Please refrain from feeding them to maintain their health.」可知，正確答案是選項 A。

|詞彙|　on a diet 正在進行節食

Q24 What is NOT allowed for visitors' safety?
為了遊客的安全，何者是不被允許的？

A. Making sudden moves　做出突如其來的動作

B. Making loud noises　製造大聲的噪音

C. Taking photos of the animals　照動物的照片

D. Climbing barriers　爬越欄杆

|詳解|　一般來說，遊客逛動物園會被告知許多禁止的事情，不過請注意本題焦點擺在「for visitors' safety」。從第三項規定的內容「Climbing barriers is not allowed for everyone's safety.」可知，正確答案是選項 D。

Questions 25-27

This is the menu of "Happy Hour Fast Food Restaurant". This restaurant is next to Kelvin's school. Kelvin and his classmates go there to have lunch frequently. Today Kelvin is going to "Happy Hour" again.

Happy Hour Menu

SOUPS		SANDWICHES	
[✓] Chicken Noodle	$1.95	[ ] Tuna	$3.25
[ ] Beef and Vegetable	$2.50	[ ] Turkey	$3.75
MAIN DISHES		[ ] Beef	$4.25
[✓] Hamburger	$2.95	**BEVERAGES**	
[ ] Fried Chicken	$3.95	[✓] Coffee	$0.75
[ ] Steak	$4.95	[ ] Tea	$0.75
SIDE ORDERS		[ ] Orange Juice	$1.00
[✓] French Fries	$1.25	[ ] Apple Juice	$1.00
Baked Potato	$1.00	[ ] Milk	$0.85
SALAD		[✓] Coke	$0.75
Italian Salad	$2.25	[ ] Mineral Water	$0.75
[✓] Caesar Salad	$2.50	Total	$10.15

| 翻譯 | 這是「快樂時光速食餐廳」的菜單。這家餐廳在凱文學校的旁邊。凱文和他的同學常常到那裡吃午餐。今天，凱文又去「快樂時光」了。

「快樂時光」菜單

湯		三明治	
[✓] 雞肉麵湯	$1.95	[ ] 鮪魚三明治	$3.25
[ ] 牛肉蔬菜湯	$2.50	[ ] 火雞三明治	$3.75
主菜		[ ] 牛肉三明治	$4.25
[✓] 漢堡	$2.95	飲料	
[ ] 炸雞	$3.95	[✓] 咖啡	$0.75
[ ] 牛排	$4.95	[ ] 茶	$0.75
副餐		[ ] 柳橙汁	$1.00
[✓] 薯條	$1.25	[ ] 蘋果汁	$1.00
[ ] 烤馬鈴薯	$1.00	[ ] 牛奶	$0.85
沙拉		[✓] 可樂	$0.75
義大利沙拉	$2.25	[ ] 礦泉水	$0.75
[✓] 凱薩沙拉	$2.50	總計	$10.15

Day 08

Day 09

Day 10

Day 11

Day 12

Day 13

Day 14

| 詞彙 | next to 在…旁邊　soup [sup] 湯　noodle [ˈnudl] 麵條　tuna [ˈtjunə] 鮪魚
turkey [ˈtɝkɪ] 火雞　main dish [men] [dɪʃ] 主菜　beverage [ˈbɛvərɪdʒ] 飲料
fried chicken [fraɪd] [ˈtʃɪkən] 炸雞　side order [saɪd] [ˈɔrdɚ] 副餐
French Fries [frɛntʃ] [fraɪz] 薯條　baked [bekt] 烤的
mineral water [ˈmɪnərəl] [ˈwɔtɚ] 礦泉水

Q25 How many items does Kelvin order?
凱文總共點了幾樣東西？

A. Seven items　七樣

B. Six items　六樣

C. Five items　五樣

D. Four items　四樣

| 詳解 | 從菜單上可以清楚看到打了六個勾（✓），所以正確答案是選項 B。

| 詞彙 | item [ˈaɪtəm] 一條，一項

Q26 How much does Kevin spend on drinks?
凱文共花多少錢在飲料上？

A. $1.50　　　　　　　　　　C. $2.95

B. $2.50　　　　　　　　　　　D. $10.15

| 詳解 | 從菜單上可以看到飲料（beverages）底下的咖啡（coffee）和可樂（coke）有打勾，
價錢皆為 $0.75，總共是 $1.50，所以正確答案是選項 A。

| 詞彙 | drinks [drɪŋks] 飲料

Q27 Which of the following combination is good for a vegetarian?
以下哪一項組合適合素食者？

A. Beef and vegetable soup, Italian salad and coke.
牛肉蔬菜湯、義大利沙拉和可樂。

B. Hamburger, baked potato and milk.
漢堡、烤馬鈴薯和牛奶。

C. Tuna sandwich, French fries, and apple juice.
鮪魚三明治、薯條和蘋果汁。

D. French fries, Caesar salad and mineral water.
薯條、凱薩沙拉和礦泉水。

| 詳解 | 題目中的 vegetarian 是 vegetable（蔬菜）的衍生字，意思是「素食主義者」（吃素的人），所以正確答案是選項 D。

| 詞彙 | **combination** [ˌkɑmbəˈneʃən] 組合　**vegetarian** [ˌvɛdʒəˈtɛrɪən] 素食主義者

Questions 28-30

Once upon a time, there were three little pigs named Peter, Paul, and Penny. They each built their own houses. Peter built his house with straw, Paul with tree branches, and Penny with bricks. One day, a big bad wolf came to their neighborhood. He made a great physical effort to blow Peter's straw house, and it fell down easily. Peter ran to Paul's house, but the wolf, deciding to have a snack, blew the tree-branch house down too. Now, the scared siblings ran to Penny's brick house. The wolf tried his hardest to blow down the strong brick house, but it didn't move at all. The three little pigs were safe. The wolf gave up and went away hungry. From that day on, Peter, Paul, and Penny knew the importance of hard work and making wise choices.

| 翻譯 | 從前，有三隻小豬，他們分別叫彼得、保羅和潘妮。他們各自建造了自己的房子。彼得用稻草，保羅用樹枝，潘妮用磚頭建造。有一天，一隻大野狼來到他們的社區。他使勁吹著彼得的稻草房，而它輕易地被吹倒了。彼得跑到保羅的房子，但野狼決定要吃點東西，也輕易地把這樹枝房吹倒了。現在，受到驚嚇的兄弟姐妹們跑到潘妮的磚房。野狼竭盡全力要吹倒堅固的磚房，但它一點都不動搖。三隻小豬安全了。野狼放棄了，餓著肚子離開了。從那天起，彼得、保羅和潘妮知道努力工作和做明智的選擇的重要性。

| 詞彙 | **once upon a time** 從前，曾幾何時　**straw** [strɔ] 稻草　**branch** [bræntʃ] 樹枝，分枝
brick [brɪk] 磚塊　**wolf** [wʊlf] 狼　**physical** [ˈfɪzɪkəl] 物理的，身體的
scared [skɛrd] 害怕的，受驚嚇的　**siblings** [ˈsɪblɪŋz] 兄弟姐妹
try one's hardest 盡全力，竭盡所能　**wise** [waɪz] 明智的

Q28 What material did the three pigs NOT use to build their houses?
三隻豬沒有使用什麼材料來建造他們的房子？

A. Tree branches　樹枝

B. Straw　稻草

C. Bricks　磚頭

D. Wood　木材

| 詳解 | 從第二句「Peter built... bricks.」可知，沒有提到的是 wood，所以正確答案是選項 D。

| 詞彙 | **material** [məˈtɪrɪəl] 材料

Q29 Whose house did the wolf fail to destroy?
野狼無法摧毀誰的房子？

A. Peter's　彼得的

B. Paul's　保羅的

C. Penny's　潘妮的

D. None of the above　以上皆非

| 詳解 | 從「The wolf tried his hardest... it didn't move at all.」這句可知，野狼無法吹倒用磚打造的房子，也就是潘妮的房子，所以正確答案是選項 C。

| 詞彙 | **fail to** 無法做到　**destroy** [dɪˋstrɔɪ] 毀壞

Q30 What does the story intend to teach us?
這故事想要教我們的是什麼？

A. The importance of working hard and making proper choices

B. The value of friendship and cooperation

C. The positive attitude toward difficulties

D. Learning from past mistakes and experiences

| 詳解 | 從最後一句「...Peter, Paul, and Penny knew the importance of...」可知，這故事要教導我們的是努力工作和做明智的選擇的重要性，所以正確答案是選項 A。

| 詞彙 | **intend to-V** 意圖要…　**cooperation** [koˌɑpəˋreʃən] 合作
positive [ˋpɑzətɪv] 積極的，正面的　**attitude** [ˋætətjud] 態度

Day 08
Day 09
Day 10
Day 11
Day 12
Day 13
Day 14

Part 1 詞彙

1. We found the restaurant _____ when we arrived for dinner last night.

   A. close　　　　　B. closing　　　　C. to close　　　D. closed

2. In his job, John is _____ for managing the company's finances and making sure everything is in order.

   A. rejected　　　　B. responsible　　C. rightful　　　D. royal

Part 2 段落填空

At the café, I went to the counter and looked at the menu. There were many choices like coffee, tea, __(3)__ , and cakes. __(4)__ The server smiled and asked __(5)__ I wanted anything else. I shook my head and paid for my order. Then, I found a table __(6)__ the window and waited for my food. Soon, the server brought my cappuccino and cake. They looked delicious and tasted __(7)__ !

3. A. sandwiches
   B. bakeries
   C. gloves
   D. watermelons

4. A. After I left the café, I saw a young
      kid riding a bicycle down the street.
   B. At the same time, I bumped into a
      magician who was eating oranges at
      another table.
   C. I decided to order a cappuccino and
      a slice of chocolate cake.
   D. I then realized I had left my umbrel-
      la at home, so I started running out
      of the café.

5. A. after
   B. if
   C. when
   D. what

6. A. as
   B. with
   C. by
   D. to

7. A. wonder
   B. wondering
   C. wonderful
   D. wonderfully

Micky, let's go watch a musical this weekend.
Do you have time to go with me?

I'm not in the mood for entertainment, Barbara.
You know, I've recently tried hard to look for a job.

 Check this out: https://www.exciting-musical/2024/lionking. Maybe you'll want to go with me.

 Q https://www.exciting-musical/2024/lionking

Exciting News!

Don't miss this opportunity to see what LION KING will bring you soon! For more, check out the following links.

➢ About the National Theater Hall
- ● The History ● Location ● Sponsors

➢ About the musical LION KING
- ● Tour ● Photo Gallery ● The Performers

➢ More
- ● Book tickets now ● Careers

---

8. What does Barbara probably want Micky to do?

   A. Look for a job
   B. Explain something for her
   C. Share an activity with her
   D. Keep her company this weekend

9. Where can we find information about the sponsors of the event?

   A. The National Theater Hall
   B. The musical LION KING
   C. The Photo Gallery
   D. The Careers section

10. According to the website, what information may Micky feel interested in?

    A. The history of National Theater Hall
    B. The photos of LION KING
    C. The famous Performers
    D. Careers

解答與詳解

Part 1 詞彙

Q1 考題重點〉過去分詞表示被動

We found the restaurant _____ when we arrived for dinner last night.

A. close   B. closing   C. to close   **D. closed**

| 翻譯 | 昨晚我們到達餐廳時，發現它已經打烊了。

| 詳解 | 關鍵在於 found（發現）的受詞是「餐廳」（the restaurant），與「打烊」這個動詞之間的語意關連，因為餐廳不會自己去做打烊這個動作，所以應選被動式，正確答案是選項 D。

| 詞彙 | **arrive** [əˋraɪv] 抵達

Q2 考題重點〉選出正確的形容詞

In his job, John is _____ for managing the company's finances and making sure everything is in order.

A. rejected   **B. responsible**   C. rightful   D. royal

| 翻譯 | 在他的工作中，約翰負責管理公司的財務並確保一切井然有序。

| 詳解 | 句意是「負責管理公司的財務並確保…」，故正確答案是選項 B。A、C、D 的意思分別是「被拒絕」、「正當的」、「高貴的」。

| 詞彙 | **finance** [faɪˋnæns] 財務   **in order** 井然有序的

Part 2 段落填空

At the café, I went to the counter and looked at the menu. There were many choices like coffee, tea, **(3) sandwiches**, and cakes. **(4) I decided to order a cappuccino and a slice of chocolate cake.** The server smiled and asked **(5) if** I wanted anything else. I shook my head and paid for my order. Then, I found a table **(6) by** the window and waited for my food. Soon, the server brought my cappuccino and cake. They looked delicious and tasted **(7) wonderful**!

| 翻譯 | 在咖啡廳，我走到櫃檯，看了看菜單。菜單上有很多選擇，像是咖啡、茶、三明治和蛋糕等。我決定點一杯卡布奇諾和一片巧克力蛋糕。服務生微笑著問我是否還要其他的。我搖了搖頭，然後付款。接著，我找到了一張靠窗的桌子，等待我的食物。不久，服務生端來了我的卡布奇諾和蛋糕。它們看起來美味，味道也很棒！ |

Q3 考題重點〉填入適當的名詞

A. sandwiches　　　B. bakeries　　　　C. gloves　　　　D. watermelons

| 詳解 | 選項中只有三明治（sandwich）才可能是咖啡廳裡會提供的，所以正確答案應為選項 A。B、C、D 的意思分別是「麵包店」、「手套」、「西瓜」。 |

Q4 考題重點〉選擇符合前後文意的句子

A. After I left the café, I saw a young kid riding a bicycle down the street.
　　我離開咖啡館後，看見一個年輕的小孩在街上騎著腳踏車。

B. At the same time, I bumped into a magician who was eating oranges at another table.　　同時，我撞到了一個在另一張桌子上吃橙子的魔術師。

C. I decided to order a cappuccino and a slice of chocolate cake.
　　我決定點一杯卡布奇諾和一片巧克力蛋糕。

D. I then realized I had left my umbrella at home, so I started running out of the café.　　接著我意識到我把雨傘忘在家裡了，於是我開始跑出咖啡館。

| 詳解 | 前面句子提到，菜單上有很多選擇，像是…等，而後面句子是服務生問是否還需要其他東西，顯然這句要告訴服務生想點些什麼東西，因此正確答案為選項 C。 |

Q5 考題重點〉選擇適當的連接詞

A. after　　　　**B. if**　　　　C. when　　　　D. what

| 詳解 | 空格前 asked 是及物動詞，顯然要填入一個可以引導後面名詞子句（I wanted anything else）的連接詞，且句意是「服務生問我是否…」，所以正確答案為選項 B。if 當「是否」時，可引導名詞子句。 |

Q6 考題重點〉介系詞 by 可表示「靠近」

A. as　　　　B. with　　　　**C. by**　　　　D. to

| 詳解 | 句意是「找了一張靠窗的桌子」，by 有相當於 close to...（靠近…）的意思，所以正確答案為選項 C。 |

Q7 考題重點〉「感官動詞 + 形容詞」的用法

A. wonder   B. wondering   **C. wonderful**   D. wonderfully

| 詳解 | 空格前的 tasted（嘗起來）是感官動詞，後面常接形容詞作為主詞補語，所以正確答案為選項 C。

Part 3 閱讀理解

> Micky, let's go watch a musical this weekend.
> Do you have time to go with me?

> I'm not in the mood for entertainment, Barbara.
> You know, I've recently tried hard to look for a job.

> Check this out: https://www.exciting-musical/2024/lionking. Maybe you'll want to go with me.

Q https://www.exciting-musical/2024/lionking

Exciting News!

Hear unforgettable songs like "Circle of Life" and "Can You Feel the Love Tonight" sung live by talented performers. Don't miss this opportunity to see what LION KING will bring you soon! For more, check out the following links.

➤ About the National Theater Hall
- The History ◉ Location ◉ Sponsors

➤ About the musical LION KING
- Tour ◉ Photo Gallery ◉ The Performers

➤ More
- Book tickets now ◉ Careers

Day 15

Day 16

Day 17

Day 18

Day 19

Day 20

Day 21

| 翻譯 |

 米奇，這個週末去看音樂會吧！
你有時間和我一起去嗎？

芭芭拉，我沒心情去娛樂活動。你知道的，
我最近一直努力在找工作。

 進去看看：https://www.exciting-musical/2024/lionking
也許你會想和我一起去。

 Q https://www.exciting-musical/2024/lionking

令人振奮的消息！

聽著才華洋溢的藝人現場演唱，像是《生命之歌》和《你感受到愛了嗎》這些令人難忘歌曲。千萬別錯過《獅子王》即將帶來的演出！想了解更多，可點選看以下連結。

➢ 關於國家劇院

　　◉ 歷史沿革　◉ 地點　◉ 贊助者

➢ 關於《獅子王》音樂劇

　　◉ 巡迴演出　◉ 照片庫　◉ 演出者

➢ 更多

　　◉ 立即訂票　◉ 工作機會

| 詞彙 | musical [`mjuzɪk!] 音樂劇，歌舞劇　have time to-V 有空（去做某事）
in the mood for... 有…的心情　entertainment [ˌɛntɚˋtenmənt] 娛樂活動
unforgettable [ˌʌnfɚˋgɛtəbl] 令人難忘的　talented [ˋtæləntɪd] 有才華的，有天賦的
performer [pɚˋfɔrmɚ] 表演者，演員　opportunity [ˌɑpɚˋtjunətɪ] 機會，良機
check out 查看，瀏覽　sponsor [ˋspɑnsɚ] 贊助商，贊助者
gallery [ˋgælərɪ] 畫廊，展覽廳　career [kəˋrɪr] 職業生涯，工作機會

Q8 What does Barbara probably want Micky to do?
芭芭拉可能想要米奇做什麼？

A. Look for a job　去找工作

B. Explain something for her　給她解釋某事

C. Share an activity with her　跟她分享一個活動

D. Keep her company this weekend　這個週末陪伴她

| 詳解 | 在第一個文本的對話中，從芭芭拉希望米奇和她一起去去看音樂會這件事來看，最接近她本意的就是希望他這個週末陪伴她，所以正確答案是選項 D。

| 詞彙 | keep sb. company 陪伴某人

Q9 Where can we find information about the sponsors of the event?
我們可以在哪裡找到關於該活動贊助者的資訊？

A. The National Theater Hall　國家劇院

B. The musical LION KING　《獅子王》音樂劇

C. The Photo Gallery　照片庫

D. The Careers section　「工作機會」區

| 詳解 | 從第二個文本（網頁）中，可看到「Sponsors」位於「About the National Theater Hall」底下，所以正確答案是選項 A。

| 詞彙 | event [ɪˋvɛnt] 盛事，活動

Q10 According to the website, what information may Micky feel interested in?
根據該網站內容，米奇可能對於什麼感興趣？

A. The history of National Theater Hall　國家劇院的歷史

B. The photos of LION KING　《獅子王》的照片

C. The famous Performers　有名的演出者

D. Careers　工作機會

| 詳解 | 這個題目要綜合兩篇文章來解題。首先，從第一個文本（對話）中 Micky 說的「I've recently tried hard to look for a job.」可知，他最近一直心繫著找工作這件事，接著在第二個文本（網頁）最底下可以看到「Careers」這個選項，推知這部分也許會是 Micky 想去了解一下的，所以正確答案是選項 D。

| 詞彙 | (be) interested in 對…感興趣

Day 16

月　　日

我的完成時間＿＿＿＿＿分鐘
標準作答時間 10 分鐘

Day 15
Day 16
Day 17
Day 18
Day 19
Day 20
Day 21

Part 1 詞彙

1. I brush my teeth every morning and night to keep them healthy, just like the ＿＿＿＿＿＿＿＿＿ told me.
   A. artist　　　B. dentist　　　C. pianist　　　D. scientist

2. I'm sorry I've made you wait, ＿＿＿＿＿＿＿＿＿ I'm late because of a serious traffic jam.
   A. and　　　B. before　　　C. after　　　D. but

Part 2 段落填空

David walked proudly across the stage __(3)__ his family cheered loudly. Receiving his high school diploma felt __(4)__ a huge success. After that, they celebrated with a big dinner and __(5)__ . David expressed his thanks to his teachers and friends for their __(6)__ . Looking ahead, he felt both excited and nervous about __(7)__ the future held, but he was ready to go on this new journey.

3. A. though
   B. since
   C. unless
   D. while

4. A. as if
   B. like
   C. as
   D. for

5. A. took many photos to capture the moment
   B. shared stories about what they have experienced in the kindergarten.
   C. talked about the entrance exam they've just taken
   D. stepped down the stage with flying colors

6. A. entertainment
   B. agreement
   C. encouragement
   D. employment

7. A. why
   B. when
   C. what
   D. which

Take a look at this upcoming special offer! You can choose a birthday gift for our son.

Let me see... Oh no! I just bought a golf club in an Adidas shop yesterday!

 Oh yeah? No wonder you have the money. Yesterday was May 5, your pay day!

Adidas Sports Equipment

Limited Time Offer   Only on this weekend (May 9-10)

Product Item	Original Price	Special Price
Basketball Shoes	NT$2,800	NT$2,500
Soccer Ball	NT$ 1,000	NT$ 800
Golf Club	NT$8,500	NT$7,000
Gym Glove (a pair)	NT$450	NT$400

NOTE: For large orders, we offer lower prices for each item. Please call 02-6698-9922 for more details.

8. What does the first speaker suggest?

A. Go to an Adidas store   C. Go window shopping together

B. Choose a gift   D. Hand in the pay right away

9. What is NOT true about this Limited Time Offer?

A. You can save NT$200 if you purchase an Adidas soccer on this weekend.

B. The "limited time" here means only two days.

C. The soccer ball offers a 20% discount.

D. If you want to buy 100 pairs of gym gloves, you only need to pay NT$40,000.

10. According to the dialogue, how much did the second speaker pay on his golf club?

A. NT$ 7,000   C. NT$ 9,000

B. NT$ 8,500   D. NT$ 10,000

💡 **解答與詳解** | 上頁簡答 | 1. (B)　2. (D)　3. (D)　4. (B)　5. (A)
　　　　　　　　　　　　6. (C)　7. (C)　8. (B)　9. (D)　10. (B)

Part 1 詞彙

Q1 考題重點〉選出正確的名詞

I brush my teeth every morning and night to keep them healthy, just like the ＿＿＿＿＿＿＿＿＿＿ told me.

A. artist　　**B. dentist**　　C. pianist　　D. scientist

| 翻譯 | 我每天早晚都刷牙，就像牙醫告訴我的那樣，以保持牙齒健康。

| 詳解 | 本題關鍵字是 teeth 這個名詞，且句意是「就像牙醫說的…每天早晚刷牙」，所以正確答案是選項 B。

| 詞彙 | teeth [tiθ] **n.** 牙齒（單數為 tooth）　　artist [ˋɑrtɪst] **n.** 藝術家
dentist [ˋdɛntɪst] **n.** 牙醫　　scientist [ˋsaɪəntɪst] **n.** 科學家

Q2 考題重點〉sorry… but... 的用法

I'm sorry I've made you wait, ＿＿＿＿＿＿＿＿＿ I'm late because of a serious traffic jam.

A. and　　B. before　　C. after　　**D. but**

| 翻譯 | 抱歉讓你等待了，我是因為遇上嚴重塞車才遲到。

| 詳解 | 這是考表達歉意（sorry、apologize）的基本句型。通常會先用連接 but 之後再繼續說明抱歉的原因，故正確答案是選項 D。

| 詞彙 | traffic jam 交通壅塞，塞車

Part 2 段落填空

David walked proudly across the stage **(3) while** his family cheered loudly. Receiving his high school diploma felt **(4) like** a huge success. After that, they celebrated with a big dinner and **(5) took many photos to capture the moment**. David expressed his thanks to his teachers and friends for their **(6) encouragement**. Looking ahead, he felt both excited and nervous about **(7) what** the future held, but he was ready to go on this new journey.

| 翻譯 | David 驕傲地走過舞台，而當時他的家人們大聲地歡呼著。拿到高中畢業文憑讓他感到非常成功。之後，他們用一頓豐盛的晚餐慶祝，並拍下許多照片紀念這一刻。David 表示感謝他的老師和朋友們的鼓勵。展望未來，他感到既興奮又緊張，但他已準備好踏上他的新旅程。

Q3 考題重點〉符合句意的連接詞

A. though   C. unless

B. since   **D. while**

| 詳解 | 空格前後句意分別是「驕傲地走過舞台」以及「家人大聲歡呼」，在一場畢業典禮中，應該是同時發生的，所以正確答案應為選項 D。

Q4 考題重點〉「feel like + 名詞」 的與法

A. as if   C. as

B. like   D. for

| 詳解 | 這裡的 feel 是「感官動詞」，表示「感覺起來…」，後面如果要接名詞時，須先接介系詞 like 再接名詞，所以正確答案為選項 B。

Q5 考題重點〉選擇符合前後文意的句子

A. took many photos to capture the moment
   拍下許多照片紀念這一刻

B. shared stories about what they have experienced in the kindergarten.
   他們分享了在幼稚園中所經歷的故事。

C. talked about the entrance exam they've just taken
   他們討論了他們剛參加的入學考試。

D. stepped down the stage with flying colors
   他們風風光光地從舞台上走下來。

| 詳解 | 前面的內容提到 David 在高中畢業典禮結束後，用一頓豐盛的晚餐慶祝，顯然這裡要填入的內容還是與慶祝有關，對照四個選項的內容，最適當的就是「拍照留念」，所以正確答案是選項 A。

Q6 考題重點〉填入符合句意的名詞

A. entertainment   **C. encouragement**

B. agreement   D. employment

| 詳解 | 句意是「David 表示感謝他的老師和朋友們的…」，所以正確答案為選項 C。A、B、D 的意思分別是「娛樂」、「同意」、「雇用」。

Q7 考題重點〉複合關係代名詞 what 的用法

A. why   B. when   **C. what**   D. which

| 詳解 | 空格前是介系詞 about，要填入一個可以引導名詞子句（＿＿＿＿＿＿ the future held）作為其受詞的關係代名詞，因為及物動詞 held 要有受詞，所以只有 what（= the thing which）符合文法，正確答案為選項 C。

Part 3 閱讀理解

 Take a look at this upcoming special offer!
You can choose a birthday gift for our son.

Let me see... Oh no! I just bought a golf club in an Adidas shop yesterday!

 Oh yeah? No wonder you have the money.
Yesterday was May 5, your pay day!

Adidas Sports Equipment

Limited Time Offer   Only on this weekend (May 9-10)

Product Item	Original Price	Special Price
Basketball Shoes	NT$2,800	NT$2,500
Soccer Ball	NT$ 1,000	NT$ 800
Golf Club	NT$8,500	NT$7,000
Gym Glove (a pair)	NT$450	NT$400

NOTE: For large orders, we offer lower prices for each item. Please call 02-6698-9922 for more details.

Day 15
Day 16
Day 17
Day 18
Day 19
Day 20
Day 21

看一下這張即將到來的特賣商品！你可以選一樣作為兒子的生日禮物。

我看看...。噢，不會吧！我昨天才去一家愛迪達店買了一支高爾夫球桿！

 是嗎？難怪你會有錢。昨天是5月5日，是你的領薪日呢！

愛迪達體育用品

限時優惠
僅限本週末（5/9-5/10）

品項	原價	特價
籃球鞋	NT$2,800	NT$2,500
足球	NT$ 1,000	NT$ 800
高爾夫球桿	NT$8,500	NT$7,000
運動手套	NT$450	NT$400

備註：大額訂購者可享有各品項更優惠單價。請來電 02-6698-9922 詳談

| 詞彙 | **offer** [ˈɔfɚ] 出價，提議 **club** [klʌb] 棍棒 **pay day** [ˈpeˈde] 發薪日
equipment [ɪˈkwɪpmənt] 設備，器材 **limited** [ˈlɪmɪtɪd] - 有限的
original [əˈrɪdʒənl] 原始的，最初的 **glove** [glʌv] 手套
large order [lɑrdʒ ˈɔrdɚ] 大訂單

Q8 What does the first speaker suggest? 第一位說話者建議什麼？

A. Go to an Adidas store　去一間愛迪達商店

B. Choose a gift　選個禮物

C. Go window shopping together　一起去逛街

D. Hand in the pay right away　馬上交出薪水

| 詳解 | 從第一個文本的對話內容「You can choose a birthday gift for our son.」可知，第一位說話者建議為他們的兒子選個生日禮物，所以正確答案是選項 B。

| 詞彙 | **window shopping** 逛街 **hand in** 繳交

Day 15
Day 16
Day 17
Day 18
Day 19
Day 20
Day 21

Q9 What is NOT true about this Limited Time Offer?
關於這次的限時優惠，何者為非？

A. You can save NT$200 if you purchase an Adidas soccer on this weekend.
如果你在這週末買一顆愛迪達的足球，你可以節省新台幣兩百元。

B. The "limited time" here means only two days.
這裡的「限時」是指僅僅兩天的時間。

C. The soccer ball offers a 20% discount.　　買足球可以打八折。

**D. If you want to buy 100 pairs of gym gloves, you only need to pay
NT$40,000.**　　如果你想買 100 雙運動手套，你得支付新台幣四萬元。

|詳解| 在第二個文本（促銷廣告）中，soccer ball 的原價與特價分別是 1000 和 800，所以選項 A 與 C 的敘述都是正確的；而這裡的「Only on this weekend（May 9-10）」當然就是指上一行的「Limited Time Offer」，所以選項 B 也是正確的敘述；最後一行提到「For large orders, we offer lower prices for each item.」，這表示買 100 雙手套的話，可以獲得更低的單價，所以選項 D 是錯誤的敘述，故本題答案是 D。

Q10 According to the dialogue, how much did the second speaker pay on his golf club?
根據對話內容，第二位說話者花了多少錢買了高爾夫球桿？

A. NT$ 7,000　　新台幣七千元

B. NT$ 8,500　　新台幣八千五百元

C. NT$ 9,000　　新台幣九千元

D. NT$ 10,000　　新台幣一萬元

|詳解| 這個題目要綜合兩篇文章來解題。首先，從第一個文本（對話）的「I just bought a golf club in an Adidas shop yesterday!」以及「Yesterday was May 5, your pay day!」可知，他購買高爾夫球桿的時間是 5 月 5 日。接著對照第二個文本中 Golf Club 的原價（NT$8,500）與特價（NT$7,000）可知，因為是在特價日之前買的，所以是 NT$8,500，故正確答案是選項 B。

Part 1 詞彙

1. These are my ideas and I hope you can write down ＿＿＿＿＿＿＿＿＿ .

   A. your　　　　　B. yours　　　　　C. you're　　　　D. you

2. When the clock struck seven, Jerry ＿＿＿＿＿＿＿＿＿ up from his bed.

   A. any　　　　　　B. no　　　　　　C. was waking　　D. some

Part 2 段落填空

Jenny and Sophia decided to go on a trip to Taiwan together. They visited (3) places like Taipei 101 and the National Palace Museum. They (4) took a train to Jiufen, a (5) old town with narrow streets and tasty street food. After that, they went to Nantou to see the beautiful Sun Moon Lake. (6)   (7) , they ended their trip in Kaohsiung. They relaxed on the beach and tried delicious local seafood, where they had a good time exploring Taiwan together!

3. A. ancient
   B. remote
   C. famous
   D. dirty

4. A. even
   B. then
   C. thus
   D. really

5. A. charm
   B. charming
   C. charmed
   D. charmer

6. A. But they suddenly decided to skip their Taichung trip and head straight to the airport.
   B. However, they found out that the capital city was very boring.
   C. Because of the rain, they decided to stay at the hotel all day long.
   D. They enjoyed boating and biking around the lake.

7. A. In addition
   B. At last
   C. In fact
   D. On the contrary

Day 15

Day 16

Day 17

Day 18

Day 19

Day 20

Day 21

Part **3** 閱讀理解

> Oh YA! The two-day midterm is over! Any plans for tonight, Alma?

> Not tonight, but Let's go to The Moonlight Lounge for fun tomorrow night! You have never been there, right?

Join us for Lady's Night at Joes!!

Every Wednesday, from 8:00 P.M. onwards,
Join us for an astonishing evening of fun, music,
and special show.

➢ All ladies can come in for free!
➢ Get a free drink when you arrive!
➢ We have special deals on some cocktails all night!

A DJ will play the newest songs to keep you dancing all night! Bring your friends and come to The Moonlight Lounge for a special treat on a Wednesday night. It's your time to shine!

For more information and table reservations, contact us at:

☐ Phone: 555-123-4567
☐ Location: 123 Main Street, New York, NY 10001

---

8. Why does Alma suggest going to The Moonlight Lounge?

   A. To study for exams   C. To watch a movie

   B. To relax and have fun   D. To have a candlelight dinner

9. What special offer is mentioned in the ad for ladies?

   A. Discounted entry and free snacks   C. Free entry and discounted drinks

   B. Free entry and a free drink   D. Free entry and a free meal

10. When did their midterm begin?

   A. On Monday   B. On Tuesday   C. On Wednesday   D. On Thursday

Part 1 詞彙

Q1 考題重點〉填入所有格代名詞

These are my ideas and I hope you can write down ＿＿＿＿＿＿＿＿ .

A. your　　　　**B. yours**　　　　C. you're　　　　D. you

| 翻譯 | 這些是我的想法，而我希望你能寫下你的想法。

| 詳解 | your ideas = yours，作為 write down 的受詞，所以正確答案是選項 B。

| 詞彙 | write down 寫下來

Q2 考題重點〉過去進行式的使用時機

When the clock struck seven, Jerry ＿＿＿＿＿＿＿＿ up from his bed.

A. any　　　　B. no　　　　**C. was waking**　　　　D. some

| 翻譯 | 當七點鐘響時，Jerry 正從床上醒來。

| 詳解 | 當過去某一動作發生（the clock struck seven）時，或在過去某個時間點，另一個動作（wake up）正在進行，則用過去進行式來表示，故正確答案是選項 C。

| 詞彙 | struck [strʌk]（strike 的過去式）敲擊，敲打，鳴報（時間）

Part 2 段落填空

Jenny and Sophia decided to go on a trip to Taiwan together. They visited **(3) famous** places like Taipei 101 and the National Palace Museum. They **(4) then** took a train to Jiufen, a **(5) charming** old town with narrow streets and tasty street food. After that, they went to Nantou to see the beautiful Sun Moon Lake. **(6) They enjoyed boating and biking around the lake. (7) At last**, they ended their trip in Kaohsiung. They relaxed on the beach and tried delicious local seafood, where they had a good time exploring Taiwan together!

| 翻譯 | Jenny 和 Sophia 決定一起去台灣旅行。她們搭飛機到台北，這個首都城市。她們參觀了著名的地方，像是台北 101 和故宮博物院。然後，她們搭火車到九份，這是一個迷人的古老小鎮，有窄窄的街道和美味的街頭小吃。接著，她們去了南投，看到了美麗的日月潭。她們享受在湖上划船和騎自行車的樂趣。最後，她們在高雄結束了旅行，在那裡她們在海灘上放鬆身心，品嚐美味的當地海鮮。她們一起探索台灣度過了美好的時光！

Q3 考題重點〉選擇符合前後文意的形容詞

A. ancient　　　　B. remote　　　　**C. famous**　　　　D. dirty

| 詳解 | 句意是「參觀了著名的地方，像是台北 101…」，所以正確答案應為選項 C。A、D 的意思分別是「古老的」、「遙遠的」、「骯髒的」

Q4 考題重點〉表示「接續」的副詞 then

A. even　　　　**B. then**　　　　C. thus　　　　D. really

| 詳解 | 整段文章描述的是去各個地方觀光的過程，首先是去了台北 101 和故宮博物院，而這句提到去了迷人的古老小鎮九份，顯然要填入一個表示「先後順序」的副詞，所以正確答案為選項 B。A 的意思是「甚至」，C 的意思是「因此」，D 的意思是「真正地」。

Q5 考題重點〉現在分詞作形容詞的用法

A. charm　　　　**B. charming**　　　　C. charmed　　　　D. charmer

| 詳解 | charm 當動詞表示「使受到吸引」，當名詞是「吸引力」的意思，而空格要填入的是形容詞，只有 B、C 可選。句意是「迷人的古老小鎮」，所以正確答案為選項 B。過去分詞 charmed 是「受到吸引的」意思，不合句意。

Q6 考題重點〉選擇符合前後文意的句子

A. But they suddenly decided to skip their Taichung trip and head straight to the airport.　但他們突然決定取消他們的台中之旅，直接前往機場。

B. However, they found out that the capital city was very boring.
然而，他們發現這個首都城市非常無聊。

C. Because of the rain, they decided to stay at the hotel all day long.
因為下雨的緣故，他們決定整天都待在飯店裡。

D. They enjoyed boating and biking around the lake.
她們享受在湖上划船和騎自行車的樂趣。

| 詳解 | 前面句子提到她們去了南投，看到了美麗的日月潭，所以這句應描述在明潭的活動，因此正確答案為選項 D。

Q7 考題重點〉符合文意的連接性副詞

A. In addition　　　　**B. At last**　　　　C. In fact　　　　D. On the contrary

| 詳解 | 空格後面提到「they ended their trip in Kaohsiung」，表示這是她們台灣之旅的最後一個行程，因此應填入一個作為結束的連接性副詞，正確答案為選項 B。A、C、D 意思分別是「此外」、「事實上」、「相反地」。

Oh YA! The two-day midterm is over! Any plans for tonight, Alma?

Not tonight, but Let's go to The Moonlight Lounge for fun tomorrow night! You have never been there, right?

Join us for Lady's Night at Joes!!

Every Wednesday, from 8:00 P.M. onwards,
Join us for an astonishing evening of fun, music,
and special show.

➢ All ladies can come in for free!
➢ Get a free drink when you arrive!
➢ We have special deals on some cocktails all night!

A DJ will play the newest songs to keep you dancing all night! Bring your friends and come to The Moonlight Lounge for a special treat on a Wednesday night. It's your time to shine!

For more information and table reservations, contact us at:
☐ Phone: 555-123-4567
☐ Location: 123 Main Street, New York, NY 10001

| 翻譯 |

 喔耶！為期兩天的期中考終於結束了。愛瑪，今晚有什麼計畫？

今晚沒有，不過我們明晚可以去「月光大廳」玩一下！你還沒去過那地方吧？

Day 15
Day 16
Day 17
Day 18
Day 19
Day 20
Day 21

快來加入 Joes 的淑女之夜吧！

每週三晚上八點開始，

來感受一下我們驚喜無限的歡樂之夜，

有音樂、特別的表演。

➤ 所有女士都可免費入場！

➤ 進場可以免費獲得一杯飲料！

➤ 我們提供部分雞尾酒特別優惠，整晚都適用！

現場 DJ 將播放最新的音樂，讓你一整晚不停地舞動！邀請你的朋友一起來「月光大廳」，來點特別的享受，也讓自己閃耀一下吧！

欲了解更多資訊或訂位，請聯繫我們：

☐ 電話：555-123-4567

☐ 地址：紐約市，123 號主街，郵編 10001

| 詞彙 | **lounge** [laʊndʒ] 休息室，閒逛的地方　**midterm** [ˈmɪdˌtɚm] 期中考試
onwards [ˈɑnwɚdz] 往後，以後　**astonishing** [əˈstɑnɪʃɪŋ] 令人驚訝的，驚人的
deal [dil] 交易，協議　**treat** [trit] 款待，招待　**shine** [ʃaɪn] 閃耀，發光
reservation [ˌrɛzɚˈveʃən] 預訂，訂位

Q8 Why does Alma suggest going to The Moonlight Lounge?
為什麼愛瑪建議去「月光大廳」？

A. To study for exams　去準備考試

B. To relax and have fun　去放鬆好好玩一下

C. To watch a movie　去看電影

D. To have a candlelight dinner　去吃燭光晚餐

| 詳解 | 從第一個文本的對話內容「The two-day midterm is over!」以及「Let's go to The Moonlight Lounge for fun tomorrow night!」可知，結束了期中考試，Alma 建議去 The Moonlight Lounge 這地方玩一下，所以正確答案是選項 B。

| 詞彙 | **candlelight** [ˈkændlˌlaɪt] 燭光

Q9 What special offer is mentioned in the ad for ladies?
廣告宣傳中提到給予女士們什麼特別的優惠？

A. Discounted entry and free snacks　折扣入場和免費小吃

B. Free entry and a free drink　免費入場和一杯免費飲料

C. Free entry and discounted drinks　免費入場和折扣飲料。

D. Free entry and a free meal　免費入場和一餐免費餐點

| 詳解 | 從第二個文本（宣傳廣告）中的「All ladies can come in for free!」以及「Get a free drink when you arrive!」可知，所有女士都可免費入場，且可以免費獲得一杯飲料，所以正確答案是選項 B。

| 詞彙 | **special offer** 特別的優惠　**mention** [ˋmɛnʃən] 提及　**discounted** [ˋdɪskauntɪd] 折扣的　**entry** [ˋɛntrɪ] 進入，入場　**snack** [snæk] 小吃，點心

Q10 When did their midterm begin? 他們的期中考何時開始的？

A. On Monday　在星期一

B. On Tuesday　在星期二

C. On Wednesday　在星期三

D. On Thursday　在星期四

| 詳解 | 這個題目要綜合兩篇文章來解題。首先，從第二個文本（宣傳廣告）中提到「Join us for Lady's Night ... Every Wednesday」、「come to The Moonlight Lounge for a special treat on a Wednesday night」可知，The Moonlight Lounge 的「淑女之夜」是在每週三晚上。接著對照第一個文本（對話）內容中「The two-day midterm is over! Any plans for tonight」以及「The Moonlight Lounge for fun tomorrow night!」可知，「明晚」＝「週三晚上」，而為期兩天的期中考是「今晚」（＝週二晚上）結束，意即期中考是週一開始的，所以正確答案是選項 A。

Day **18**

月　　　日

我的完成時間＿＿＿＿＿ 分鐘
標準作答時間 10 分鐘

Day 15
Day 16
Day 17
Day 18
Day 19
Day 20
Day 21

Part **1** 詞彙

1. The couple visited the museum and the zoo during their vacation, ＿＿＿＿＿＿＿＿＿＿ ?

   A. aren't they　　　B. did they　　　C. did not they　　D. didn't they

2. Would you please give me ＿＿＿＿＿＿＿＿＿ coffee?

   A. too much　　　B. a few more　　　C. little　　　D. some more

Part **2** 段落填空

Nowadays, people eat too much meat and forget __(3)__ enough portions of fruit and vegetables in their __(4)__ . The health advantages of eating fruit and vegetables are endless, but __(5)__ . They are __(6)__ in cellulose, minerals and vitamins A, C and E. As a person consumes more fruit and vegetables, they feel full and thus eats less meat, which reduces the __(7)__ of fat and calories.

3. A. including
   B. to include
   C. to including
   D. included

4. A. diets
   B. menu
   C. body
   D. dinner

5. A. sometimes a juicy steak just hits the spot
   B. you may still need pizza and burgers now and then
   C. reducing the chance of cancer is the most notable
   D. nothing beats the satisfaction of a hearty bacon cheeseburger

6. A. rich
   B. full
   C. filled
   D. plenty

7. A. addition
   B. intake
   C. number
   D. amount

Boss, I'm not feeling well now, though I went see a doctor last night.

So you need to take today off, right?

 Yes, ... but actually I'd like to have one more day off.

Malcolm Clinic

➢ Patient's Name: Jane Doe
➢ Age: 32
➢ Date: March 24, 2024
➢ Medication
   PainX - Take 1 tablet every 6 hours.
   ReliefZ - Take 10 c.c. after each meal daily.
➢ Instructions
   Take PainX with enough warm water. Three times a day for 7 days. Avoid alcohol while taking these medications.
➢ Follow-up:
   Return for a follow-up appointment in 7 days.

If you have any concerns or side effects, please contact us immediately.

8. What does the boss expect his employee to do?

   A. Go to work on time   C. Take one more day off
   B. Take a day off   D. See a doctor

9. We can we know about the clinic prescription?

   A. The boss' name is Jane Doe.

   B. Take 1 tablet of ReliefZ every 6 hours.

   C. Take ReliefZ mixed enough warm water.

   D. Jane needs to come back to the clinic on 3/30.

10. When did the employee want to be back to work?

   A. On March 24   C. On March 26
   B. On March 25   D. On March 27

解答與詳解

1. (D)	2. (D)	3. (B)	4. (A)	5. (C)
6. (A)	7. (B)	8. (B)	9. (D)	10. (D)

Part 1 詞彙

Q1 考題重點〉附加問句的用法

The couple visited the museum and the zoo during their vacation, ＿＿＿＿＿＿?

A. aren't they　　　B. did they　　　C. did not they　　　**D. didn't they**

| 翻譯 | 那對夫妻在假期期間參觀了博物館和動物園，對吧？ |

| 詳解 | 本題考附加問句的用法。主詞是複數的 The couple，動詞為過去簡單式（visited），語態為主動，因此附加問句主詞必須用 they 以及否定的助動詞 didn't，所以正確答案是選項 D。 |

| 詞彙 | museum [mju`zɪəm] 博物館 |

Q2 考題重點〉可數名詞與不可數名詞的區別

Would you please give me ＿＿＿＿＿＿＿ coffee?

A. too much　　　B. a few more　　　C. little　　　**D. some more**

| 翻譯 | 可以請您在給我一些咖啡嗎？ |

| 詳解 | coffee（咖啡）屬不可數名詞，a few more 只用在可數名詞前，所以選項 B 錯誤。little 如果要用在不可數名詞前而且表示肯定時，必須加上冠詞 a，所以選項 C 不符。too much 的原意是「太多」，不符合題目內容，所以本題正確答案為選項 D。 |

Part 2 段落填空

Nowadays, people eat too much meat and forget **(3) to include** enough portions of fruit and vegetables in their **(4) diets**. The health advantages of eating fruit and vegetables are endless, but **(5) reducing the chance of cancer is the most notable**. They are **(6) rich** in cellulose, minerals and vitamins A, C and E. As a person consumes more fruit and vegetables, they feel full and thus eats less meat, which reduces the **(7) intake** of fat and calories.

| 翻譯 | 現今，人們吃太多肉類而忘了在他們的日常飲食中納入足夠份量的蔬果。吃蔬果的健康益處不勝枚舉，不過其中最顯著的是降低罹癌機率。它們含有豐富的纖維素、礦物質以及維生素 A、C、E。當人們多吃蔬果，他們會有飽足感而因此少吃點肉，這樣可以減少脂肪和卡路里的攝取。 |

Q3 考題重點〉forget 接不定詞與動名詞的區別

A. including   **B. to include**   C. to including   D. included

| 詳解 | 和 stop、remember... 等動詞一樣，forget 後面接動名詞的話，表示「忘記已經做了某事」，後面接不定詞的話表示「忘記要去做某事」，而句意是「忘了要納入足夠份量的蔬果」，應使用不定詞，故正確答案應為選項 B。

Q4 考題重點〉符合前後文意 的名詞

A. diets   B. menu   C. body   D. dinner

| 詳解 | 這整段內容探討的是在日常生活飲食中要多蔬果少肉才會健康，所以應選 diets（飲食），正確答案為選項 A。其餘 menu、body、dinner 雖然單以空格所在句子來看也沒有錯，但不符整體文意。

Q5 考題重點〉選擇符合前後文意的句子

A. sometimes a juicy steak just hits the spot
有時候，一塊多汁的牛排正好符合口味

B. you may still need pizza and burgers now and then
你可能還是常常會需要披薩及漢堡

C. reducing the chance of cancer is the most notable
最顯著的是降低罹癌機率

D. nothing beats the satisfaction of a hearty bacon cheeseburger
沒有什麼比一份豐盛的培根起司漢堡的滿足感更好了

| 詳解 | 前面句子提到「吃蔬果的健康益處不勝枚舉，不過…」，而後面句子提到「它們含有豐富的纖維素…」，顯然 but 後面這半句還是在說明吃蔬果的好處，因此正確答案為選項 C。

Q6 考題重點〉形容詞與介系詞的正確搭配

A. rich   B. full   C. filled   D. plenty

| 詳解 | 句意是「它們含有豐富的纖維素、礦物質以及維生素 A、C、E」，而四個選項單字都有「充滿、豐富」的意思，不過不同的形容詞要搭配不同的介系詞。意即 (be) rich in = full of = filled with = plenty of，所以正確答案為選項 A。

Q7 考題重點〉選擇符合語意的名詞

A. addition   **B. intake**   C. number   D. amount

Day 15
Day 16
Day 17
Day 18
Day 19
Day 20
Day 21

| 詳解 | number 不可形容脂肪的量，因為 fat（脂肪）是不可數名詞，所以選項 C 不對。amount（量）以及 addition（額外的量），就詞性及意思而言，都可能是答案，不過 intake（吸收）更貼近內文之意，所以正確答案為選項 B。

Part 3 閱讀理解

Boss, I'm not feeling well now, though I went see a doctor last night.

So you need to take today off, right?

Yes, ... but actually I'd like to have one more day off.

Malcolm Clinic

➢ Patient's Name: Jane Doe

➢ Age: 32

➢ Date: March 24, 2024

➢ Medication

PainX - Take 1 tablet every 6 hours.

ReliefZ - Take 10 c.c. after each meal daily.

➢ Instructions

Take PainX with enough warm water. Three times a day for 7 days. Avoid alcohol while taking these medications.

➢ Follow-up:

Return for a follow-up appointment in 7 days.

If you have any concerns or side effects, please contact us immediately.

| 翻譯 |

老闆，我現在感覺不舒服，雖然昨晚去看了醫生。

所以你今天需要請假，對吧？

是的…但實際上我想再多請一天假。

馬爾科姆診所

➢ 病患姓名：Jane Doe

➢ 年齡：32 歲

➢ 日期：2024 年 3 月 24 日

➢ 藥物

PainX - 每 6 小時服用 1 片。

ReliefZ - 每日飯後服用 10 c.c.。

➢ 服藥說明

使用足夠的溫開水服用 PainX。一天三次七日份。在服用這些藥物期間請避免飲酒。

➢ 後續追蹤：七天後回診。

若您有任何疑慮或副作用，請立即與我們聯繫。

| 詞彙 | take... off 請...（幾天）假　clinic [ˈklɪnɪk] 診所
medication [ˌmɛdɪˈkeʃən] 藥物，藥品　tablet [ˈtæblɪt] 藥片　capsule [ˈkæpsjul] 膠囊
instruction [ɪnˈstrʌkʃən] 指示，說明　avoid [əˈvɔɪd] 避免，防止
alcohol [ˈælkəˌhɔl] 酒精，酒類　follow-up [ˈfɑloˌʌp] 後續追蹤，跟進
appointment [əˈpɔɪntmənt] 預約，約會　concern [kənˈsɜ-n] 擔憂，關心
side effect [ˈsaɪd ɪ ˈfɛkt]：副作用，不良反應　immediately [ɪˈmidɪətlɪ] 立即，馬上

Q8 What does the boss expect his employee to do?
老闆預期他的員工要做什麼？

A. Go to work on time　準時去上班

B. Take a day off　請一天假

C. Take one more day off　再多請一天假

D. See a doctor　去看醫生

| 詳解 | 從第一個文本的對話內容「Boss, I'm not feeling well now...」以及「So you need to take today off, right?」可知，老闆認為這位員工今天想請假，所以正確答案是選項 B。

| 詞彙 | expect [ɪkˈspɛkt] 預計，預期

Day 15

Day 16

Day 17

Day 18

Day 19

Day 20

Day 21

$\text{Q}9$ We can we know about the clinic prescription?
從診所的處方籤中我們可以知道什麼？

A. The boss' name is Jane Doe.
那位老闆的名字是 Jane Doe.

B. Take 1 tablet of ReliefZ every 6 hours.
每六小時服用一顆 ReliefZ。

C. Take ReliefZ mixed enough warm water.
以足夠的溫開水混和 ReliefZ 來服用。

D. Jane needs to come back to the clinic on 3/30.
Jane 必須在 3/30 回到該診所。

| 詳解 | 從第二個文本（處方籤）中的「Patient's Name: Jane Doe」，我們知道 Jane 就是這名員工。接著從看病的日期「Date: March 23, 2024」以及「Return for a follow-up appointment in 7 days」可知，Jane 必須在 3/30 回診，所以正確答案是選項 D。

| 詞彙 | prescription [prɪˋskrɪpʃən] 處方

$\text{Q}10$ When did the employee want to be back to work?
該名員工想要何時回去上班？

A. On March 24　在 3 月 24 日
B. On March 25　在 3 月 25 日
C. On March 26　在 3 月 26 日
D. On March 27　在 3 月 27 日

| 詳解 | 這個題目要綜合兩篇文章來解題。首先，從第一個文本（對話）的「I went see a doctor last night」可知，這位員工昨晚去看醫生，接著對照第二個文本（處方）的「Date: March 24, 2024」可知，昨天是 3 月 24 日，那麼「今天」就是 3 月 25 日。然後我們再回到對話中看到老闆問「So you need to take today off, right?」以及員工回答「actually I'd like to have one more day off」可推知，這位員工（Jane Doe）希望「後天」才回公司上班，所以正確答案是選項 D。

Part 1 詞彙

1. Henry _____ to Australia. He is coming back this weekend.

   A. will go
   B. has been
   C. has gone
   D. is going

2. Mr. Chen has two sons. One of _____ to junior high school.

   A. them go
   B. they go
   C. them goes
   D. they goes

Part 2 段落填空

Animal __(3)__ is very important. For the purpose of keeping the balance of nature, we need to protect some animals. Like tigers and elephants, __(4)__ are in danger because of hunting and habitat loss. We can do something useful __(5)__ not buying products made from endangered animals and __(6)__ conservation organizations. We should also learn about animals and the places where they live, so __(7)__ . Everyone can do something to help save animals!

3. A. emotion
   B. description
   C. science
   D. protection

4. A. any
   B. some
   C. much
   D. all

5. A. so that
   B. for example
   C. because of
   D. such as

6. A. support
   B. supporting
   C. to support
   D. supported

7. A. we can have delicious meat to eat
   B. we can understand how to help them
   C. we can understand how to take care of our pets
   D. we can appreciate their beauty from afar

Part 3 閱讀理解

 Hi, Peter. Good to hear you've left prison. As you're still young and look healthy, what are you going to do?

Take a look at this job ad. I need a stable job first. Plans for other things will be made later.

⋯⋯⋯⋯⋯⋯⋯⋯⋯⋯⋯⋯⋯⋯⋯⋯⋯⋯⋯⋯⋯⋯⋯⋯

Security Guard Wanted

➢ Requirements:
  1. A police criminal record certificate is a must.
  2. Senior high school graduate or above
  3. Male under forty
  4. Good health and strong body required

➢ Working hours & holidays:
  1. 42 hours per week
  2. Need to take shifts, including night shifts and national holidays

➢ Duty:
  Look over all computer screens and make sure no other people except staff and workers enter the company

---

8. What is Peter going to do first?

   A. Serve in the prison   C. Look for a full-time job

   B. Seek a part-time job   D. Have a mate and get married

9. Which of the following persons might get the job?

   A. Ellen graduated from the university. He is 38 but seldom exercises.

   B. Donald was a soccer player. He is 41. He only finished high school.

   C. Shawn is 30. He is skinny and short. He has a master degree.

   D. Mike is 33. He has a bachelor degree. He taught PE before.

10. What requirement listed in the job ad does Peter probably fail to meet?

   A. Police criminal record certificate   C. Male under forty

   B. Senior high school graduate or above   D. Good health and strong body

Day 15 | Day 16 | Day 17 | Day 18 | Day 19 | Day 20 | Day 21

Part 1 詞彙

Q1 考題重點〉現在完成式 have gone 與 have been 區別

Henry _____ to Australia. He is coming back this weekend.

A. will go　　　B. has been　　　**C. has gone**　　　D. is going

| 翻譯 | 亨利已經去了澳洲。他這週末就會回來了。

| 詳解 | 根據題目所指亨利目前人還在澳洲，所以他「已經去了澳洲」，格要用完成式「have/ has + 過去分詞」，所以正確答案為選項 C。選項 B 是指「曾經去過」，但題目是人已經回來 了，不合邏輯。未來式的 will go 和現在進行式 is going 也會產生語意上的矛盾。

Q2 考題重點〉主詞動詞一致性

Mr. Chen has two sons. One of _____ to junior high school.

A. them go　　　B. they go　　　**C. them goes**　　　D. they goes

| 翻譯 | 陳先生有兩個兒子。他們其中一個唸國中。

| 詳解 | one of 後面要用「受格」的代名詞，所以 B、C 錯誤；而主詞是「One of them」，為 單數的主詞，要搭配單數動詞，所以 A 錯誤，故正確答案為選項 C。

Part 2 段落填空

Animal **(3) protection** is very important. For the purpose of keeping the balance of nature, we need to protect some animals. Like tigers and elephants, **(4) some** are in danger because of hunting and habitat loss. We can do something useful **(5) such as** not buying products made from endangered animals and **(6) supporting** conservation organizations. We should also learn about animals and the places where they live, so **(7) we can understand how to help them**. Everyone can do something to help save animals!

| 翻譯 | 動物保護非常重要。我們保護一些動物的目的是要維持自然界的平衡。像是老虎和大 象，一些動物正面臨著獵捕和棲息地喪失的威脅。我們可以做些有用的事，像是不購 買來自瀕臨絕種動物的產品，並支持保育組織。我們也應該學習有關動物及其棲息地 的知識，這樣我們才能了解如何幫助牠們。每個人都可以做一些事情來幫助拯救動物!

146

Q3 考題重點〉填入符合語境的名詞

A. emotion   B. description   C. science   **D. protection**

| 詳解 | 本題無法單從空格所在句子去判斷答案，關鍵在下一句的「we need to protect some animals」，所以正確答案應為選項 D。A、B、C 的意思分別是「情緒」、「描述」、「科學」。

Q4 考題重點〉代名詞的正確使用

A. any   **B. some**   C. much   D. all

| 詳解 | 從空格後面的 are 來看，選項 A、C 都不符文法規則；而句意是「像是老虎和大象，一些動物…」，故正確答案為選項 B。all 雖然符合文法規則，但不合語意與邏輯。

Q5 考題重點〉填入符合句意的介系詞

A. so that   B. for example   C. because of   **D. such as**

| 詳解 | 空格後面是「not buying products...」，是個「動名詞」片語，所以要填入一個介系詞，連接詞的選項 A 以及副詞的 B 顯然都是錯誤的；句意是「我們可以做些有用的事，像是不購買…」，故正確答案為選項 D。

Q6 考題重點〉and 連結對等結構

A. support   **B. supporting**   C. to support   D. supported

| 詳解 | 空格前的介系詞 and 連接「not buying products made from...」以及「_____ conservation organizations」兩個結構，所以應填入動名詞的 supporting，正確答案為選項 B。

Q7 考題重點〉選擇符合前後文意的句子

A. we can have delicious meat to eat   我們可以有美味的肉食來享用

B. we can understand how to help them   我們才能了解如何幫助它們

C. we can understand how to take care of our pets
    我們可以了解如何照顧我們的寵物

D. we can appreciate their beauty from afar
    我們可以遠遠地欣賞牠們的美

| 詳解 | 前面句子提到「我們也應該學習有關動物及其棲息地的知識」，而後面句子提到「每個人都可以做一些事情來幫助拯救動物」，顯然 so 後面這半句英語如何幫助動物有關，因此正確答案為選項 B。

Hi, Peter. Good to hear you've left prison. As you're still young and look healthy, what are you going to do?

Take a look at this job ad. I need a stable job first. Plans for other things will be made later.

Security Guard Wanted

➢ Requirements:

1. A police criminal record certificate is a must.

2. Senior high school graduate or above

3. Male under forty

4. Good health and strong body required

➢ Working hours & holidays:

1. 42 hours per week

2. Need to take shifts, including night shifts and national holidays

➢ Duty:

Look over all computer screens and make sure no other people except staff and workers enter the company

| 翻譯 |

 嗨，彼得。很高興聽到你已經出獄了。你還年輕，看起來身體健康，你打算做什麼呢？

看看這個求職廣告。我需要先找到一份穩定的工作。其他的事，以後再做打算。

Day 15
Day 16
Day 17
Day 18
Day 19
Day 20
Day 21

誠徵警衛

➤ 條件：
  1. 需提供良民證（刑事犯罪紀錄）
  2. 高中以上畢業
  3. 限男性，四十歲以下
  4. 身體健康，體格佳

➤ 工時及休假：
  1. 每週工作 42 小時
  2. 需輪班，包括夜班及國定假日

➤ 職責：
  留意所有監視螢幕，確保除了員工以外，沒有其他人進入公司

| 詞彙 | **prison** [ˈprɪzn] 監獄，指收容罪犯的地方　**stable** [ˈstebl] 穩定的，不變動的
security guard 保安人員，警衛　**requirement** [rɪˈkwaɪrmənt] 要求，條件
criminal record 犯罪記錄，前科　**certificate** [sɚˈtɪfəket] 證書
must [mʌst] n. 必要條件　**shift** [ʃɪft] 輪班　**additional** [əˈdɪʃənl] 附加的，額外的

Q8 What is Peter going to do first? 彼得首先將要做什麼？

　　A. Serve in the prison　去坐牢

　　B. Seek a part-time job　找個兼職工作

　　C. Look for a full-time job　找一份全職工作

　　D. Have a mate and get married　找個伴結婚

| 詳解 | 從第一個文本的對話內容「I need a stable job first. Plans for other things will be made later」可知，他首先需要一份穩定的工作，所以正確答案是選項 C。

| 詞彙 | **serve** [sɝv] 服務，服役

Q9 Which of the following persons might get the job?
以下哪一位人士可能會得到此工作?

A. Ellen graduated from the university. He is 38 but seldom exercises.
艾倫從大學畢業了。他三十八歲但不常運動。

B. Donald was a soccer player. He is 41. He only finished high school.
唐那以前是足球員。他四十一歲。他只有高中畢業。

C. Shawn is 30. He is skinny and short. He has a master degree.
夏恩今年三十歲。他身材矮小瘦削。他有碩士學歷。

D. Mike is 33. He has a bachelor degree. He taught PE before.
麥克今年三十三歲。他有 學士學位。他以前是體育老師。

| 詳解 | 求才廣告中清楚說明應徵者必須是四十歲以下,所以 B 不符。選項 A 的 Ellen 年齡及學歷都沒問題,但他 seldom(偶爾,很少)運動,可能不符「體格 佳」的條件。而 Shawn 跟 Ellen 的一樣,年齡學歷都符合,但身材不合格。故本題正確答案為選項 D。

| 詞彙 | **graduate** [ˈɡrædʒuet] 畢業　**seldom** [ˈsɛldəm] 很少(指發生的頻率很低)
skinny [ˈskɪnɪ] 體型纖瘦的　**master degree** 碩士學位　**bachelor degree** 學士學位

Q10 What requirement listed in the job ad does Peter probably fail to meet? 彼得可能無法符合求職廣告中哪一項要條件?

A. Police criminal record certificate　良民證

B. Senior high school graduate or above　高中以上畢業

C. Male under forty　四十歲以下男性

D. Good health and strong body　身體健康,體格佳

| 詳解 | 這個題目要綜合兩篇文章來解題。首先,從第一個文本(對話)的「Hi, Peter. Good to hear you've left prison.」可知,Peter 剛出獄,意即有刑事案件的前科紀錄,接著對照第二個文本(求職廣告)上方 Requirements 列出的條件,有「A police criminal record certificate is a must.」,顯然 Peter 可能會因為這一項而無法錄取該工作,所以正確答案是選項 A。

Part 1 詞彙

1. I wish I _____ a small truck. It would help me a lot.

   A. have
   B. am having
   C. had
   D. would have

2. We _____ a chance to perform in the show.

   A. have given
   B. were given
   C. were giving
   D. will give

Part 2 段落填空

Everyone knows we should brush our teeth after a meal. (3) , most of us naturally brush our teeth as soon as getting up in the morning and in fact, (4) There is a method to (5) the teeth clean. Squeeze a lemon, then (6) a tissue in the lemon juice and wipe the surface of the teeth. Try it! It does (7) !

3. A. Awfully
   B. Interestingly
   C. Thankfully
   D. Lastly

4. A. some people prefer to brush their teeth before breakfast
   B. no one thinks brushing teeth with soda is better than using toothpaste
   C. many people seldom do it later after breakfast
   D. a few people think it's no big deal to brush their teeth once a week

5. A. waste
   B. wipe
   C. wave
   D. widen

6. A. dip
   B. dipping
   C. dipped
   D. to dip

7. A. good
   B. not
   C. useful
   D. work

Whether you're relaxing at the beach or working out on your favorite exercise machine, it's important to drink enough water. The PK-20 bottle keeps your drinks cool, and is very easy to clean. It holds up to 1200 c.c. of any drink. The bottle is made from good-quality steel. We deliver for free by the end of this month. You can now pick red, green, blue and yellow.

Best regards,

Marketing director
Rick Hung
LINE: @cshung88
Mobile: 0968-987897
15/Dec./2023

••

Hi Rick,

I'd like to know first if the bottle is suitable for both hot and cold drinks.

Thanks,
Kevin Wang
5/Jan./2024

8. What is the purpose of the first letter?

    A. To advertise a new exercise machine

    B. To promote a useful water container

    C. To introduce a new brand of sports drink

    D. To offer discounts on beach accessories

9. According to the second email, what does Kevin want to know?

    A. One of the PK-20's functions

    B. Any more special discounts for the bottle

    C. The suitable amount of cold and hot water for the bottle

    D. The time free delivery is offered

10. Which of the following is NOT true about the PK-20 bottle?

    A. There are four colors for customers to choose.

    B. It is good to hold cold water.

    C. It holds more than 1 liter of any drink.

    D. Kevin can enjoy free shipment if he place an order for it.

Day 15
Day 16
Day 17
Day 18
Day 19
Day 20
Day 21

解答與詳解

Part 1 詞彙

Q1 考題重點〉**假設語氣的動詞時態**

I wish I _____ a small truck. It would help me a lot.

A. have
C. **had**

B. am having
D. would have

| 翻譯 | 我希望我有一台小貨車。它可以幫我很多的忙。

| 詳解 | 本題考假設語氣。題目中說話者「希望（wish）」有小貨車，但實際上是沒有的，所以是「與現在事實相反」，wish 子句內的動詞必須用過去式，所以正確答案為選項 C。

Q2 考題重點〉**授予動詞的被動式**

We _____ a chance to perform in the show.

A. have given
C. were giving

B. were given
D. will give

| 翻譯 | 我們獲得在節目中表演的機會。

| 詳解 | 空格要填入的動詞是 give，而後面只有一個受詞（a chance），如果 give 當完全及物動詞的話，通常是「舉辦」的意思，但套入句中顯然不合邏輯，所以這裡 give 是最簡單的「給」意思，語態應為被動，故正確答案為選項 B。

Part 2 段落填空

Everyone knows we should brush our teeth after a meal. **(3) Interestingly**, most of us naturally brush our teeth as soon as getting up in the morning and in fact, **(4) many people seldom do it later after breakfast.** There is a method to **(5) wipe** the teeth clean. Squeeze a lemon, then **(6) dip** a tissue in the lemon juice and wipe the surface of the teeth. Try it! It does **(7) work**!

| 翻譯 | 每個人都知道我們應該在餐後刷牙。有趣的是，我們大部分人很自然地都會在早上起床後刷牙，且事實上，很多人在之後吃完早餐就不太會去做這件事了。有一個方法可以把牙齒擦乾淨。擠一顆檸檬，然後用衛生紙沾一點檸檬汁刷洗牙齒表面。試試看吧！真的很有用！

Q3 考題重點〉填入符合語境的連接性副詞

A. Awfully   C. Thankfully

B. Interestingly   D. Lastly

| 詳解 | 前一句說「我們應該在餐後刷牙」，後面句子卻說是「大部分人很自然地都會在早上起床後刷牙」，顯然兩句有相反或矛盾之意，所以正確答案應為選項 B。A、C、D 的意思分別是「可怕地」、「幸好」、「最後」。

Q4 考題重點〉選擇符合前後文意的句子

A. some people prefer to brush their teeth before breakfast
有些人喜歡在早餐前刷牙

B. no one thinks brushing teeth with soda is better than using toothpaste
沒有人認為用蘇打水刷牙比使用牙膏好

C. many people seldom do it later after breakfast
許多人在之後吃完早餐後就不太會去做這件事了

D. a few people think it's no big deal to brush their teeth once a week
有些人認為每週刷牙一次並不是什麼大問題

| 詳解 | 空格這句前面有連接詞 and，顯然要與前面的「most of us... in the morning」相呼應或作為補充說明，也就是說，大部分人早上起床後會刷牙，但吃完早餐後就不會刷了，因此正確答案為選項 C。

Q5 考題重點〉填入符合句意的動詞

A. waste   C. wave

B. wipe   D. widen

| 詳解 | 句意是「有一個方法可以把牙齒擦乾淨。」故正確答案為選項 B。A、C、D 的意思分別是「浪費」、「揮手」、「加寬」。

Q6 考題重點〉and 連結對等結構

A. dip   C. dipped

B. dipping   D. to dip

| 詳解 | 選項中的 dip（浸泡）是個動詞，即使不知道這個字的意思，只要從文中「Squeeze a lemon, then _____ a tissue... and wipe the surface...」這個應連接三個原形動詞的對等結構，即可判斷答案，故正確答案為選項 A。

Day 15
Day 16
Day 17
Day 18
Day 19
Day 20
Day 21

Q7 考題重點〉助動詞後面接原形動詞

A. good

C. useful

B. not

D. work

| 詳解 | 空格前的 does 是個助動詞，表示「的確」，為強調用法，因此後面需接原形動詞，所以正確答案為選項 D。

Part 3 閱讀理解

Whether you're relaxing at the beach or working out on your favorite exercise machine, it's important to drink enough water. The PK-20 bottle keeps your drinks cool, and is very easy to clean. It holds up to 1200 c.c. of any drink. The bottle is made from good-quality steel. We deliver for free by the end of this month. You can now pick red, green, blue and yellow.

Best regards,

Marketing director
Rick Hung
LINE: @cshung88
Mobile: 0968-987897
15/Dec./2023

....

Hi Rick,

I'd like to know first if the bottle is suitable for both hot and cold drinks.

Thanks,
Kevin Wang
5/Jan./2024

無論您是在沙灘上放鬆還是在您喜愛的運動機器上運動，保持足夠的水分很重要。PK-20 水壺可以保持您的飲料冰冷，且非常容易清潔。它可以容納 1200 c.c. 的任何飲料。這個瓶子是用優質的鋼材製成的。我們在本月底前有免運服務。現在您可以選擇紅色、綠色、藍色及黃色的。

謹啟

行銷總監

Rick Hung

LINE: @cshung88

手機: 0968-987897

2023 年 12 月 15 日

．．．

嗨 Rick，

我想先問一下，嗎？

謝謝，

Kevin Wang

2024 年 1 月 5 日

| 詞彙 | **work out** 運動，鍛煉　**drink** [drɪŋk] 飲料，飲品　**be made from** 由…製成 **good-quality** 優質的　**steel** [stil] 鋼材，鋼鐵　**deliver** [dɪˈlɪvɚ] 交付，送達 **for free** 免費地　**marketing director** 行銷總監　**suitable** [ˈsutəbl] 合適的

Q8 What is the purpose of the first letter?
第一封信件的目的為何？

A. To advertise a new exercise machine　為了宣傳一款新的運動器材

B. To promote a useful water container　推廣一款好用的水容器

C. To introduce a new brand of sports drink　一個新的運動飲料品牌

D. To offer discounts on beach accessories　提供海灘配件的折扣

| 詳解 | 從「The PK-20 bottle keeps... It holds up to... The bottle is made from...」的內容可知正確答案是選項 B。

| 詞彙 | **purpose** [ˋpɝpəs] 目的　**advertise** [ˋædvɚˌtaɪz] 廣告，宣傳 **container** [kənˋtenɚ] 容器　**accessory** [ækˋsɛsərɪ] 配件

Q9 According to the second letter, what does Kevin want to know?
根據第二封信件內容，凱文想知道什麼事？

A. One of the PK-20's functions

　　PK-20 的一項功能

B. Any more special discounts for the bottle

　　這水壺是否還有任何折扣優惠

C. The suitable amount of cold and hot water for the bottle

　　這水壺合適的冷熱水容量

D. The time free delivery is offered

　　提供免運的時間

| 詳解 | 第二封信件中，Kevin 只問了一個問題：I'd like to know first if the bottle is suitable for both hot and cold drinks.，亦即這個 PK-20 水壺是否適用熱飲和冷飲，表示它的一項功能，故本題正確答案為選項 A。

| 詞彙 | function [ˋfʌŋkʃən] 功能　discount [ˋdɪskaʊnt] 折扣，優惠

Q10 Which of the following is NOT true about the PK-20 bottle?
關於這款 PK-20 水壺，以下何者為非？

A. There are four colors for customers to choose.

　　顧客可以有四種顏色可選。

B. It is good to hold cold water.

　　它的保冷效果很不錯。

C. It holds more than 1 liter of any drink.

　　它可以填裝超過一公升的任何飲料。

D. Kevin can enjoy free shipment if he place an order for it.

　　如果 Kevin 下訂單的話，可以享有免運服務。

| 詳解 | 第一個文本提到「You can now pick red, green, blue and yellow」、「The PK-20 bottle keeps your drinks cool」、「It holds up to 1200 c.c. of any drink」，所以選項 A、B、C 都是正確的敘述；選項 D 的部分要綜合兩篇文章來解題。首先，從第一封信中「We deliver for free by the end of this month.」以及下面的日期「15/Dec./2023」可知，免運服務提供到十二月底，接著在第二個文本的顧客回覆信件下方可知，發信日期是「5/Jan./2024」，顯然 Kevin Wang 如果要買的話，已無法獲得免運優惠了，所以選項 D 是錯誤的敘述，故本題正確答案是 D。

Part 1 詞彙

1. It is no use ＿＿＿＿＿＿＿＿＿＿ . I won't forgive you.
   A. begging　　　　B. to beg　　　　C. to begging　　D. begged

2. That's so nice of you to give me a ＿＿＿＿＿＿＿＿＿ to the airport.
   A. drive　　　　B. drink　　　　C. ride　　　　D. try

Part 2 段落填空

We would love to believe everything other people tell us or __(3)__ they promise to keep, but experience tells us that __(4)__ . In some situations, they mean __(5)__ and have good intentions, but they overestimate their ability to fulfill their promises. While there are others who intend to cheat us __(6)__ gain some advantages. At the end of the day, however, it is actions and deeds, __(7)__ promises or excuses, that have the true meaning.

3. A. which
   B. that
   C. what
   D. X

4. A. what they say usually can match what they do
   B. sometimes people promise things that they cannot deliver
   C. nothing is a big deal if they fail to keep a promise
   D. many of us may sometimes break a promise

5. A. well
   B. good
   C. bad
   D. badly

6. A. in order to
   B. for the purpose of
   C. with a view to
   D. so that

7. A. together with
   B. because of
   C. instead of
   D. in addition to

A+ Broadband Internet Services

Looking for better Internet? Try our Internet Services!

We offer fast, reliable Internet for work or home. Plus, our security system keeps your computer safe. Visit *www.a+internet.com* for details on our Regular, Business, and Highest-quality packages. Show this flyer when you place an order for our best service by the end of July and get 60% off your first bill!

Hello,

I got your Internet service for my studio last month. The speed and connection have been good. But yesterday, I got my first bill and was surprised. It was for the full amount of the monthly fee. Your ad said I'd only pay 40% for the first month. What's wrong? Please tell me soon.

Thanks,
Brian Chang

8. How can you find more information on different Internet packages?

    A. By reading the flyer

    B. By visiting the company's website

    C. By calling a phone number

    D. By going to the local store

9. How was Brian's experience of making this purchase?

    A. He wasn't satisfied with the connection speed.

    B. He complained about the bad connection.

    C. He thinks the Internet service is very cheap.

    D. He doubted about the bill he's just received.

10. What kind of packages did Brian place an order for?

    A. Regular packages   C. Highest quality packages

    B. Business packages   D. We don't know.

Day 15
Day 16
Day 17
Day 18
Day 19
Day 20
Day 21

Part 1 詞彙

Q1 考題重點〉「no use + Ving」的用法

It is no use _____ . I won't forgive you.

A. begging　　　B. to beg　　　C. to begging　　　D. begged

| 翻譯 | 用求的也沒用。我不會原諒你的。

| 詳解 | 本題考的是「It/There is no use（沒有用）」後面接現在分詞（Ving）的用法，此為固定句型，所以正確答案為選項 A。

Q2 考題重點〉選擇符合句意的名詞

That's so nice of you to give me a _____ to the airport.

A. drive　　　B. drink　　　**C. ride**　　　D. try

| 翻譯 | 你人真好，還載我去機場。

| 詳解 | 空格後面是 to the airport（去機場），所以跟 drink 以及 try 完全扯不上關係，而 drive 雖然有「開車」的意思，但以這個句子的意思，drive 要當動詞用，應該是「... to drive me to the airport」，故本題正確答案為選項 C。

Part 2 段落填空

We would love to believe everything other people tell us or **(3) what** they promise to keep, but experience tells us that **(4) sometimes people promise things that they cannot deliver**. In some situations, they mean **(5) well** and have good intentions, but they overestimate their ability to fulfill their promises. While there are others who intend to cheat us **(6) in order to** gain some advantages. At the end of the day, however, it is actions and deeds, **(7) instead of** promises or excuses, that have the true meaning.

| 翻譯 | 我們很樂意相信別人告訴我們的每件事，或是他們承諾做到的事，但經驗告訴我們，有時候人們會許下他們無法堅持的承諾。在某些情況下，他們的出發點是善意的，但卻高估了自己實現諾言的能力。而還有其他人意圖欺騙我們以取得某些好處。不過，到頭來，真正具有意義的是行動與作為，而非承諾與藉口。

Day 15
Day 16
Day 17
Day 18
Day 19
Day 20
Day 21

Q3 考題重點〉複合關係代名詞 what 的使用

A. which

C. what

B. that

D. X

| 詳解 | 空格後面是「they promise to keep」，顯然缺少了 keep 的受詞，雖然 which 和 that 也可以作為其受詞，但沒有先行詞，所以 A、B 也是錯誤的選項，正確答案為選項 C。複合關係代名詞 what 引導名詞子句，作為動詞 believe 的受詞。

Q4 考題重點〉選擇符合前後文意的句子

A. what they say usually can match what they do

他們說的話通常會與他們的行為相符

B. sometimes people promise things that they cannot deliver

有時候人們會許下他們無法堅持的承諾

C. nothing is a big deal if they fail to keep a promise

如果他們未能遵守承諾，那也沒有什麼大不了的

D. many of us may sometimes break a promise

我們許多人有時可能也會違背承諾

| 詳解 | 空格這句前面有連接詞 but，顯然要與前面的「We would love to believe everything other people tell us...」具有相反意義，也就是說，要與下一句 but 後面的「they overestimate their ability to fulfill their promises」相呼應，因此正確答案為選項 B。

Q5 考題重點〉填入符合句意的副詞

A. well

C. bad

B. good

D. badly

| 詳解 | 空格前的動詞 mean 意思是「展現意圖」，所以要用副詞來修飾它，形容詞的 B、C 可直接刪除；而句意是「他們的出發點是好的，但高估了自己實現諾言的能力」，故正確答案為選項 A。

Q6 考題重點〉表示「目的」的 in order to 用法

A. in order to

C. with a view to

B. for the purpose of

D. so that

| 詳解 | 空格後面是原形動詞，所以 B、D 都是明顯錯誤的（of 要接 Ving，so that 後面要有主詞，引導完整的句子），故正確答案為選項 A。with a view to 其實和 in order to 是一樣，都是「為了要…」的意思，只是後面要接動名詞才行。

Q7 考題重點〉「是…而不是…」的表達

A. together with   **C. instead of**

B. because of   D. in addition to

| 詳解 | 句意是「真正具有意義的是行動與作為，而非承諾與藉口」，所以正確答案為選項 C，instead of 是「而不是…」的意思。選項 A、B、D 分別表示「連同…」、「因為…」、「除了…之外」。

Part3 閱讀理解

A+ Broadband Internet Services

Looking for better Internet? Try our Internet Services!

We offer fast, reliable Internet for work or home. Plus, our security system keeps your computer safe. Visit *www.a+internet.com* for details on our Regular, Business, and Highest-quality packages. Show this flyer when you place an order for our best service by the end of July and get 60% off your first bill!

Hello,

I got your Internet service for my studio last month. The speed and connection have been good. But yesterday, I got my first bill and was surprised. It was for the full amount of the monthly fee. Your ad said I'd only pay 40% for the first month. What's wrong? Please tell me soon.

Thanks,
Brian Chang

A+ 寬頻網路服務

還在尋找更好的網路嗎？試試我們的網路服務吧！

我們提供快速、可靠的工作或家用網路。此外，我們的安全系統可保護您的電腦安全。請上 www.a+internet.com，以了解我們的一般、商用和最高品質方案的詳細資訊。若在七月底前訂購我們最頂級的套餐並出示此傳單，您首月費用將可享有四折優惠！

您好，

上個月我為我的工作室購買了您的網路服務。速度和連線一直都很好。但是昨天，我收到我的第一筆帳單，且感到有些驚訝。帳單金額是全額的月費。您的廣告說我第一個月只需支付 40%。所以是出了什麼問題？請盡快告訴我。

謝謝，

Brian Chang

| 詞彙 | **broadband** [ˈbrɔdbænd] 寬頻　**reliable** [rɪˈlaɪəbl] 可靠的，可信賴的、不易出錯的
plus [plʌs] 此外，再者　**security** [sɪˈkjʊrətɪ] 安全性
regular [ˈrɛgjələ] 常規的，標準的，一般性的　**flyer** [ˈflaɪə] 傳單
place an order 下訂單（購買商品或服務）　**studio** [ˈstjudɪo] 工作室
connection [kəˈnɛkʃən] 連線

Q8 How can you find more information on different Internet packages？ 你可以如何找到更多關於網路服務方案的資訊？

A. By reading the flyer　在傳單上即可看到

B. By visiting the company's website　去上該公司網站

C. By calling a phone number　透過撥打電話號碼

D. By going to the local store　當地商店

| 詳解 | 題目關鍵字是 packages，所以從「Visit *www.a+internet.com* for details on our Regular, Business, and Highest-quality packages.」這句話即可了解，可以點進該公司網站去了解網路服務方案的資訊，故本題正確答案是選項 B。

Day 15
Day 16
Day 17
Day 18
Day 19
Day 20
Day 21

Q9 How was Brian's experience of making this purchase?
布萊恩對於此次購物的體驗如何？

A. He wasn't satisfied with the connection speed.
他對連線速度不滿意。

B. He complained about the bad connection.
他抱怨連線品質不好。

C. He thinks the Internet service is very cheap.
他認為網路服務非常便宜。

D. He doubted about the bill he's just received.
他對他剛收到的帳單感到懷疑。

| 詳解 | 在第二個文本的信件中，Brian 提到「It was for the full amount of the monthly fee. Your ad said I'd only pay 40% for the first month. What's wrong?」表示他認為他的第一期帳單應該要給四折優惠，但卻上面卻顯示一個正常月費的金額，故本題正確答案為選項 D。

| 詞彙 | doubt [daʊt] 對…存疑

Q10 What kind of packages did Brian place an order for?
布萊恩訂購的是什麼服務？

A. Regular packages　一般方案

B. Business packages　企業方案

C. Highest quality packages　最高品質方案

D. We don't know.　無法得知

| 詳解 | 這個題目要綜合兩篇文章來解題。首先，Brian 在信件中提到「I got my first bill... Your ad said I'd only pay 40% for the first month.」表示他收到第一筆帳單時發現被索取的金額並非該公司廣告中說的第一筆帳單有四折優惠；接著我們對照第一個文本（廣告）中的「...our Regular, Business, and Highest-quality packages...」以及「when you place an order for our best service by the end of July and get 60% off your first bill」，表示訂購最高級服務可享有第一期帳單四折優惠，所以 Brian 訂購的就是最高品質的方案，正確答案是選項 C。

Day 22

月　　日

我的完成時間＿＿＿分鐘
標準作答時間 10 分鐘

Day 22

Day 23

Day 24

Day 25

Day 26

Day 27

Day 28

Part 1 詞彙

1.　The carton is ＿＿＿＿＿＿＿＿ heavy ＿＿＿＿＿＿＿＿ no one can move it.
　　A. too... to...　　　　B. very... as...　　　C. so... that...　　D. such... that...

2.　The express train comes in ＿＿＿＿＿＿＿＿ 30 minutes.
　　A. all　　　　　　B. once　　　　　　C. nearly　　　　D. every

Part 2 段落填空

Pizza Hut is a big business because you can see it almost everywhere. Believe it or not, it got __(3)__ by two college students in 1958 with a $600 __(4)__ . They were trying to earn some money so that __(5)__ . In the beginning, they had to __(6)__ free pizza to draw customers. __(7)__ But now, it is the one of the biggest pizza chain stores in the world.

3.　A. starting
　　B. started
　　C. to start
　　D. to starting

4.　A. money
　　B. loan
　　C. interest
　　D. dollars

5.　A. they can pay their way through
　　　college
　　B. the school could buy new books for
　　　the library
　　C. their future career would be earlier
　　　decided
　　D. work can be a part of life and can
　　　bring satisfaction

6.　A. take in
　　B. give away
　　C. carry on
　　D. fight for

7.　A. In addition
　　B. No wonder
　　C. Of course
　　D. But now

Fisherman Film Festival

October 12-15 at the Panda Theater
Scheduled Screenings:
Time of Fantasy, Oct. 12, 8 P.M.
The Spring King, Oct. 13, 7 P.M.
Diamond Dolls, Oct. 14, 8 P.M.
Up the Ladder, Oct. 15, 9 P.M.

* There will be a Q&A talk with a world famous director after the screenings are over.

Taipei, Oct. 5 (CNA) The famous film director Vincent Lau has been expected to spoke about his new film he's making now during a talk at the Fisherman Film Festival. "I really have high expectations for it," he said. Vincent will be at the festival showing his last film, *Up the Ladder*, which has gained an important success.

8. What is true about the film festival?

    A. The movies will be made in October.

    B. All the movie directors will attend the festival.

    C. The film festival will last for 4 days.

    D. Diamond Dolls will be screened on October 15.

9. What is NOT true about Vincent Lau?

    A. He will show up at the end of the movie festival.

    B. He will talk about his new film at the festival.

    C. His new movie will be screened at the end of the festival.

    D. He has high expectations for his newest film.

10. At what time will Mr. Lau's film be screened during the festival?

    A. At 7 o'clock   C. At 9 o'clock

    B. At 8 o'clock   D. At 10 o'clock

Day 22

Day 23

Day 24

Day 25

Day 26

Day 27

Day 28

解答與詳解

上頁簡答	1. (C)　2. (D)　3. (B)　4. (B)　5. (A)
	6. (B)　7. (D)　8. (C)　9. (C)　10. (C)

Part 1　詞彙

Q1　考題重點〉「so... that...」的句型

The carton is _____ heavy _____ no one can move it.

A. too... to...

C. so... that...

B. very... as...

D. such... that...

| 翻譯 | 這紙箱如此地重而沒有人能搬動它。 |

| 詳解 | 本題考的是「如此…以致於…」的句型，too... to... 以及 so... that... 都可以用來表示此句型，但空格後面是個完整句（no one can move it），所以正確答案為選項 C。 |

Q2　考題重點〉every + 一段時間

The express train comes in _____ 30 minutes.

A. all

C. nearly

B. once

D. every

| 翻譯 | 快速列車每三十分鐘一班。 |

| 詳解 | 句意是「每三十分鐘一班」，所以正確答案為選項 D。nearly（幾乎，將近）雖然可以表達「差不多三十分鐘之後來到」，似乎也沒什麼不對，但必須用未來式（will come）才行。至於 all 與 once 則完全不合邏輯。 |

Part 2　段落填空

Pizza Hut is a big business because you can see it almost everywhere. Believe it or not, it got **(3) started** by two college students in 1958 with a $600 **(4) loan**. They were trying to earn some money so that **(5) they can pay their way through college**. In the beginning, they had to **(6) give away** free pizza to draw customers. **(7) But now**, it is the one of the biggest pizza chain stores in the world.

| 翻譯 | 必勝客是一家規模龐大的企業，因為你幾乎到處都可以看到它。信不信，它是在 1958 年由兩名大學生用 600 美金的貸款開始創立的。他們努力想賺些錢以支付大學學費。一開始時，他們得免費送披薩來招攬客人。但時至今日，必勝客已經成為全球最大的披薩連鎖店之一。 |

Q3 考題重點〉「get + P.P.」的被動式用法

A. starting　　**B. started**　　C. to start　　D. to starting

| 詳解 | 本句主詞 it 是指 Pizza Hut，動詞 got 相當於 be 動詞（連綴動詞）的功能，公司不會自己創立，而是被創立，所以動詞 start 應用過去分詞 started 表示被動，正確答案為選項 B。

Q4 考題重點〉填入符合句意的名詞

A. money　　**B. loan**　　C. interest　　D. dollars

| 詳解 | 兩個大學生創業金是 $600，美金的寫法不是在數字前直接寫 $ 的符號，就是直接在數字後加 dollar(s)，所以選項 D 不對。money 是「錢」，而 interest 是指「利息」，$600 不可能是利息，而是本金，所以正確答案為選項 B。

Q5 考題重點〉選擇符合前後文意的句子

A. they can pay their way through college　他們才可以支付大學學費

B. the school could buy new books for the library　學校可以為圖書館購買新的書籍

C. their future career would be earlier decided　他們未來的職業可以更早確立

D. work can be a part of life and can bring satisfaction
　　工作可以成為生活的一部分且能帶來滿足感

| 詳解 | 空格這句前面有連接詞 so that，表示前面「They were trying to earn some money」是因，而空格這句是果，但以一般大學生打工的動機而言，只有選項 A 的敘述（支付大學學費）是比較合情合理的，因此正確答案為選項 A。

Q6 考題重點〉填入符合句意的動詞片語

A. take in　　**B. give away**　　C. carry on　　D. fight for

| 詳解 | 句意是「他們得免費送披薩來招攬客人」，故正確答案為表示「分發，贈送」的選項 B。A、C、D 的意思分別是「接受」、「繼續進行」、「為…抗爭」，皆不符語意。

Q7 考題重點〉符合前後文語意的轉折語

A. In addition　　B. No wonder　　C. Of course　　**D. But now**

| 詳解 | 前面提到「一開始時，他們得免費送披薩來招攬客人」，這一句則是「它已是全球最大的披薩連鎖店之一」，顯然前後有很大的不同與轉變，所以正確答案應為選項 D，表示「但如今…」。A、B、C 的意思分別是「此外」、「難怪」、「當然」。

Day 22

Day 23

Day 24

Day 25

Day 26

Day 27

Day 28

Fisherman Film Festival

October 12-15 at the Panda Theater

Scheduled Screenings:

Time of Fantasy, Oct. 12, 8 P.M.

The Spring King, Oct. 13, 7 P.M.

Diamond Dolls, Oct. 14, 8 P.M.

Up the Ladder, Oct. 15, 9 P.M.

* There will be a Q&A talk with a world famous director after the screenings are over.

Taipei, Oct. 5 (CNA) The famous film director Vincent Lau has been expected to spoke about his new film he's making now during a talk at the Fisherman Film Festival. "I really have high expectations for it," he said. Vincent will be at the festival showing his last film, *Up the Ladder*, which has gained an important success.

| 翻譯 |

漁夫電影節
十月十二至十五日在熊貓劇院舉辦

排定播映：

《幻想時刻》，十月十二日，晚上八點

《春天之王》，十月十三日，晚上七點

《鑽石玩偶》，十月十四日，晚上八點

《平步青雲》，十月十五日，晚上九點

* 放映結束後將有一場與一位世界知名導演的問答交流。

台北，10 月 5 日（中央社）知名電影導演劉文森預計在「漁夫電影節」的一場談話講座上談論他正在拍攝的新電影。他說：「我對這部新片影確實有很高的期許。」文森將在電影節上展示了他上一部電影《平步青雲》，該片已獲得重要的成就。

| 詞彙 | **festival** [ˈfɛstəvl] 節日，節慶　**scheduled** [ˈskɛdʒuld] 預定的，安排好的
screening [ˈskrinɪŋ] 放映　**fantasy** [ˈfæntəsɪ] 幻想　**doll** [dɑl] 玩偶
ladder [ˈlædə] 梯子，階梯　**expectation** [ˌɪkspɛkˈteʃən] 期望，預期　**gain** [gen] 獲得

Q8 What is true about the film festival? 關於這場電影節，何者為真？

A. The movies will be made in October.　這些電影將於十月分拍攝。

B. All the movie directors will attend the festival.
這些電影的所有導演都將出席電影節。

C. The film festival will last for 4 days.　電影節將維期四天。

D. *Diamond Dolls* will be screened on October 15.
《鑽石玩偶》將於十月十五日播映。

| 詳解 | 本題針對第一個文本（schedule）內容答題。首先，make a movie 是指「拍電影」或「製作電影」，因此選項 A 顯然錯誤；從「a Q&A talk with a world famous director」可知，只有一位導演會到現場，因此選項 B 錯誤；從「October 12-15 at the Panda Theater」可知，電影節將維期四天，因此正確答案是選項 C；從「*Diamond Dolls*, Oct. 14, 8 P.M.」可知，選項 D 錯誤。

Q9 What is NOT true about Vincent Lau?
關於劉文森，何者為非？

A. He will show up at the end of the movie festival.
他將於電影節的最後現身。

B. He will talk about his new film at the festival.
他將在電影節上談談他的新片。

C. His new movie will be screened at the end of the festival.
他的新電影將在電影節的最後播映。

D. He has high expectations for his newest film.
他對他最新的電影期望很高。

| 詳解 | 在第二個文本的新聞報導中提到「Vincent will be at the festival showing his last film, *Up the Ladder*, which...」表示文森將在電影節上展示了他上一部電影《平步青雲》，顯然 C 的敘述是錯誤的，故本題正確答案為選項 C。

| 詞彙 | **show up** 出現，現身　**screen** [skrin] 播映

Day 22

Day 23

Day 24

Day 25

Day 26

Day 27

Day 28

$Q10$ At what time will Mr. Lau's film be screened during the festival?
劉先生的電影將在電影節中的什麼時間播映？

A. At 7 o'clock　在七點鐘

B. At 8 o'clock　在八點鐘

C. At 9 o'clock　在九點鐘

D. At 10 o'clock　在十點鐘

| 詳解 | 這個題目要綜合兩篇文章來解題。首先，第二個文本的新聞報導提到「Vincent will be at the festival showing his last film, *Up the Ladder...*」表示，《平步青雲》這部電影是他所執導的，接著我們看到第一個文本中「Up the Ladder, Oct. 15, 9 P.M.」可知，《平步青雲》是在 10/15 的晚上九點播映，所以正確答案是選項 C。

Part 1 詞彙

1. _____ interesting it is to see your face suddenly turn old!
   A. What   C. Where
   B. How   D. Which

2. He is moving to Singapore _____ the end of this year.
   A. in   C. by
   B. on   D. for

Part 2 段落填空

A man reported to have mental (3) cruelly killed a man and injured four other people in Taipei with a pair of scissors before he was (4) by police yesterday morning. This local news underlined the fact (5) treatment and care of people with mental illness indeed needs better resources and (6) efforts. Let's now work together to support those who (7) .

3. A. problems   6. A. enough
   B. behavior   B. good
   C. health   C. more
   D. ages   D. less

4. A. accepted   7. A. have been ill in bed for many years
   B. arrested   B. are always hard up for money
   C. admitted   C. do not have good living conditions
   D. adopted   D. need more close friends to get along

5. A. because
   B. with
   C. which
   D. that

You are invited to the yearly Special Events Exhibition!

Food makers, suppliers and event planners and other party-related experts will have their products and services on display.

The special event will be held at Nichol Public Park from Friday, June 11 to Sunday, June 13, between 10 A.M. and 6 P.M.

All planned events will include cake making skills in Section A, cookie baking tools in Section B, and various parties planning in Section C and special arrangements for parent-child activities in Section D.

To attend the event, simply present this invitation at the entrance. We look forward to seeing you.

Local Baker Shows Off Skills at Expo

Kaoshiung, May. 15

Trevor Gates is famous all over the world for his amazing cooking skills. He's from a bakery in Manchester. Guess what? He's going to be at the Special Events Exhibition next month! Trevor will show his yummy food and teach people about cooking. You should come and meet Trevor. Try his tasty treats yourself!

8. What will happen on June 13?
   A. The special event will begin.
   B. The exhibition will come to an end.
   C. The guest list will be completed.
   D. One of the halls will close temporarily.

9. What do we know about Mr. Gates?
   A. He is good at making cookers.
   B. He works for a famous a bakery in Manchester.
   C. His father is also a famous baker.
   D. He learned baking skills in Manchester.

10. Where is Mr. Gates expected to meet his fans?
    A. In Section A
    B. In Section B
    C. In Section C
    D. In Section D

Day 22
Day 23
Day 24
Day 25
Day 26
Day 27
Day 28

解答與詳解

Part 1　詞彙

Q1　考題重點〉疑問詞（5W1H）開頭的感嘆句結構

_____ interesting it is to see your face suddenly turn old!

A. What　　　　　　　　　C. Where

B. How　　　　　　　　　D. Which

| 翻譯 | 看見你的臉突然變老了真是有趣啊！

| 詳解 | 本題考的是感嘆句的句型。一般來說有「What + N + S + V...」以及「How + Adj/Adv + S + V...」這兩種句型。空格後面 interesting 是個形容詞，所以正確答案為選項 B。

| 詞彙 | **suddenly** [ˋsʌdn̩l̩ɪ] 突然地　**turn old** 變老

Q2　考題重點〉表示時間的介系詞 by

He is moving to Singapore _____ the end of this year.

A. in　　　　　　　　　　　**C. by**

B. on　　　　　　　　　　　D. for

| 翻譯 | 他將在年底前移居新加坡。

| 詳解 | end 可以表示一個「時間點」，因此正確答案是選項 C。「by + 時間點」的意思是「在某個時間點之前」，意義上會比用 before 表達的時間距離更為靠近。

Part 2　段落填空

A man reported to have mental **(3) problems** cruelly killed a man and injured four other people in Taipei with a pair of scissors before he was **(4) arrested** by police yesterday morning. This local news underlined the fact **(5) that** treatment and care of people with mental illness indeed needs better resources and **(6) more** efforts. Let's now work together to support those who **(7) do not have good living conditions**.

| 翻譯 | 據報台北昨日早晨一名患有精神問題的男子在被警方逮捕前，利用剪刀殘殺一名男性，並傷及其他四人。這條當地新聞事件突顯一個事實：精神異常患者的治療與照顧確實需要更好的資源及更多的努力。現在就讓我們一起來支持那些失去良好生活條件的人吧。

Day 22

Day 23

Day 24

Day 25

Day 26

Day 27

Day 28

Q3 考題重點〉填入符合句意的名詞

A. problems   B. behavior   C. health   D. ages

|詳解| 句意是「患有精神問題的男子殘殺一名男性…」，所以正確答案為選項 A。選項 B、C、D 的意思分別是「行為」、「健康」、「年齡」。

Q4 考題重點〉填入符合句意的動詞

A. accepted   C. admitted

B. arrested   D. adopted

|詳解| 句意是「…被警方逮捕前，利用剪刀殘殺一名男性，並傷及其他四人」，所以正確答案為選項 B。選項 A、C、D 的意思分別是「接受」、「承認」、「採用，領養」。

Q5 考題重點〉「the fact + that 子句」的用法

A. because   C. which

B. with   **D. that**

|詳解| 空格前後都是完整句，顯然應填入一個連接詞連接兩句，故選項 B 可直接排除。「the fact」後面接「that 子句」表示「…的事實」，是對於 fact 作補充說明，以文法結構來說，that 子句是 fact 的同位語，故正確答案為選項 D。

Q6 考題重點〉and 前後對等的概念

A. enough   **C. more**

B. good   D. less

|詳解| 本題關鍵字是對等連接詞 and 前面的 better，因此在 efforts 前填入同樣是比較級地 more 是最適當的，所以正確答案為選項 C。雖然 less 也是比較級，但不符語意。

Q7 考題重點〉選擇符合前後文意的句子

A. have been ill in bed for many years   長年臥病在床

B. are always hard up for money   總是缺錢

C. do not have good living conditions   沒有良好的生活條件

D. need more close friends to get along   需要更多可以好好相處的朋友

|詳解| 空格這半句前面關係代名詞 who，顯然是用來形容需要給予支持的……人，我們可以從整篇前文的大意了解，是罹患精神異常、在外面傷害他人的人，所以只有選項 C 是最接近的答案。

You are invited to the yearly Special Events Exhibition!

Food makers, suppliers and event planners and other party-related experts will have their products and services on display.

The special event will be held at Nichol Public Park from Friday, June 11 to Sunday, June 13, between 10 A.M. and 6 P.M.

All planned events will include cake making skills in Section A, cookie baking tools in Section B, and various parties planning in Section C and special arrangements for parent-child activities in Section D.

To attend the event, simply present this invitation at the entrance. We look forward to seeing you.

Local Baker Shows Off Skills at Expo

Kaoshiung, May. 15

Trevor Gates is famous all over the world for his amazing cooking skills. He's from a bakery in Manchester. Guess what? He's going to be at the Special Events Exhibition next month! Trevor will show his yummy food and teach people about cooking. You should come and meet Trevor. Try his tasty treats yourself!

| 翻譯 |

Day 22
Day 23
Day 24
Day 25
Day 26
Day 27
Day 28

敬邀前來一年一度的特別活動展！

食品製造商、供應商、活動策劃人以及其他與派對相關的專家將展示他們的產品和服務。

這場特別活動將於 6 月 11 日（星期五）至 6 月 13 日（星期日）在尼科爾公園舉行，每天上午 10 點至下午 6 點。

所有排定的活動將包括在 A 區展示蛋糕製作技巧，在 B 區展示餅乾烘焙工具，以及在 C 區舉辦的各種派對規劃，還有 D 區親子活動的特別安排。

想要參加活動，只需在入口處出示這張邀請函即可。

我們期待著您的光臨。

當地麵包師傅在博覽會展現技藝

高雄，5 月 15 日

特雷弗・蓋茲以其驚人的烹飪技巧聞名於世界各地。他來自曼徹斯特一家麵包店。你知道嗎？下個月他將出席一場特別活動展覽！特雷弗將展示他美味的食物，並教大家烹飪。你應該來見見特雷弗。親自品嚐他美味的點心吧！

| 詞彙 | **yearly** [ˈjɪrlɪ] 一年一度的，每年的　　**exhibition** [ˌɛksəˈbɪʃən] 展覽會，展覽
supplier [səˈplaɪɚ] 供應商，提供者　　**event** [ɪˈvɛnt] 事件，活動
on display 展示中，展出　　**cookie** [ˈkʊkɪ] 餅乾　　**section** [ˈsɛkʃən] 區域，地段
various [ˈværɪəs] 各種各樣的　　**arrangement** [əˈrendʒmənt] 安排，整理
parent-child [pəˈrɛnt-tʃaɪld] 親子的　　**invitation** [ˌɪnvəˈteʃən] 邀請，邀請函
entrance [ˈɪntrəns] 入口處　　**look forward to** 期待，盼望
baker [ˈbekɚ] 麵包師傅，烘焙師　　**shows off** 炫耀，展示
bakery [ˈbekərɪ] 麵包店，烘焙坊　　**treat** [trit] 款待，招待

Q8 What will happen on June 13? 在 6 月 13 日將發生什麼事？

A. The special event will begin.　這場特別的活動將開始。

B. The exhibition will come to an end.　這場展覽將要結束。

C. The guest list will be completed.　將要完成顧客名單。

D. One of the halls will close temporarily.　將臨時關閉一間大廳。

Q9 What do we know about Mr. Gates?
關於蓋茲先生，我們可以知道什麼？

A. He is good at making cookers.　他善於製造烹飪器具。

B. He works for a famous a bakery in Manchester.

他在曼徹斯特一家麵包店工作。

C. His father is also a famous baker.　他的父親也是個有名的烘培師。

D. He learned baking skills in Manchester.　他在曼徹斯特學習烘培技術。

|詳解| 從第二個文本的「He's from Manchester Bakery.」可知，他來自曼徹斯特一家麵包店，故正確答案為選項 B。選項 A 刻意以 cookers 來混淆答題，而選項 C 與 D 都是沒有提及的。

|詞彙| **cooker** [`kʊkɚ] 烹飪器具

Q10 Where is Mr. Gates expected to meet his fans?
蓋茲先生預計在哪裡和他的粉絲們會面？

A. In Section A　在 A 區

B. In Section B　在 B 區

C. In Section C　在 C 區

D. In Section D　在 D 區

|詳解| 這個題目要綜合兩篇文章來解題。首先，第二個文本的新聞報導提到「He's from a bakery in Manchester... Trevor will show his yummy food and teach people about cooking.」，這表示他是曼徹斯特一家麵包店的師傅，且展示他美味的食物，並教大家烹飪。接著我們可以看到第一個文本（邀請函）中的「All planned events will include cake making skills in Section A」提到，在 A 區展示蛋糕製作技巧，可見蓋茲先生會出現在 A 區，所以正確答案是選項 A。

Day 22

Day 23

Day 24

Day 25

Day 26

Day 27

Day 28

Day 24

月　　　日

Part 1 詞彙

1. I suggest you read some books ＿＿＿＿＿＿＿＿＿＿ TG Miller. That would be help-ful.

   A. from

   B. of

   C. by

   D. with

2. Would you mind ＿＿＿＿＿＿＿＿＿ off the air conditioner? It's a cold.

   A. turn

   B. turning

   C. to turn

   D. turned

Part 2 段落填空

  (3) . Some like to run, some like to walk, and (4) like to dance or play ball games. Why do people like to exercise? It makes them feel good. They feel (5) so they sleep better at night. They feel energetic after exercising so they feel recharged at work. Walking or running is very good exercise, and it's more (6) if you go with a friend. Find an exercise that you like, (7) you'll soon know how wonderful it is.

3. A. In fact, there are many popular indoor activities

   B. Some people easily suffer from sleeplessness at night.

   C. The favorite form of exercise is jogging, based on the survey.

   D. Many people nowadays love to do exercise.

4. A. other

   B. others

   C. the other

   D. another

5. A. relax

   B. relaxing

   C. relaxed

   D. to relax

6. A. fun

   B. funny

   C. funner

   D. funnest

7. A. or

   B. but

   C. and

   D. X

179

FunZone Toys and Games

FunZone makes toys and games for kids that are fun and help them learn. You can pick from hundreds of different things online. Click on the links below to see more about each item that's on sale for a limited period.

Musical toys (under 3 years old)
Wooden blocks (3 - 6 years old)
Board games (6 years old and older)

NOTE: Shipping and taxes are not included in the prices listed on our website.

A Visit to the Zoo

Product Description:
1. Children can learn to develop problem-solving skills, and improve memory ability as they need to remember rules.
2. NT$350, without shipping
3. Product carton size: 27.5 x 13 x 10.5 cm
4. Weight: 1.1 kg

8. What products does FunZone NOT sell?

   A. A baby doll   C. Pull-along toys
   B. Toy vehicles   D. Pencils and backpacks

9. Which of the following is NOT true about A Visit to the Zoo?

   A. Children can be trained to solve problems by themselves.

   B. The product costs NT$350 that does not include shipping.

   C. Its weight is more than 1 kg.

   D. The product includes a free ticket to the zoo.

10. What age is the product A Visit to the Zoo suitable for?

   A. Under 3 years old   C. 6 years old and older
   B. 3 - 6 years old   D. Older than 10 years old

解答與詳解

1. (C)　2. (B)　3. (D)　4. (B)　5. (C)
6. (A)　7. (C)　8. (D)　9. (D)　10. (C)

Part 1　詞彙

Q1　考題重點〉表示「著作者」的介系詞 by

I suggest you read some books ＿＿＿＿＿＿＿ TG Miller. That would be helpful.

A. from　　　　B. of　　　　**C. by**　　　　D. with

| 翻譯 | 我建議你讀些 TG Miller 的書。那會很有幫助。

| 詳解 | TG Miller 是一名作家（author、writer），他寫的書籍我們會說「books written by TG Miller」，所以正確答案為選項 C。介系詞 of 是「…的」，雖然「some books of TG Miller」聽起來好像行得通，但這是指「TG Miller 的書」（可能是他買的或別人給他的），與本題語意不符。

| 詞彙 | helpful [ˋhɛlpfəl] 有幫助的

Q2　考題重點〉mind + Ving 的用法

Would you mind ＿＿＿＿＿＿＿ off the air conditioner? It's a cold.

A. turn　　　　**B. turning**　　　　C. to turn　　　　D. turned

| 翻譯 | 你可以把冷氣關掉嗎？有點冷。

| 詳解 | mind 當動詞時表示「介意」，後面必須接動名詞（Ving）作為其受詞，因此正確答案是選項 B。

| 詞彙 | air conditioner 冷氣機

Part 2　段落填空

(3) Many people nowadays love to do exercise. Some like to run, some like to walk, and **(4) others** like to dance or play ball games. Why do people like to exercise? It makes them feel good. They feel **(5) relaxed** so they sleep better at night. They feel energetic after exercising so they feel recharged at work. Walking or running is very good exercise, and it's more **(6) fun** if you go with a friend. Find an exercise that you like, **(7) and** you'll soon know how wonderful it is.

| 翻譯 | 現今很多人都喜歡運動。有些人喜歡跑步，有些人喜歡散步，而其他人則喜歡跳舞或打球。人們為什麼喜歡運動呢？因為運動讓他們感覺很好。他們覺得放鬆，所以晚上睡得比較好。運動後他們覺得充滿活力，因此上班更有精神。走路或跑步都是很好的運動，如果你跟朋友一起去運動會更有趣。試著找一項你喜歡的運動，你很快就會知道它是多麼美妙。

Q3 考題重點〉選擇符合前後文意的句子

A. In fact, there are many popular indoor activities
事實上，有許多受歡迎的室內活動。

B. Some people easily suffer from sleeplessness at night.
有些人晚上很容易失眠。

C. The favorite form of exercise is jogging, based on the survey.
根據調查，最受喜愛的運動是慢跑。

D. Many people nowadays love to do exercise.
現今很多人都喜歡運動。

| 詳解 | 開頭這一句等於是整段的主旨，基本上參考指標就是後面「Some like to run... games」這句，因 為散步、跳舞、打球都是運動（exercise）的一種，且並不限於室內的運動，所以正確答案是選項 D。

Q4 考題重點〉選擇正確的人稱代名詞

A. other　　　　**B. others**　　　　C. the other　　　　D. another

| 詳解 | 空格這句話當中的兩個 some 都是指 some people（有些人），句意是「有些人…，有些人…，而其他人…」所以正確答案為選項 B。others = other people。

Q5 考題重點〉過去分詞用來形容「人的感受」

A. relax　　　　B. relaxing　　　　**C. relaxed**　　　　D. to relax

| 詳解 | 當我們要表達「（人）感到…」時，要用過去分詞當形容詞，若是要表達某事物「令人…的」時，要用現在分詞（V-ing），所以正確答案為選項 C。

Q6 考題重點〉fun 當名詞時的用法

A. fun　　　　B. funny　　　　C. funner　　　　D. funnest

| 詳解 | 空格前雖然有 more，看似比較級的用法，很容易選了 B 的 funny，但 funny 的比較級是 funnier 不是 more funny，所以是錯誤答案。其實 fun（樂趣）當名詞也很常見，是個不可數名詞，可以被 more 修飾，此時的 more 是形容詞，不是副詞，故正確答案為選項 A。

Q7 考題重點〉「祈使句, + and...」句型

A. or
B. but

C. and
D. X

| 詳解 | 這個句子是以原形動詞 Find 開頭，是個祈使句，後面的「you'll soon know how wonderful it is」表示這個祈使句的「結果」或同時會發生的事，所以正確答案為選項 C。「Find..., and you'll...」=「If you find..., you'll...」。

Part 3 閱讀理解

FunZone Toys and Games

FunZone makes toys and games for kids that are fun and help them learn. You can pick from hundreds of different things online. Click on the links below to see more about each item that's on sale for a limited period.

Musical toys (under 3 years old)
Wooden blocks (3 - 6 years old)
Board games (6 years old and older)

NOTE: Shipping and taxes are not included in the prices listed on our website.

A Visit to the Zoo

Product Description:
1. Children can learn to develop problem-solving skills, and improve memory ability as they need to remember rules.
2. NT$350, without shipping
3. Product carton size: 27.5 x 13 x 10.5 cm
4. Weight: 1.1 kg

Day 22

Day 23

Day 24

Day 25

Day 26

Day 27

Day 28

FunZone 玩具與遊戲

FunZone 專門製造趣味且有助於孩子學習的玩具和遊戲。您可以在線上挑選數各式各樣的品項。請點擊以下連結,可以看到更多限時特賣產品的資訊。

音樂玩具(3 歲以下)
木製積木(3 - 6 歲)
棋盤遊戲(6 歲及以上)

注意:網站上列出的價格為未稅且不包含運費。

參觀動物園

產品描述:

1. 孩子們能夠學習培養解決問題的技巧,並提升記憶能力,因為他們必須記住一些規則。

2. 新台幣 350 元(不含運費)

3. 產品包裝盒尺寸 27.5 x 13 x 10.5 cm

4. 重量:1.1 公斤

| 詞彙 | **online** [ˈɑnˌlaɪn] 在線上,透過網路　**click on** (用滑鼠)點擊
link [lɪŋk](網路)連結　**below** [bɪˈlo] 在下面,以下　**on sale** 特價中
wooden [ˈwʊdn̩] 木製的　**block** [blɑk] 方塊,積木　**board** [bɔrd] 板;棋盤
description [dɪˈskrɪpʃən] 描述;說明　**problem-solving** [ˈprɑbləmˌsɑlvɪŋ] 解決問題的
improve [ɪmˈpruv] 改善;提高　**memory** [ˈmɛmərɪ] 記憶;記憶力
carton [ˈkɑrtən] 紙盒,紙箱　**weight** [wet] 重量,體重

Q8 What products does FunZone NOT sell?
什麼產品是 FunZone 沒有賣的?

A. A baby doll　嬰兒玩偶

B. Toy vehicles　玩具車

C. Pull-along toys　拖拉玩具

D. Pencils and backpacks　鉛筆與後背包

| 詳解 | 從第一個文本中第一句話「FunZone makes toys and games for kids that are fun and help them learn.」可知，FunZone 主要賣的是製造趣味且有助於孩子學習的玩具和遊戲，因此正確答案是選項 D。

| 詞彙 | **pull-along** [pul əˋlɔŋ] 拖拉的　　**backpack** [ˋbækͺpæk] 後背包

Q9 Which of the following is NOT true about A Visit to the Zoo?
關於「參觀動物園」，以下何者為非？

A. Children can be trained to solve problems by themselves.
孩子們可以被訓練自己解決問題。

B. The product costs NT$350 that does not include shipping.
產品售價為 NT$350，不包括運費。

C. Its weight is more than 1 kg.　產品的重量超過 1 公斤。

D. The product includes a free ticket to the zoo.　產品包含一張免費入園券。

| 詳解 | 從第二個文本的「Product Description」下方的內容「develop problem-solving skills」、「NT$350, without shipping」、「Weight: 1.1 kg」可知，選項 A、B、C 都是正確的敘述，而內容中並沒有提到贈送入園券，故正確答案為選項 D。

Q10 What age is the product A Visit to the Zoo suitable for?
「參觀動物園」這項產品適合幾歲的孩童使用？

A. Under 3 years old　3 歲以下

B. 3 - 6 years old　3 - 6 歲

C. 6 years old and older　6 歲及以上

D. Older than 10 years old　十歲以上

| 詳解 | 這個題目要綜合兩篇文章來解題。首先，第二個文本「Product Description」下方內容提到這項產品可以培養孩子解決問題，並提升記憶能力，因為他們必須記住一些規則，接著再對照第一個文本 FunZone 列出正在特價的三項產品（Musical toys、Wooden blocks、Board games）可知，「A Visit to the Zoo」屬於「棋盤遊戲（Board games）」，適合 6 歲及以上孩童，所以正確答案是選項 C。

Part **1** 詞彙

1. During the school play, Emily ＿＿＿＿＿＿＿＿ confidently on stage.

   A. greeted
   B. treated
   C. equaled
   D. behaved

2. My phone is ＿＿＿＿＿＿＿＿, so it doesn't have the latest apps and features like my friends' phones do.

   A. in the past
   B. on the way
   C. out of date
   D. at the stage

Part **2** 段落填空

Patty was excited and nervous to try ballet (3) . She wore her pink tight clothes and ballet shoes. In class, the teacher showed them how to stand (4) and point their (5) . Patty tried her best but (6) . She liked learning the plié and tendu moves. At the end of class, she felt tired but satisfied. Patty (7) wait to go back and learn more ballet!

3. A. to date
   B. by no means
   C. for the time being
   D. for the first time

4. A. high
   B. highly
   C. tall
   D. tally

5. A. fingers
   B. toes
   C. knees
   D. noses

6. A. nothing seemed very difficult
   B. sometimes failed to move well
   C. she felt a bit bored sometimes
   D. of course, she was already able to dance perfectly

7. A. should
   B. shouldn't
   C. could
   D. couldn't

Notice for Residents

The Seemiao Apartment Complex is planning two talks held in the meeting room for parents who have little kids next month. The first one is scheduled for Sept. 12 about early childhood education, and the second one is about home safety for kids under age 3 on Sept. 14. If you want to join, call Susan Hong at (02) 555-8249 to sign up before the end of this month.

 Did you see the notice posted on the bulletin?

Yes, and we were just talking about how to teach our kids well yesterday! I thought we could attend together.

8. What is the purpose of the notice?

   A. To let residents know about an event

   B. To encourage residents to do a free health checkup

   C. To advertise a sale at the apartment complex

   D. To hold a year-end party

9. According to the dialogue, what does the second speaker suggest doing?

   A. Discussing how to teach their kids well

   B. Taking their kids to attend an activity

   C. Attending an event

   D. Waiting for more information

10. On what date will they most likely attend the meeting?

   A. Sept. 9

   B. Sept. 11

   C. Sept. 12

   D. Sept. 14

Part 1 詞彙

Q1 考題重點〉選擇正確的動詞

During the school play, Emily _____ confidently on stage.

A. greeted　　　B. treated　　　C. equaled　　　**D. behaved**

| 翻譯 | 學校展演時，Emily 在舞台上表現得很有自信。

| 詳解 | 句尾的 on stage 是「登台，在舞台上」的意思，而句意是「在舞台上表現自信」，所以正確答案為選項 D。behave 意思是「（舉止、行為方面）表現…」。選項 A、B、C 的意思分別是「打招呼」、「對待」、「等同於…」。

| 詞彙 | confidently [ˈkɑnfədəntlɪ] 自信地

Q2 考題重點〉選擇正確的形容詞片語

My phone is _____ , so it doesn't have the latest apps and features like my friends' phones do.

A. in the past　　B. on the way　　**C. out of date**　　D. at the stage

| 翻譯 | 我的手機已經過時了，所以它沒有像我朋友們的手機那樣擁有最新的應用程式和功能。

| 詳解 | so 後面的主詞 it 是指前面的 My phone，而從「沒有最新的 app...」可知，就是指手機已「過時」，因此正確答案是選項 C。

| 詞彙 | lastest [ˈletɪst] 最新的　　feature [ˈfitʃɚ] 特色，功能

Part 2 段落填空

Patty was excited and nervous to try ballet **(3) for the first time**. She wore her pink tight clothes and ballet shoes. In class, the teacher showed them how to stand **(4) tall** and point their **(5) toes**. Patty tried her best but **(6) sometimes failed to move well**. She liked learning the plié and tendu moves. At the end of class, she felt tired but satisfied. Patty **(7) couldn't** wait to go back and learn more ballet!

| 翻譯 | Patty 第一次嘗試芭蕾舞時既興奮又緊張。她穿著粉紅色緊身衣和芭蕾舞鞋。在課堂上，老師教她們如何站得挺直，並將腳尖伸直向前。Patty 盡了最大努力，但有時動作不夠流暢。她喜歡學習 plié 和 tendu 的動作。課堂結束時，她感到疲憊但有滿足感。Patty 迫不及待地想要回去學習更多芭蕾舞了！

Day 22

Day 23

Day 24

Day 25

Day 26

Day 27

Day 28

Q3 考題重點〉選擇正確的副詞片語

A. to date
C. for the time being

B. by no means
D. for the first time

| 詳解 | 空格這句的前半部提到「既興奮又緊張」，所以 for the first time（第一次）是最適當的搭配，正確答案為選項 D。A、B、C 的意思分別是「迄今」、「絕不」、「暫時」。

Q4 考題重點〉選擇正確的形容詞

A. high
C.tall

B. highly
D. tally

| 詳解 | 本段內容一開始就提到跳芭蕾舞的事情，所以這裡句子要表達的當然就是「（把腳伸直）站高」的意思，正確答案為選項 C。這裡的 stand 是連綴動詞的用法，後面要接形容詞，表示一種狀態。另外，high 不可選的原因是，stand high 會變成「站在一個高高的位置」，不符語意。而 tally（帳目）並非 tall 的副詞。

Q5 考題重點〉選擇正確的名詞

A. fingers
B. toes
C. knees
D. noses

| 詳解 | 本題與前一題的答題關鍵點類似，都是以芭蕾舞的內容做為判斷，所以正確答案為選項 B。point one's toes 表示「將腳尖伸直向前」，其餘選項的 fingers（手指）、knees（膝蓋）、noses（鼻子）都與芭蕾舞步無關。

Q6 考題重點〉選擇符合前後文意的句子

A. nothing seemed very difficult　似乎沒甚麼困難的事

B. sometimes failed to move well　有時動作無法流暢

C. she felt a bit bored sometimes　她有時候感到有點無趣

D. of course, she was already able to dance perfectly
當然，她已經能夠跳得完美了

| 詳解 | 空格要填入的這半句前面有 but，表示它和「盡了最大努力」有相反的意思，所以最適當的答案應為選項 B。選項 A、D 的敘述都和「try one's best」具有一致性的關係。C 錯誤是因為後面提到她迫不及待地想要回去學習更多芭蕾舞。

Q7 考題重點〉「can't/couldn't wait to-V」句型

A. should
B. shouldn't
C. could
D. couldn't

Part3 閱讀理解

Notice for Residents

The Seemiao Apartment Complex is planning two talks held in the meeting room for parents who have little kids next month. The first one is scheduled for Sept. 12 about early childhood education, and the second one is about home safety for kids under age 3 on Sept. 14. If you want to join, call Susan Hong at (02) 555-8249 to sign up before the end of this month.

 Did you see the notice posted on the bulletin?

Yes, and we were just talking about how to teach our kids well yesterday! I thought we could attend together.

| 翻譯 |

住戶通知

Seemiao 社區計畫下個月為擁有幼兒的家長在會議室舉辦兩場講座。第一場定於 9 月 12 日舉行，主題是「幼兒教育」；第二場將於 9 月 14 日舉行，主題為「3 歲以下幼童的居家安全」。如有興趣參加，請於本月底之前致電（02）555-8249 向 Susan Hong 報名。

 你看過貼在布告欄上的公告了嗎？

有啊，而且我們昨天才談論過如何把我們的小孩教好呢！我想我們可以一起去參加。

| 詞彙 | notice [ˋnotɪs] 通知，告示　resident [ˋrɛzədənt] 住戶，居民
complex [ˋkɑmplɛks] 建築群　schedule [ˋskɛdʒul] 排定　sign up 報名，註冊
post [post] 張貼　bulletin [ˋbʊlɪtɪn] 布告欄　attend [əˋtɛnd] 參加，出席

Day 22
Day 23
Day 24
Day 25
Day 26
Day 27
Day 28

Q8 What is the purpose of the notice? 這項通知的目的為何？

A. To let residents know about an event　為了告知住戶社區的一項活動

B. To encourage residents to do a free health checkup
為鼓勵住戶做一項免費的健康檢查

C. To advertise a sale at the apartment complex　為該社區的特賣活動打廣告

D. To hold a year-end party　為舉辦一場尾牙活動

| 詳解 | 從第一個文本（通知）第一句話「The Seemiao Apartment Complex is planning two talks for parents who have little kids next month.」可知，這是住宅社區管委會通知一場為幼兒家長舉辦的講座，因此正確答案是選項 A。

| 詞彙 | **encourage** [ɪnˈkɝɪdʒ]　**checkup** [ˈtʃɛkʌp]　**advertise** [ˈædvɚtaɪz]
year-end party 尾牙

Q9 According to the dialogue, what does the second speaker suggest doing?
根據對話內容，第二位說話者建議做什麼？

A. Discussing how to teach their kids well　討論如何把小孩教好

B. Taking their kids to attend an activity　帶他們的孩子去參加一項活動

C. Attending an event　出席一場活動

D. Waiting for more information　等待更多資訊

| 詳解 | 從第二位說話者最後一句話「I thought we could attend together.」可知，建議一起去參加一場活動，但並未提到帶小孩子去，所以正確答案為選項 C。

Q10 On what date will they most likely attend the meeting?
他們最有可能在哪一天出席這場會議？

A. Sept. 9　九月九日

B. Sept. 11　九月十一日

C. Sept. 12　九月十二日

D. Sept. 14　九月十四日

| 詳解 | 這個題目要綜合兩篇文章來解題。首先，在第一個文本（通知）中，我們知道有兩場座談會，一場在 9 月 12 日，另一場在 9 月 14 日，分別是關於幼兒教育（early childhood education）與幼童居家安全（home safety）。接著再看對話中說話者談到他們昨天談論過如何把的小孩教好（...how to teach our kids well...），因此我們可以推斷他們最有可能去參加的是關於「幼兒教育」這一場，時間是 Sept. 12，所以正確答案是選項 C。

Part 1 詞彙

1. The bus arrives at the stop at a ＿＿＿＿＿＿＿＿＿ past ten every morning.

   A. second
   B. quarter
   C. clock
   D. time

2. I ＿＿＿＿＿＿＿＿＿ to my friend that I couldn't make it to her birthday party because I was sick.

   A. complained
   B. apologized
   C. expressed
   D. insisted

Part 2 段落填空

In the history of television around the world, there have been many changes. (3) , televisions were large and (4) , and they only showed black and white pictures. People would gather around to watch their favorite shows together. Then, (5) , televisions became smaller and lighter, and they could show colorful images. (6) Nowadays, with the internet, we can watch shows and movies on our phones, notebooks or computers too. Television has really changed a lot (7) it was first invented!

3. A. At first
   B. So far
   C. For good
   D. From now on

4. A. light
   B. tall
   C. thin
   D. heavy

5. A. over time
   B. at times
   C. in no time
   D. from time to time

6. A. That way, buying TV became much easier.
   B. Because of this, there were more and more TV channels.
   C. But some people still enjoy watching black-and-white pictures.
   D. This made watching TV even more fun!

7. A. because
   B. so
   C. since
   D. when

CAREFREE RESTAURANT

Want yummy food and drinks with your family or friends
in a cool and relaxing place with breathtaking sea view?
Come to Carefree Restaurant.
Call 555-5789 or add us on LINE with the ID: @cf_rest
to book a table and each of you will get a free drink of your choice
during our newly-opening period between 3/1-3/3!

Hi, I'd like to book a table for 8 at 12:30 p.m.
on March 5. My name is Bernard Garcia.

Good afternoon, Mr. Garcia! Let me take a look... OK.
No problem. May I have your cellphone number, please?

8. Which of the following is NOT true about Carefree Restaurant?

   A. It serves both food and drinks.

   B. You can use your cellphone to book a table.

   C. It's just started business recently.

   D. It is located in a busy city.

9. Who might be the speakers?

   A. Patient and nurse

   B. Employee and employer

   C. Customer and hair-dresser

   D. Customer and waiter

10. What is NOT true about Bernard?

   A. He will get a drink free of charge.

   B. He will go to Carefree Restaurant shortly.

   C. He will have lunch with his friends or family on March 5.

   D. His last name is Garcia.

Part 1 詞彙

Q1 考題重點〉選擇正確的名詞

The bus arrives at the stop at a _____ past ten every morning.

A. second   **B. quarter**   C. clock   D. time

| 翻譯 | 這輛巴士每天早上十點十五分到站。

| 詳解 | 本題考 quarter（四分之一）這個字用於時間表示法。「a quarter past ten」就是十點十五分，所以正確答案是選項 B。

| 詞彙 | arrive [əˈraɪv] 抵達

Q2 考題重點〉選擇正確的動詞

I _____ to my friend that I couldn't make it to her birthday party because I was sick.

A. complained   **B. apologized**   C. expressed   D. insisted

| 翻譯 | 我向我的朋友道歉，因為我生病了，無法參加她的生日派對。

| 詳解 | 本題 that 子句內容是答題關鍵，其中提到「因為生病了，無法去參加生日派對」，所以向朋友「表示歉意」的說法是最適當的答案，正確答案是選項 B。其餘 A、C、D 意思分別是「抱怨」、「表達」、「堅持」。

| 詞彙 | make it to... 前往…赴約

Part 2 段落填空

In the history of television around the world, there have been many changes. **(3) At first**, televisions were large and **(4) heavy**, and they only showed black and white pictures. People would gather around to watch their favorite shows together. Then, **(5) over time**, televisions became smaller and lighter, and they could show colorful images. **(6) This made watching TV even more fun!** Nowadays, with the internet, we can watch shows and movies on our phones, notebooks or computers too. Television has really changed a lot **(7) since** it was first invented!

Day 22
Day 23
Day 24
Day 25
Day 26
Day 27
Day 28

| 翻譯 | 在世界各地的電視歷史中，發生了許多變化。起初，電視機又大又重，只能顯示黑白影像。人們會聚在一起觀看他們喜愛的節目。然後，隨著時間的過去，電視機變得越來越小、越來越輕，並且能夠顯示彩色影像。這讓看電視變得更加有趣！如今，有了網際網路，我們也可以在手機、筆電或電腦上觀看節目和電影了。電視從最初發明以來確實發生了很大的變化！

Q3 考題重點〉選擇正確的副詞片語

A. At first　　　B. So far　　　C. For good　　　D. From now on

| 詳解 | 從後面提到的「televisions were large and... only showed black and white pictures」可知，這是在描述電視機一開始時的樣子，所以正確答案為選項 A。選項 B、C、D 的意思分別是「目前為止」、「永遠地」、「從現在起」。

Q4 考題重點〉選擇正確的形容詞

A. light　　　B. tall　　　C. thin　　　**D. heavy**

| 詳解 | 從空格前的「televisions were large and...」以及後面的「only showed black and white...」可知，這句話在描述電視機一開始時的樣子，也就是「又大又重」，所以正確答案為選項 D。

Q5 考題重點〉選擇正確的副詞片語

A. over time　　　B. at times　　　C. in no time　　　D. from time to time

| 詳解 | 句意是「然後，…，電視機變得越來越小、越來越輕」，因此「隨著時間過去，電視機變得…」是最符合邏輯的說法，正確答案為選項 A。其餘選項的 at times（有時候）、in no time（立即）、from time to time（時常）都不符語意。

Q6 考題重點〉選擇符合前後文意的句子

A. That way, buying TV became much easier.
　　如此一來，買電視變得容易多了。

B. Because of this, there were more and more TV channels.
　　因為如此，電視頻道變得越來越多了。

C. But some people still enjoy watching black-and-white pictures.
　　但有些人還是比較喜歡看黑白畫面。

D. This made watching TV even more fun!　　這讓看電視變得更加有趣！

| 詳解 | 前一句提到「...televisions became smaller and lighter... colorful images」，表示後來的彩色電視變得更加輕巧，可推知這句話是要呼應電視機的變革，因此「看電視變得更加有趣」是最適當的接續語，故正確答案是選項 D。

Q7 考題重點〉since 與完成式連用

A. because   B. so   **C. since**   D. when

| 詳解 | 主句的動詞時態是「現在完成式」（has changed），且副詞子句動詞用過去式，表示從過去某個時間點持續的現在，所以只能有 since（自從）來連接兩句，正確答案為選項 C。

Part 3 閱讀理解

CAREFREE RESTAURANT

Want yummy food and drinks with your family or friends
in a cool and relaxing place with breathtaking sea view?
Come to Carefree Restaurant.
Call 555-5789 or add us on LINE with the ID: @cf_rest
to book a table and each of you will get a free drink of your choice
during our newly-opening period between 3/1-3/3!

 Hi, I'd like to book a table for 8 at 12:30 p.m. on March 5. My name is Bernard Garcia.

Good afternoon, Mr. Garcia! Let me take a look... OK. No problem. May I have your cellphone number, please?

| 翻譯 |

忘憂餐廳

想和家人或朋友們在一個舒適、放鬆又有絕讚海景的地方，
享受美味的食物和飲料嗎？來忘憂餐廳吧。
請來電 555-5789 或加入我們的 LINE，ID 是 @cf_rest
訂位，開幕期間（3/1-3/3）每一位客人都可以自選一杯免費的飲料喔！

嗨！我想訂位，時間是 3/5 中午十二點半，8 位。我的名字是伯納德・賈西亞。

午安，賈西亞先生。我看一下…。好的，沒問題。請問您的手機號碼？

| 詞彙 | **carefree** [ˈkɛrˌfri] 無憂無慮的　**yummy** [ˈjʌmɪ] 美味的
relaxing [rɪˈlæksɪŋ] 輕鬆的，令人放鬆的
breathtaking [ˈbrɛθˌtekɪŋ] 令人屏息的，極美的　**night view** 夜景
add... on LINE 加入…的 LINE　**book a table** 訂位　**newly-opening** 新開張的
period [ˈpɪrɪəd] 期間

Q8 Which of the following is NOT true about Carefree Restaurant?
關於「忘憂餐廳」，何者為非？

A. It serves both food and drinks.　它提供食物及飲料的販售。

B. You can use your cellphone to book a table.　你可以使用手機來訂位。

C. It's just started business recently.　它最近才開始營業。

D. It is located in a busy city.　它位在一個都市鬧區。

| 詳解 | 從第一個文本（廣告）第一句話「a cool and relaxing place with breathtaking sea view」可知，這間餐廳應該是在高山上或近海邊的位置上，可推知選項 D 是錯誤的敘述，故本題正確答案是選項 D。

| 詞彙 | **business** [ˈbɪznɪs] 營業，生意　**locate** [loˈket] 使座落於…

Q9 Who might be the speakers?
對話者是誰？

A. Patient and nurse　病患與護士

B. Employee and employer　員工與雇主

C. Customer and hair-dresser　顧客與美髮師

D. Customer and waiter　顧客與服務員

| 詳解 | 第一位說話者表示「I'd like to book a table for 8」，即要訂八個人的位子，顯然是打電話到餐廳去訂位，所以正確答案為選項 D。

Q10 What is NOT true about Bernard?
關於伯納德，何者為非？

A. He will get a drink free of charge.　他將免費獲得一杯飲料。

B. He will go to Carefree Restaurant shortly.　他不久之後會去「忘憂餐廳」。

C. He will have lunch with his friends or family on March 5.
　　他將於三月五日和朋友或家人共進午餐。

D. His last name is Garcia.　他的姓是賈西亞。

| 詳解 | 這個題目要綜合兩篇文章來解題。首先，在第二個文本（對話）中，我們知道伯納德想預約三月五日「忘憂餐廳」的位子，接著在第一個文本（廣告）中的「you will get a free drink... between 3/1-3/3」可知，在開幕期間（3/1-3/3）每一位客人都可以自選一杯免費的飲料。由此可見，當伯納德一行人去開餐廳用餐時，已經過了開幕期間，所以無法獲得免費的飲料了，因此本題正確答案是選項 A。其餘選項都可以在對話內容中確認是正確的敘述。

Day 22
Day 23
Day 24
Day 25
Day 26
Day 27
Day 28

Part 1 詞彙

1. My teacher asked me to stay after school so I could ＿＿＿＿＿＿＿＿＿ the lesson I missed yesterday.

   A. look forward to　B. get used to　　C. catch up on　D. come up with

2. Many people dream of traveling the world, but ＿＿＿＿＿＿＿＿＿ actually save money and plan trips.

   A. some　　　　B. others　　　C. little　　　D. few

Part 2 段落填空

Brian has a special __(3)__ . He loves collecting stamps from all over the world. Every weekend, __(4)__ . Brian finds pleasure in learning about different countries and cultures by __(5)__ stamps. He carefully organizes his stamps in albums, arranging them __(6)__ country and year. Sometimes, Brian trades stamps with his friends to expand his collection even more. More importantly, collecting stamps __(7)__ him a sense of joy and knowledge to the wider world.

3. A. plan
   B. hobby
   C. lesson
   D. talent

4. A. he almost has no time hunting for rare stamps
   B. he goes online to eBay to buy new stamps
   C. some of his stamps would look a bit old
   D. there are always some thankless tasks for him

5. A. gathering
   B. drawing
   C. exporting
   D. judging

6. A. with
   B. by
   C. in
   D. from

7. A. bring
   B. brings
   C. will bring
   D. brought

| Bianchi Cycles | Order No. 45987 | Date: Aug. 1 | Name: Karl Miler |

123 Zhongda Road, Zhongli District, Taoyuan City, Taiwan

ITEM	MODEL NO.	QUNT.	COST
Water bottle	WB59918	2	NT$780
Biking shorts	BS91054	1	NT$800
Bike lock	BL45097	1	NT$250
Phone holder	PH41952	1	NT$350

TOTAL: NT$1,880

Thanks for your purchase from Bianchi Cycles. If there're any problems, contact us right away at 03-6664-5897 or send us a message at cs@bianchi.net.

••

Dear customer service,

I got my order (##45987) today and found I was charged for the phone holder! In fact, it was to take the place of something that got broken when it was sent to me before. I hope you could fix this mistake and hope to hear from you soon.

Thanks,

Karl Miler

8. What can we know about the order form?

   A. A water bottle costs NT$780.

   B. The Bianchi Cycles shop is located in southern Taiwan.

   C. Service staff can be contacted to report damage.

   D. There's a problem with the total amount of this order.

9. What is indicated about Mr. Miler?

   A. He thinks he doesn't need to pay for one of the items.

   B. One of the items he purchased was found broken.

   C. He complained about the late delivery.

   D. He wanted to change the phone holder for something else.

10. How much was Mr. Miler wrongly charged?

   A. NT$250   B. NT$350   C. NT$390   D. NT$800

💡 **解答與詳解** 上頁簡答

1. (C) 2. (D) 3. (B) 4. (B) 5. (A)
6. (B) 7. (B) 8. (C) 9. (A) 10. (B)

Part 1 詞彙

Q1 考題重點〉選擇正確的動詞片語

My teacher asked me to stay after school so I could _____ the lesson I missed yesterday.

A. look forward to B. get used to **C. catch up on** D. come up with

| 翻譯 | 我的老師要求我放學後留下來，讓我補昨天沒有上到的課。

| 詳解 | 句子大意是「放學後留下來補沒有上到的課」，catch up on 有「趕上進度」的意思，所以正確答案是選項 C。選項 A、B、D 的意思分別是「期待」、「習慣於」、「提出」。

| 詞彙 | after school 放學後 miss [mɪs] 錯過

Q2 考題重點〉不定代名詞 few 用法

Many people dream of traveling the world, but _____ actually save money and plan trips.

A. some B. others C. little **D. few**

| 翻譯 | 許多人夢想著環遊世界，但很少人確實在存錢及計畫旅行。

| 詳解 | 空格前有連接詞 but，顯然後半句應與「許多人夢想著環遊世界」的作為相反，因此後半句最通順的說法應該是「很少人」在為環遊世界存錢與計畫，故正確答案是選項 D。C 的 little 後面要接不可數名詞。

| 詞彙 | actually [ˈæktʃʊəlɪ] 實際上

Part 2 段落填空

Brian has a special **(3) hobby**. He loves collecting stamps from all over the world. Every weekend, **(4) he goes online to eBay to buy new stamps**. Brian finds pleasure in learning about different countries and cultures by **(5) gathering** stamps. He carefully organizes his stamps in albums, arranging them **(6) by** country and year. Sometimes, Brian trades stamps with his friends to expand his collection even more. More importantly, collecting stamps **(7) brings** him a sense of joy and knowledge to the wider world.

| 翻譯 | Brian 有一項特別的嗜好。他喜歡從世界各地蒐集郵票。每週末，他會上 eBay 網站買新的郵票。Brian 透過集郵的方式來了解不同國家和文化，這讓他感到愉悅。他會把郵票仔細地整理在集郵冊裡，並按照國家和年份排列。有時，Brian 會和朋友交換郵票，以增廣他的收藏。更重要的是，集郵讓他感到快樂並認識到更廣闊的世界。

Q3 考題重點〉選擇符合語境的名詞

A. plan　　　　　**B. hobby**　　　　　C. lesson　　　　　D. talent

| 詳解 | 從下一句的「Every weekend, ...」以及最後的「...collecting stamps... a sense of joy...」可知，整篇短文在描述「集郵」習慣、興趣或嗜好，所以正確答案為選項 B。選項 A、C、D 的意思分別是「計畫」、「課程」、「天賦」，皆不符整篇文意的內容。

Q4 考題重點〉選擇符合前後文意的句子

A. he almost has no time hunting for rare stamps
因此，他幾乎沒有時間找尋罕見的郵票

B. he goes online to eBay to buy new stamps　　他上 eBay 網站買新的郵票

C. some of his stamps would look a bit old　　他有些郵票會看起來有點舊

D. there are always some thankless tasks for him
總會有一些吃力不討好的工作給他

| 詳解 | 前兩句提到，Brian 有個集郵的嗜好，而這句以 Every weekend 開頭，顯然後面應該接他如何為了這項嗜好去做一些事情，且後面句子也提到在這項嗜好中找到的樂趣（Brian finds pleasure in...）因此上網找新的郵票，會是最適當的連接，正確答案是選項 B。

Q5 考題重點〉選擇正確的動詞

A. gathering　　　B. drawing　　　　C. exporting　　　　D. judging

| 詳解 | 這個短文講的是「集郵」，且前面出現了 collecting stamps，這裡只是再用另一個相同意思的動詞表達，所以正確答案為選項 A。選項 B、C、D 的意思分別是「畫畫」、「輸出」、「判斷」。

Q6 考題重點〉介系詞 by 表示「方法」

A. with　　　　　**B. by**　　　　　C. in　　　　　D. from

| 詳解 | 表達「以…方式」的介系詞用 by，這裡的「arranging them **by** country and year」表示「以年、月來編排郵票」，所以正確答案為選項 B。with 雖然也有類似意義，但主要強調的是用實體的工具來做什麼事。一般來說，可以記住一個基本原則：「by + 方法」中的 by 後面不會有冠詞，而「with + 工具」中的 with 後面會有冠詞。

Day 22
Day 23
Day 24
Day 25
Day 26
Day 27
Day 28

Q7 考題重點〉動名詞當主詞視為第三人稱單數

A. bring

C. will bring

B. brings

D. brought

| 詳解 | 全文以現在式敘述 Brain 的集郵興趣，以及從中獲得的樂趣，因此未來式的 C 及過去式的 D 皆不可選。句子主詞是「collecting stamps」，表示「集郵」這件事，主詞為第三人稱單數，應搭配動詞 brings，可別被空格前的複數名詞（stamps）誤導了，正確答案為選項 B。

Part 3 閱讀理解

Bianchi Cycles   Order No. 45987   Date: Aug. 1   Name: Karl Miler

123 Zhongda Road, Zhongli District, Taoyuan City, Taiwan

ITEM	MODEL NO.	QUNT.	COST
Water bottle	WB59918	2	NT$780
Biking shorts	BS91054	1	NT$800
Bike lock	BL45097	1	NT$250
Phone holder	PH41952	1	NT$350

TOTAL: NT$1,880

Thanks for your purchase from Bianchi Cycles. If there're any problems, contact us right away at 03-6664-5897 or send us a message at cs@bianchi.net.

Dear customer service,

I got my order (##45987) today and found I was charged for the phone holder! In fact, it was to take the place of something that got broken when it was sent to me before. I hope you could fix this mistake and hope to hear from you soon.

Thanks,

Karl Miler

Bianchi Cycles	訂單編號：45987	日期：8月1日	姓名：Karl Miler

台灣桃園市中壢區中大路 123 號

品項	型號	數量	價格
水壺	WB59918	2	NT$780
單車短褲	BS91054	1	NT$800
單車鎖	BL45097	1	NT$250
手機支架	PH41952	1	NT$350

TOTAL: NT$1,880

感謝您購買 Bianchi Cycles 的商品。如有任何問題，請立即致電 03-6664-5897 或發送郵件至cs@bianchi.net與我們聯繫。

．．

客服部 您好：

我今天收到了我的訂貨（##45987），且發現我被收取了手機架的費用！事實上，這東西是要取代之前運送給我時損壞的東西。希望您能夠修正此錯誤，並期待您盡快回覆。

謝謝，

Karl Miler

| 詞彙 | **order** [ˈɔrdə] 訂單，訂貨　**biking** [ˈbaɪkɪŋ] 自行車　**shorts** [ʃɔrts] 短褲
holder [ˈholdə] 支架，支托物　**purchase** [ˈpɝtʃəs] 購買　**contact** [ˈkɑntækt]
right away 立刻，馬上　**customer** [ˈkʌstəmə] 顧客
charge [tʃɑrdʒ] 向…（某人）索取費用　**take the place of** 取代…
broken [ˈbrokən] 壞掉的，破損的　**fix** [fɪks] 修理，修正

Q8 What can we know about the order form?
我們可以從這訂貨單上得知什麼？

A. A water bottle costs NT$780.　一個水壺要價 NT$780。

B. The Bianchi Cycles shop is located in southern Taiwan.
　　這間 Bianchi Cycles 店家位於南台灣。

C. Service staff can be contacted to report damage.
　　可以聯繫服務人員來通報物品受損狀況。

D. There's a problem with the total amount of this order.
　　這張訂貨單的總額有問題。

Day 22

Day 23

Day 24

Day 25

Day 26

Day 27

Day 28

| 詳解 | 從第一個文本（訂貨單）下方的「If there're any problems, contact us right away at...」可知，收到貨品時，如有任何問題都可以打電話或發 email 聯繫客服，故正確答案就是選項 C。選項 A 應修正為 1 個水壺 NT$390；選項 B 應修正為北台灣；選項 D 是第一個文本未提及的。

| 詞彙 | **damage** [ˈdæmɪdʒ] 受損，損壞

Q9 What is indicated about Mr. Miler?
關於 Miler 先生，有指出了什麼？

A. He thinks he doesn't need to pay for one of the items.
　　他認為他沒有必要支付其中一個品項的費用。

B. One of the items he purchased was found broken.
　　他發現購買的其中一個品項破損了。

C. He complained about the late delivery.　　他抱怨到貨延遲。

D. He wanted to change the phone holder for something else.
　　他想將手機支架換成別的東西。

| 詳解 | 在第二個文本中，Miler 先生提到「... I was charged for the phone holder... it was to take the place of something... before」，這表示他不該支付手機支架的費用，因為它是用來彌補先前某一件訂貨的受損，所以正確答案為選項 A。

Q10 How much was Mr. Miler wrongly charged?
Miler 先生被誤收了多少錢？

　　A. NT$250　　新台幣 250 元

　　B. NT$350　　新台幣 350 元

　　C. NT$390　　新台幣 390 元

　　D. NT$800　　新台幣 800 元

| 詳解 | 這個題目要綜合兩篇文章來解題。首先，在第二個文本中，Miler 說「it（= the phone holder）was to take the place of something that got broken when it was sent to me before」，這表示店家不該向他索取手機支架的費用。接著我們再對照第一個文本（訂貨單）品項（item）中的 Phone holder 可知，其價錢是 NT$350，因此正確答案是選項 B。

Part 1　詞彙

1. I wish I ＿＿＿＿＿＿＿＿ an eagle that can fly very high above the high mountains.

   A. am

   B. will be

   C. can be

   D. were

2. You have every ＿＿＿＿＿＿＿＿ of getting the job if you are well-prepared.

   A. event

   B. chance

   C. image

   D. direction

3. Sarah has difficulty ＿＿＿＿＿＿＿＿ people's names, so she writes them down in her notebook.

   A. remembered

   B. to remember

   C. to remembering

   D. remembering

4. A: Who took out the garbage tonight?

   B: I ＿＿＿＿＿＿＿＿.

   A. do

   B. did

   C. am

   D. took

5. Summer vacation is ＿＿＿＿＿＿＿＿, and I can't wait to go to the beach and play under the sun.

   A. on the other hand

   B. from time to time

   C. few and far between

   D. around the corner

6. No one knows ＿＿＿＿＿＿＿＿.

   A. how could this happen

   B. when will she come

   C. what happened to her

   D. where she is going to

7. Take a look at that sign! It ＿＿＿＿＿＿＿＿ "Danger! Deep Water!"

   A. says

   B. speaks

   C. talks

   D. tells

8. When you leave the house, remember _____ your keys with you.

   A. bringing

   B. brought

   C. to bring

   D. to bringing

9. She cooked a big meal, but nobody was hungry, so she cooked _____.

   A. in no time

   B. as soon as possible

   C. without doubt

   D. for nothing

10. My mom made me _____ my room before I could go out to play.

   A. to clean

   B. cleaning

   C. clean

   D. cleaned

Part 2 段落填空

Questions 11-14

In movies, sharks are often shown as (11) killers, but in real life, human beings may be (12) crueler in killing these animals. A well-known fact is that (13) . Once the sharks are caught and fins are removed, their useless bodies are thrown into the ocean by fishermen. Not only has the number of sharks (14) rapidly but also the balance of ecology has been destroyed as a result.

11. A. open-minded

    B. far-sighted

    C. cold-blooded

    D. short-lived

12. A. very

    B. more

    C. much

    D. most

13. A. more and more people are trying hard to protect sharks

    B. many people like to eat shark fins

    C. sharks have early been an endangered animal

    D. it is more difficult than before for fishermen to catch sharks

14. A. decrease

    B. decreasing

    C. to decrease

    D. decreased

Day 22
Day 23
Day 24
Day 25
Day 26
Day 27
Day 28

Questions 15-18

We may be willing to believe everything people tell us or what they promise to (15) , but experience tells us that sometimes they promise things that they cannot (16) deliver, even though you know they don't mean (17) that. In some situations, they indeed want to help, but in fact they just think they have the ability to. Anyway, through past experiences, we should learn to (18) , and to value actions and results more.

15. A. notice
    B. realize
    C. accept
    D. reject

16. A. ever
    B. never
    C. quite
    D. more

17. A. to do
    B. doing
    C. to doing
    D. to be done

18. A. easily trust what others say
    B. consider what others promise a lie
    C. rely only on ourselves no matter what happens
    D. think more carefully about promises and words

Part 3 閱讀理解

Questions 19-21

Reading is an activity some people enjoy a lot during their leisure. Some of them like reading newspapers, and some others enjoy novels or comic books. I like reading about the lives of great people. This always gives me a lot of ideas on how to make my own life better.

Great people are remembered not because how handsome or beautiful they are, but because they never say die during hard times. They use every opportunity to change their lives and make the world better instead. When I feel sad or unhappy, stories of famous people always cheer me up and help me move forward.

19. What does "this" mean in the last sentence of the first paragraph?

   A. Being a famous person

   B. Reading a lot of books

   C. Enjoying one's free time

   D. Reading about the lives of successful people

20. According to the article, which is NOT true about the great people?

   A. They have perfect appearance.

   B. They can survive through difficult times.

   C. They make good use of every chance and possibility.

   D. They always have the thought of improving.

21. What is in closest meaning to "say die" in the second paragraph?

   A. Die hard

   B. Give up

   C. Become angry

   D. Blame others

Questions 22-24

Notice for All Teachers

Huanan University will soon be attending several recruitment fairs next month to find new students. We'd like to emphasize that we are different from general universities because we always focus on giving students more personal attention from teachers. To let more students know about this, we want at least one teacher at each event. The location and time of each event is shown below:

- Tue, Apr. 10: Marsha Hotel, Taichung
- Sat, Apr. 14: Yehda College, Kaohsiung
- Tue, Apr. 17: World Trade Center, Taipei

If you can attend any of the fairs, please let me know at jocelyn_yang@huanan_university.org.edu. Working overtime at weekends will surely be paid for.

Day 22
Day 23
Day 24
Day 25
Day 26
Day 27
Day 28

From:	michelle_chang@huanan_university.org.edu
To:	jocelyn_yang@huanan_university.org.edu
Subject:	Recruitment fairs

Hello Jocelyn,

I was happy to see the notice you posted, and I'd like to tell you that I can go to the event on April 14. One of my uncles lives nearby, so I plan to visit him on that weekend. Please send me all the details of the event as soon as possible.

Cheers,
Teacher Andrew Hu

22. What job has Jocelyn Yang probably been given to do?

    A. Ask some teachers to participate in an event

    B. Make travel plans for some teachers

    C. Make a list of some upcoming events

    D. Find some suitable places for an event

23. What makes Huanan University different from other universities?

    A. Holding recruitment fairs more often

    B. Having more foreign teachers than any other university

    C. Giving students more educational resources

    D. More personal guidance and support for students from their teachers

24. Where does Teacher Andrew's uncle live?

    A. In Taipei

    B. In Taichung

    C. In Kaohsiung

    D. Near Huanan University

Questions 25-27

Richard Trevithick was very clever since he was still a young kid. In the 19th century, he made something very important in the history: the steam train. Before him, people relied on horses for moving from one place to another. However, Richard always had something different in mind from others: he wanted to create a machine that could move on its own. In 1804, he built the first steam train called the "Puffing Devil." This train was special because it could carry heavy loads and travel faster than horses. Richard's invention has changed the way people travel, making it quicker and more convenient. Even today, trains remain one of the primary parts of transportation thanks to him. What Richard Trevithick had left for people is a reminder that an idea, though involving risk and danger, can sometimes change the world. What's more, what he had left for later generations continues to inspire other inventions and progress in technology and transportation, shaping a different future for generations to come.

25. What is the main idea of this article?

    A. Richard Trevithick's childhood

    B. Encouragement for inventions involving danger

    C. The influence of Richard Trevithick's invention

    D. The importance of changing the world

26. What kind of moving machine did Trevithick invent?

A.

C.

B.

D.

Day 22

Day 23

Day 24

Day 25

Day 26

Day 27

Day 28

27. In this article, what is NOT true about Trevithick's invention?

   A. It can move faster than any horses people took in the past.

   B. It was first created in the early 19th century.

   C. He thought his invention is quite safe before it came into being.

   D. People thought it had paved way for many following inventions.

Questions 28-30

Sandra was walking down the street when suddenly someone pulled away her purse quickly. She felt angry, frightened and nervous then. Quickly, she went to the police station to report what had happened to her. She told the police officer that the thief was a man aged about 40, wearing a black face mask and blue shorts. He also wore sunglasses from which his eyes can be seen through. She said that he had big eyes. Sandra also remembered that he smelled like cigarettes. The police officer listened carefully and told Sandra that they would do everything they could to catch the thief. Sandra felt a bit better knowing that the police were helping her. She hoped that they would find the thief soon and that her purse would be returned safely. In the meantime, she told herself that she must be more careful in the future when walking alone on the streets.

28. What caused Sandra to feel frightened?
   A. A car accident
   B. A robbery
   C. A fire
   D. A very loud thunder

29. What lesson did Sandra learn from what happened to her?
   A. Do not bring too much money when going outside
   B. Always keep calm after being robbed of something
   C. Try not to walk alone on the streets in the future
   D. Pay more attention when walking alone outside

30. According to Sandra, what is NOT true about the thief?
   A. He wore a black face mask and a pair of sunglasses.
   B. He wore blue pants with a cigarette in his mouth.
   C. He looks middle-aged.
   D. His big eyes can be seen through his sunglasses.

Day 22

Day 23

Day 24

Day 25

Day 26

Day 27

Day 28

解答與詳解

上頁簡答

1. (D) 2. (B) 3. (D) 4. (B) 5. (D) 6. (C) 7. (A) 8. (C) 9. (D)
10. (C) 11. (C) 12. (C) 13. (B) 14. (D) 15. (B) 16. (A)
17. (A) 18. (D) 19. (D) 20. (A) 21. (B) 22. (A) 23. (D)
24. (C) 25. (C) 26. (D) 27. (C) 28. (B) 29. (D) 30. (B)

Part 1 詞彙

Q1 考題重點〉wish 的假設語氣用法

I wish I _____ an eagle that can fly very high above the high mountains.

A. am   C. can be

B. will be   **D. were**

| 翻譯 | 我希望我是一隻老鷹，無憂無慮且高高地飛在高山上。

| 詳解 | 本題考「wish 假設語氣」用法。題目用現在式，所以是「與現在事實相反」的假設，而假設語氣中的 be 動詞不分人稱，一律用 were，所以正確答案是選項 D。

| 詞彙 | eagle [`igl] 老鷹

Q2 考題重點〉選擇符合句意的名詞

You have every _____ of getting the job if you are well-prepared.

A. event   C. image

B. chance   D. direction

| 翻譯 | 如果你準備充分，你完全有機會獲得這份工作。

| 詳解 | 這個句子大意是，如果好好準備，完全有機會得到這份工作，因此正確答案是選項 B。A、C、D 的意思分別是「事件」、「影像」、「方向」，皆不符句意。

| 詞彙 | well-prepared [`wɛl prɪ`pɛrd] 充分準備的

Q3 考題重點〉「have difficulty + Ving」句型

Sarah has difficulty _____ people's names, so she writes them down in her notebook.

A. remembered   C. to remembering

B. to remember   **D. remembering**

| 翻譯 | Sarah 很難記住大家名字，所以她用筆記本寫了下來。

| 詳解 | 「have difficulty + Ving」是個常見的句型，表示「在…（方面）有困難」，類似用法還有「have a hard time + Ving」，其實只要記住一個概念：動名詞（Ving）表示「同時發生」，而不定詞（to-V）表示「不同時發生」，就可以輕易理解這句不能用不定詞（to-V），本題正確的答案是選項 D。

Q4 考題重點〉簡答時用助動詞

A: Who took out the garbage tonight?

B: I _____ .

A. do   **B. did**   C. am   D. took

| 翻譯 | A：今天晚上誰倒了垃圾？B：是我。

| 詳解 | 對話中 A 用的動詞時態是過去式，所以 B 的回答當然也要用過去式，因此 A、C 不可選，而從對話內容來看，B 用「簡答」，所以要用過去式助動詞 did，故正確答案是選項 B。如果要用 took，就必須詳答了，要說「I took it out.」或「I took out the garbage.」。

Q5 考題重點〉選擇符合句意的主詞補語

Summer vacation is _____ , and I can't wait to go to the beach and play under the sun.

A. on the other hand   C. few and far between

B. from time to time   **D. around the corner**

| 翻譯 | 暑假就要到了，而我已等不及要去海邊及在太陽底下玩耍了。

| 詳解 | 空格前面有 is，顯然要填入的是主詞（Summer vacation）的補語，而後面提到已經等不及要去海邊玩耍，因此 and 前的句意是「暑假就快要到了」，正確答案是選項 D。A、B、C 的意思分別是「另一方面來說」、「經常性地」、「人煙稀少的」。

| 詞彙 | **can't wait to-V** 等不及…

Q6 考題重點〉名詞子句當受詞時的語序

No one knows _____ .

A. how could this happen   **C. what happened to her**

B. when will she come   D. where she is going to

| 翻譯 | 沒有人知道她發生了什麼事。

| 詳解 | 疑問詞引導的名詞子句當動詞的受詞時，該名詞子句主詞與動詞的排列比照肯定句，因此 A、B 都是錯誤的，而 D 的主詞、動詞雖然是肯定句的結構，但 where 是地方副詞，本身就是「介系詞+地方」的概念，因此句尾不應再有 to，所以正確答案是選項 C。

Q7 考題重點〉表示「說」的動詞比較

Take a look at that sign! It _____ "Danger! Deep Water!"

A. says   B. speaks   C. talks   D. tells

| 翻譯 | 看看那標誌上面的！它寫說「水深勿近！」

Day 22
Day 23
Day 24
Day 25
Day 26
Day 27
Day 28

| 詳解 | tell 和 speak 主要都是用在「人」身上，即主詞通常是人，而 talk 是不及物動詞。後面必須有介系詞 about，因此，正確答案是選項 A。say 除了可以用來表示「某人說」，其主詞也可以是非生命事物，像是文章、報導、告示、訊息…等。

| 詞彙 | **sign** [saɪn] 標誌，牌子

Q8 考題重點〉remember + 不定詞（to-V）的意義

When you leave the house, remember ＿＿＿＿＿＿＿＿＿ your keys with you.

A. bringing   **C. to bring**

B. brought   D. to bringing

| 翻譯 | 當你離開這屋子時，記得把鑰匙帶在身上。

| 詳解 | remember 後面接不定詞時，表示「記得要去做某事」（事情還沒做），如果要表示「記得已經做了某事」，則後面要接動名詞（Ving），故正確答案是選項 C。像是 forget、stop、try…等動詞，後面接 to-V 或 Ving，也都有不同的意義。

| 詞彙 | **bring sth. with sb.** （某人）將某物帶在身上

Q9 考題重點〉選擇符合句意的副詞片語

She cooked a big meal, but nobody was hungry, so she cooked ＿＿＿＿＿＿＿＿＿.

A. in no time   C. without doubt

B. as soon as possible   **D. for nothing**

| 翻譯 | 她煮了一頓大餐，但沒有人肚子餓，所以她白煮了。

| 詳解 | so 表示一個「結果」，那麼前面的句子應該表示一個「原因」，句子大意是，煮了大餐卻沒人想吃，等於是白煮了，正確答案是選項 D。for nothing 字面意思是「沒有為了任何原因」，即「毫無意義地」。A、B、C 的意思分別是「立即」、「盡快」、「毫無疑慮地」。

Q10 考題重點〉使役動詞的用法

My mom made me ＿＿＿＿＿＿＿＿＿ my room before I could go out to play.

A. to clean   **C. clean**

B. cleaning   D. cleaned

| 翻譯 | 我母親要我先整理房間才能出去玩。

| 詳解 | 「使役動詞 + 受詞 + 原形動詞」是固定的句型，所以正確答案是選項 C。雖然使役動詞接受詞之後，也有可能接過去分詞（p.p.），但語意必須是被動，例如：I made/had my car fixed.（我將我的車送修了。）

Questions 11-14

In movies, sharks are often shown as **(11) cold-blooded** killers, but in real life, human beings may be **(12) much** crueler in killing these animals. A well-known fact is that **(13) many people like to eat shark fins**. Once the sharks are caught and fins are removed, their useless bodies are thrown into the ocean by fishermen. Not only has the number of sharks **(14) decreased** rapidly but also the balance of ecology has been destroyed as a result.

| 翻譯 | 在電影中，鯊魚常被呈現為冷血殺手，但實際上，人類在殺害這些動物方面可能更加殘忍多了。眾所周知，許多人喜歡吃魚翅。一旦捕獲鯊魚且取走魚翅後，漁民會將它們無用的身體拋入海洋。這不僅導致鯊魚數量已經迅速減少，結果還已讓生態平衡遭到破壞。

Q11 考題重點〉選擇正確的複合形容詞

A. open-minded   **C. cold-blooded**

B. far-sighted   D. short-lived

| 詳解 | 如果不清楚電影中描繪的鯊魚是何種形象，那麼從後面的「human beings may be... crueler in killing...」亦可推斷，電影中描繪的鯊魚也是跟 cruel（殘忍的）相近，所以正確答案為選項 C（冷血的）。A、B、D 意思分別是「心胸開放的」、「遠視的」、「短命的」，皆不符句意與邏輯。

Q12 考題重點〉修飾比較級的副詞

A. very   **C. much**

B. more   D. most

| 詳解 | 空格後面是形容詞比較級（crueler），所以要填入的是可以修飾形容詞比較級的副詞，故正確答案為選項 C。(A) very 只能修飾原級形容詞，而 crueler 本身就是比較級了，不需要再加 (B) more；(D) most 用來構成最高級形容詞。

Q13 考題重點〉選擇符合前後文的句子

A. more and more people are trying hard to protect sharks
越來越多人正試圖努力要保護鯊魚

B. many people like to eat shark fins   許多人喜歡吃魚翅

C. sharks have early been an endangered animal　鯊魚早已是一種瀕臨絕種的動物

D. it is more difficult than before for fishermen to catch sharks
　　對於漁夫來說現在比過去更難捕捉沙魚了

|詳解| 後面句子提到「Once the sharks are caught and fins are removed...（一旦捕獲鯊魚，取走魚翅後…）」，所以空格句子應與人們捕獲鯊魚、取走魚翅的動機有關，故正確答案為選項 B。

Q14 考題重點〉注意倒裝句中的動詞時態

A. decrease

B. decreasing

C. to decrease

D. decreased

|詳解| 空格所在的這個句子以 Not only 開頭，是個倒裝句，而從 has 這個助動詞來看，句子動詞時態是完成式，所以 decrease 這個動詞必須用過去分詞的 decreased，故正確答案是選項 D。

Questions 15-18

We may be willing to believe everything people tell us or what they promise to **(15) realize**, but experience tells us that sometimes they promise things that they cannot **(16) ever** deliver, even though you know they don't mean **(17) to do** that. In some situations, they indeed want to help, but in fact they just think they have the ability to. Anyway, through past experiences, we should learn to **(18) think more carefully about promises and words**, and to value actions and results more.

|翻譯| 雖然我們可能願意相信人們告訴我們的一切，或是他們承諾要實現的事情，但經驗告訴我們，有時候他們會承諾他們永遠無法兌現的事情，即使你知道他們並非有意如此。在某些情況下，他們確實想要幫忙，但實際上他們只是以為自己有能力這麼做。無論如何，透過過往的經驗，我們應學會更加審慎思考承諾和言語，並更加珍惜行動和成果。

Q15 考題重點〉選擇符合語境的動詞

A. notice

B. realize

C. accept

D. reject

|詳解| 本題關鍵在後面的「they promise things that they cannot... deliver（承諾他們…無法兌現的事情）」，這句話等於是把前面的「what they promise to...」再說一次，所以在這裡和 deliver 這動詞概念類似的只有 realize（實現），故正確答案是選項 B。A、C、D 的意思分別是「注意到」、「接受」、「拒絕」。

Day 22
Day 23
Day 24
Day 25
Day 26
Day 27
Day 28

Q16 考題重點〉選擇正確的副詞

A. ever

B. never

C. quite

D. more

| 詳解 | 空格所在句子「experience tells us that sometimes they promise things that they cannot... deliver」意思是「有時候他們會承諾他們…無法兌現的事情」，句子為否定，所以填入 ever（從來都…，在任何時候）是最適當的，故正確答案是選項 A。not ever = never，所以 B 不可選，其餘 quite、more 也都不符合語意。

Q17 考題重點〉「mean + to-V」表示「故意…」

A. to do

B. doing

C. to doing

D. to be done

| 詳解 | 句意是「即使你知道他們並非故意這麼做」，mean 用來表示「故意…（做某事）」時，後面需用不定詞（to-V），所以正確答案是選項 A。空格後面有 that，作為 do 的受詞，所以表被動的不定詞（D）to be done 不可選。

Q18 考題重點〉選擇符合前後文意的句子

A. easily trust what others say　輕易相信別人所說

B. consider what others promise a lie　將別人的承諾視為謊言

C. rely only on ourselves no matter what happens
無論發生任何事只要靠自己就好了

D. think more carefully about promises and words
更加審慎思考承諾和言語

| 詳解 | 前面提到有時候人們高估自己的能力而無法實現其承諾，即使他們的出發點可能是好的，因此空格這句要強調的是，學習對於他人的言語或承諾審慎評估，因此正確答案是選項 D。輕易相信別人所說（選項 A）、將別人的承諾一律視為謊言（選項 B）或是凡事靠自己（選項 C）都不是本文的主旨。

Part 3 閱讀理解

Questions 19-21

Reading is an activity some people enjoy a lot during their leisure. Some of them like reading newspapers, and some others enjoy novels or comic books. I like reading about the lives of great people. This always gives me a lot of ideas on how to make my own life better.

Day 22

Day 23

Day 24

Day 25

Day 26

Day 27

Day 28

Great people are remembered not because how handsome or beautiful they are, but because they never say die during hard times. They use every opportunity to change their lives and make the world better instead. When I feel sad or unhappy, stories of famous people always cheer me up and help me move forward.

| 翻譯 |

閱讀是一項閒暇時許多人喜愛的活動。有些人喜歡看報紙，而有些人則喜歡小說或漫畫。我喜歡閱讀偉大人物的生平事蹟。這一直給我許多如何讓我自己的生活變得更好的靈感。

偉人之所以被懷念不是因為他們多麼英俊或美麗，而是因為他們在艱困時期永不放棄。他們把握每一次的機會改變自己的人生，並讓世界變得更美好。當我感到傷心或心情不悅時，這些知名人士的故事總是讓我振作起來，且幫助我向前邁進。

| 詞彙 | leisure [ˈliʒɚ] 閒暇，休閒時　novel [ˈnɑvəl] 小說　comic book [ˈkɑmɪk bʊk] 漫畫書
remember [rɪˈmɛmbɚ] 記得，紀念　never say die 永不言敗，永不放棄
hard time 困難時期，艱苦時刻　opportunity [ˌɑpɚˈtjunətɪ] 機會
famous [ˈfeməs] 著名的，出名的　cheer up 振作起來

Q19 What does "this" mean in the last sentence of the first paragraph?
第一段最後一句的「This」是指什麼？

A. Being a famous person　成為有名的人

B. Reading a lot of books　讀很多的書

C. Enjoying one's free time　享受空閒時間

D. Reading about the lives of successful people　閱讀關於成功者的生平

| 詳解 | 這句開頭的 This 是指前一句「我喜歡閱讀偉大人物的生平事蹟（I like reading about the lives of great people）」這件事，所以正確答案是選項 D。

| 詞彙 | sentence [ˈsɛntəns] 句子　paragraph [ˈpærəˌgræf] 段落

Q20 According to the article, which is NOT true about the great people?
根據本文，關於偉人的敘述何者為非？

A. They have perfect appearance.
他們擁有完美的外貌。

B. They can survive through difficult times.
他們能夠熬過艱困時期。

C. They make good use of every chance and possibility.
他們能夠善加利用每一次機會與可能。

D. They always have the thought of improving.
他們總是有上進的想法。

| 詳解 | 選項 B 的 survive 指「生存，活下來」，也就是文中所說的「they never say die during hard times」，選項 C 的「make good use of every chance」也就是文中所說的「use every opportunity」，選項 D 的 improving 是「改善，改進」，正呼應文中的「change their lives and make the world better」，只有選項 A 的敘述不符合作者對於偉人的觀點，因為文中提到「Great people are remembered not because how handsome or beautiful they are...」，故本題正確答案為選項 A。

| 詞彙 | **perfect** [ˈpɝfɪkt] 完美的，無缺點的　**appearance** [əˈpɪrəns] 外表，外貌
survive [səˈvaɪv] 生存　**improve** [ɪmˈpruv] 改善，提升

Q21 What is in closest meaning to "say die" in the second paragraph?
第二段的「say die」與何者意思最接近？

A. Die hard　不易戒掉

B. Give up　放棄

C. Become angry　發脾氣

D. Blame others　責怪別人

| 詳解 | 第二段第一句後半的「never say die」是個常見的慣用語，字面意思是「從不提及去死」，其實就是「不輕言放棄（人生）」的意思，所以正確答案是選項 B。

| 詞彙 | **blame** [blem] 責怪

Day 22

Day 23

Day 24

Day 25

Day 26

Day 27

Day 28

Questions 22-24

Notice for All Teachers

Huanan University will soon be attending several recruitment fairs next month to find new students. We'd like to emphasize that we are different from general universities because we always focus on giving students more personal attention from teachers. To let more students know about this, we want at least one teacher at each event. The location and time of each event is shown below:

- Tue, Apr. 10: Marsha Hotel, Taichung
- Sat, Apr. 14: Yehda College, Kaohsiung
- Tue, Apr. 17: World Trade Center, Taipei

If you can attend any of the fairs, please let me know at jocelyn_yang@huanan_university.org.edu. Working overtime at weekends will surely be paid for.

···

From:	michelle_chang@huanan_university.org.edu
To:	jocelyn_yang@huanan_university.org.edu
Subject:	Recruitment fairs

Hello Jocelyn,

I was happy to see the notice you posted, and I'd like to tell you that I can go to the event on April 14. One of my uncles lives nearby, so I plan to visit him on that weekend. Please send me all the details of the event as soon as possible.

Cheers,
Teacher Andrew Hu

請所有教師注意

下個月華南大學即將去參加幾場招生博覽會，以招攬新生。我們想強調，我們與一般大學不同，因為我們始終著眼於讓學生得到老師更多的個人關注。為了讓更多學生知道，我們希望每個活動至少有一位老師參與。以下是各場地點與時間：

4 月 10 日（週二）：台中瑪莎酒店
4 月 14 日（週六）：高雄葉達學院
4 月 17 日（週二）：台北世界貿易中心

如果您能參加任何一個招生博覽會，請告知我，電子郵箱為 jocelyn_yang@huanan_university.org.edu。週末加班當然支薪。

....

寄件人：	michelle_chang@huanan_university.org.edu
收件人：	jocelyn_yang@huanan_university.org.edu
主題：	招生博覽會

Jocelyn 您好：

我看到您張貼的通知感到很開心，我想告訴你我可以參加4 月11 日那一場。我有一個叔叔住在附近，所以我計劃那個週末上去拜訪他。請盡快將活動所有細節發送給我。

祝好，
老師 Andrew Hu

| 詞彙 | **notice** [ˈnotɪs] 注意，通知　**recruitment** [rɪˈkrutmənt] 招生，徵募
fair [fɛr] 博覽會，展覽　**emphasize** [ˈɛmfəˌsaɪz] 強調，著重
(be) different from 與…不同　**focus on** 專注於，著重於
personal [ˈpɜsənəl] 個人的，私人的　**attention** [əˈtɛnʃən] 注意，關注
event [ɪˈvɛnt] 活動，事件　**overtime** [ˈovəˌtaɪm] 加班，超時　**pay for** 支付…的費用
nearby [ˈnɪrˌbaɪ] 在附近，鄰近地　**detail** [ˈdiˌtel] 細節，詳情

Day 22
Day 23
Day 24
Day 25
Day 26
Day 27
Day 28

Q22 What job has Jocelyn Yang probably been given to do?
Jocelyn Yang 可能被賦予了什麼工作？

A. Ask some teachers to participate in an event 徵求一些老師加入一項活動

B. Make travel plans for some teachers 為一些老師做旅行計畫

C. Make a list of some upcoming events 列出一些即將到來的活動

D. Find some suitable places for an event 為一項活動找出適當的地點

| 詳解 | 從第一個文本（通知）的「If you can attend any of the fairs, please let me know at jocelyn_yang@huanan_university.org.edu.」可知，她徵求幾位願意前往招生博覽會的老師，所以正確答案是選項 A。

| 詞彙 | **participate in** 參加　**make a list of** 條列出…　**suitable** [ˈsutəbl] 適合的

Q23 What makes Huanan University different from other universities?
華南大學與其他大學不同之處為何？

A. Holding recruitment fairs more often 更常舉辦招生博覽會

B. Having more foreign teachers than any other university
比其他大學有更多外籍老師

C. Giving students more educational resources 給學生更多教育資源

D. More personal guidance and support for students from their teachers
學生可以從老師那獲得更多個人指導及支援

| 詳解 | 從第一個文本（通知）的「we are different from general universities because we always focus on giving students personal attention from teachers」可知，該校與一般大學不同的原因在於始終著眼於讓學生得到老師更多的個人關注，所以正確答案是選項 D。

| 詞彙 | **educational** [ˌɛdʒʊˈkeʃənl] 教育的　**resource** [rɪˈsɔrs] 資源
guidance [ˈgaɪdn̩s] 指導，指引

Q24 Where does Teacher Andrew's uncle live?
Andrew 老師的叔叔住在哪裡？

A. In Taipei 在台北

B. In Taichung 在台中

C. In Kaohsiung 在高雄

D. Near Huanan University 在華南大學附近

| 詳解 | 本題應綜合兩個文本才能找到答案。首先，從提到 Teacher Andrew's uncle 的第二個文

本來看。從「I'd like to tell you that I can go to the event on April 14. One of my uncles lives nearby...」可知，Andrew 老師想要去參加 4 月 14 日那一場招生博覽會，因為他叔叔住在博覽會場所附近，想順道去拜訪他。接著我們再看到第一個文本（通知）的「Sat, Apr. 14: Yehda College, Kaohsiung」可知，4 月 14 日的招生博覽會是在高雄，所以正確答案是選項 C。

Questions 25-27

Richard Trevithick was very clever since he was still a young kid. In the 19th century, he made something very important in the history: the steam train. Before him, people relied on horses for moving from one place to another. However, Richard always had something different in mind from others: he wanted to create a machine that could move on its own. In 1804, he built the first steam train called the "Puffing Devil." This train was special because it could carry heavy loads and travel faster than horses. Richard's invention has changed the way people travel, making it quicker and more convenient. Even today, trains remain one of the primary parts of transportation thanks to him. What Richard Trevithick had left for people is a reminder that an idea, though involving risk and danger, can sometimes change the world. What's more, what he had left for later generations continues to inspire other inventions and progress in technology and transportation, shaping a different future for generations to come.

| 翻譯 |

理查・特理維西克（Richard Trevithick）從小就非常聰明。19 世紀時，他創造了歷史上一件非常重要的東西：蒸汽火車。在他之前，人們依靠馬匹從某個地方移動到另一個地方。然而，理查總是有與別人不一樣的想法：他想創造一台能夠自行移動的機器。1804 年，他建造了第一輛蒸汽火車，名為「噴氣魔鬼」。這輛火車很特別，因為它可以載運重物，比馬匹跑得更快。理查的發明改變了人們的旅行方式，使其更快捷、更方便。即使在今天，火車仍然是交通運輸的主要部分之一，這都要歸功於他。除此之外，他留給後代的東西是一種提醒，即使是含有危險與風險的想法，有時也可以改變世界。此外，他留給後代的東西繼續激勵著其他在科技與運輸界的發明和進步，同時為後代塑造出一個不一樣的未來。

| 詞彙 | clever [ˈklɛvɚ] 聰明的　steam [stim] 蒸汽　rely on 依賴
have... in mind 心中惦記著…　load [lod] 負載　invention [ɪnˈvɛnʃən] 發明
primary [ˈpraɪˌmɛri] 主要的　transportation [ˌtrænspɔrˈteɪʃən] 交通運輸
thanks to 由於，幸好有…　reminder [rɪˈmaɪndɚ] 提醒　involve [ɪnˈvɑlv] 涉及，包含
risk [rɪsk] 風險　generation [ˌdʒɛnəˈreʃən] 世代　inspire [ɪnˈspaɪɚ] 激勵，啟發
progress [ˈprɑgrɛs] 進步　technology [tɛkˈnɑlədʒɪ] 科技，技術
shape [ʃep] 形塑，塑造

Day 22
Day 23
Day 24
Day 25
Day 26
Day 27
Day 28

Q25 What is the main idea of this article?
這篇文章的主要概念為何？

A. Richard Trevithick's childhood　理查‧特理維西克的童年

B. Encouragement for inventions involving danger　鼓勵危險性的發明

C. The influence of Richard Trevithick's invention
　　理查‧特理維西克的發明所造成的影響

D. The importance of changing the world　改變世界的重要性

| 詳解 | 本題應從整段文章的內容來看，也就是理查‧特理維西克發明了蒸氣火車，並對後世人們帶來的影響，相關文字包括「...he made something very important in the history: the steam train... inspire other inventions and progress in technology and transportation...」所以正確答案是選項 C。

| 詞彙 | encouragement [ɪnˈkɝɪdʒmənt] 鼓勵　influence [ˈɪnflʊəns] 影響
importance [ɪmˈpɔrtəns] 重要性

Q26 What kind of moving machine did Trevithick invent?
特理維西克發明了什麼樣的移動式機器？

A.

C.

B.

D.

| 詳解 | 題目中 invent 是「發明」的意思，可以直接指向第二句的「he made something very important in the history: the steam train」，所以正確答案是選項 D。

| 詞彙 | machine [məˈʃin] 機器　invent [ɪnˈvɛnt] 發明

Q27 In this article, what is NOT true about Trevithick's invention?
在本文中，關於特理維西克的發明，何者為非？

A. It can move faster than any horses people took in the past.
   它比人們過去乘坐的馬車移動速度更快。

B. It was first created in the early 19th century.
   它在十九世紀初首度被創造出來。

C. He thought his invention is quite safe before it came into being.
   在他這項發明問世之前，他認為它非常安全。

D. People thought it had paved way for many following inventions.
   人們認為它造就了後來許多發明物。

| 詳解 | 文中「What Richard Trevithick had left for people... an idea, though involving risk and danger, can sometimes change the world.」這句話已清楚暗示著特理維西克先有大膽的想法才能在後來發明了火車，因此他並非一開始時認為這項發明是非常安全的，顯然 C 的敘述是錯誤的，故正確答案是選項 C。

| 詞彙 | **come into being** 存在，成立　**pave way for** 為⋯鋪路，造就⋯

Questions 28-30

Sandra was walking down the street when suddenly someone pulled away her purse quickly. She felt angry, frightened and nervous then. Quickly, she went to the police station to report what had happened to her. She told the police officer that the thief was a man aged about 40, wearing a black face mask and blue shorts. He also wore sunglasses from which his eyes can be seen through. She said that he had big eyes. Sandra also remembered that he smelled like cigarettes. The police officer listened carefully and told Sandra that they would do everything they could to catch the thief. Sandra felt a bit better knowing that the police were helping her. She hoped that they would find the thief soon and that her purse would be returned safely. In the meantime, she told herself that she must be more careful in the future when walking alone on the streets.

| 翻譯 |

當 Sandra 走在街上時，突然有人迅速地拉走了她的皮包。她感到生氣、驚恐又緊張。她迅速地去了警察局報案。她告訴警官，小偷是一名戴著黑色口罩和藍色短褲的男人，大約 40 歲左右。他還戴著太陽眼鏡，但可以透過它看到他的眼睛。她說他有大眼睛。Sandra 還記得他身上散發著菸味。警官仔細聽了後告訴 Sandra 他們會盡一切努力抓到小偷。Sandra 知道警察正在幫她，感覺好了一些。她希望他們能快速找到小偷，並安全地找回她的手提包。同時，她告訴自己以後獨自走

在街上時必須更加小心。

Day 22
Day 23
Day 24
Day 25
Day 26
Day 27
Day 28

| 詞彙 | suddenly [ˈsʌdn̩lɪ] 突然間　frightened [ˈfraɪtn̩d] 受到驚嚇的
nervous [ˈnɝvəs] 緊張的　police officer 警官　thief [θif] 小偷
face mask 口罩　sunglasses [ˈsʌnˌglæsɪz] 太陽眼鏡　see through 看穿
smell like cigarettes 身上有菸味　in the meantime 與此同時

Q28 What caused Sandra to feel frightened?
什麼事情讓 Sandra 感到驚恐？

A. A car accident　一場車禍

B. A robbery　一宗搶案

C. A fire　一場火災

D. A very loud thunder　很大的雷聲

| 詳解 | 從第一句「...when suddenly someone pulled away her purse quickly. She felt angry, frightened...」可知，她的皮包被搶走了，所以正確答案是選項 B。robbery（搶劫事件，搶劫案）是 rob（搶劫）的衍生單字。

| 詞彙 | accident [ˈæksɪdənt] 意外，偶然事件　robbery [ˈrɑbərɪ] 搶劫，搶劫
thunder [ˈθʌndɚ] 雷，雷聲

Q29 What lesson did Sandra learn from what happened to her?
Sandra 從發生在她身上的事情當中學到什麼教訓？

A. Do not bring too much money when going outside
外出時不要帶太多錢

B. Always keep calm after being robbed of something
東西被搶之後應總是保持冷靜

C. Try not to walk alone on the streets in the future
未來盡量避免獨自走在街上

D. Pay more attention when walking alone outside
在外獨自行走時多加注意

| 詳解 | 從最後一句「...she told herself that she must make sure to be more careful when walking alone on the streets」可知，她告訴自己以後獨自走在街上時必須更加小心，所以正確答案是選項 D。

| 詞彙 | lesson [ˈlɛsn̩] 課程，教訓　calm [kɑm] 冷靜的
rob sb. of sth. 從某人身上搶走某物

Q30 According to Sandra, what is NOT true about the thief?
根據 Sandra 的說法，以下關於這名小偷的敘述，何者為非？

A. He wore a black face mask and a pair of sunglasses.
他戴著黑色口罩和一副太陽眼鏡。

B. He wore blue pants with a cigarette in his mouth.
他穿著一條藍色的短褲，嘴裡叼著一根菸。

C. He looks middle-aged.
他看似個中年人。

D. His big eyes can be seen through his sunglasses.
可以透過他的太陽眼鏡看見他的大眼睛。

| 詳解 | 從「...wearing a black face mask and blue shorts...」以及「...he smelled like cigarettes...」可知，這名小偷穿著藍色短褲，且身上有菸味（並非嘴裡叼著一根菸），所以 B 的敘述是錯誤的，本題正確答案是選項 B。

| 詞彙 | **pants** [pænts] 長褲　**middle-aged** [`mɪdl͵edʒd] 中年的

聽力測驗答對題數與分數對照表

答對題數	分數	答對題數	分數	答對題數	分數
30	120	20	80	10	40
29	116	19	76	9	36
28	112	18	72	8	32
27	108	17	68	7	28
26	104	16	64	6	24
25	100	15	60	5	20
24	96	14	56	4	16
23	92	13	52	3	12
22	88	12	48	2	8
21	84	11	44	1	4

閱讀測驗答對題數與分數對照表

答對題數	分數	答對題數	分數	答對題數	分數
30	120	20	80	10	40
29	116	19	76	9	36
28	112	18	72	8	32
27	108	17	68	7	28
26	104	16	64	6	24
25	100	15	60	5	20
24	96	14	56	4	16
23	92	13	52	3	12
22	88	12	48	2	8
21	84	11	44	1	4

備考全民英檢、多益測驗、雅思

無論是單字、文法、聽力、閱讀、解題策略、

語言檢定

托福、新日檢JLPT、韓檢TOPIK
題庫，你需要的都在國際學村！

唯一選擇！

台灣廣廈 國際出版集團
Taiwan Mansion International Group

國家圖書館出版品預行編目（CIP）資料

GEPT 全民英檢初級閱讀測驗初試1次過／國際語言中心委員會 著
; -- 初版 -- 新北市：
國際學村, 2024.04
　　面；　公分
978-986-454-347-2 (平裝)
1. CST: 英語 . 2. CST: 檢定

805.1892　　　　　　　　　　　　　　　　113002043

 國際學村

GEPT 全民英檢初級閱讀測驗初試1次過
每日刷題 **10 分鐘**，**1 天 2 頁**，一個月後高分過關！

作　　　者／國際語言中心委員會

編輯中心編輯長／伍峻宏・**編輯**／許加慶
封面設計／陳沛涓・**內頁排版**／菩薩蠻數位文化有限公司
製版・印刷・裝訂／皇甫・秉成

行企研發中心總監／陳冠蒨
媒體公關組／陳柔彣
綜合業務組／何欣穎

線上學習中心總監／陳冠蒨
產品企製組／顏佑婷
企製開發組／江季珊

發　行　人／江媛珍
法律顧問／第一國際法律事務所 余淑杏律師・北辰著作權事務所 蕭雄淋律師
出　　　版／國際學村
發　　　行／台灣廣廈有聲圖書有限公司
　　　　　　地址：新北市 235 中和區中山路二段 359 巷 7 號 2 樓
　　　　　　電話：（886）2-2225-5777・傳真：（886）2-2225-8052

代理印務・全球總經銷／知遠文化事業有限公司
　　　　　　地址：新北市 222 深坑區北深路三段 155 巷 25 號 5 樓
　　　　　　電話：（886）2-2664-8800・傳真：（886）2-2664-8801
郵 政 劃 撥／劃撥帳號：18836722
　　　　　　劃撥戶名：知遠文化事業有限公司（※單次購書金額未達 1000 元，請另付 70 元郵資。）
讀者服務信箱／cs@booknews.com.tw

■ 出版日期：2024 年 04 月

ISBN：978-986-454-347-2